A BOY AT
THE EDGE OF
THE WORLD

Essential Prose Series 146

Canada Council for the Arts   **Conseil des Arts du Canada**

ONTARIO ARTS COUNCIL
CONSEIL DES ARTS DE L'ONTARIO

an Ontario government agency
un organisme du gouvernement de l'Ontario

Canada

Guernica Editions Inc. acknowledges the support of the Canada Council
for the Arts and the Ontario Arts Council. The Ontario Arts Council
is an agency of the Government of Ontario.

We acknowledge the financial support of the Government of Canada.

A BOY AT THE EDGE OF THE WORLD

DAVID KINGSTON YEH

GUERNICA EDITIONS
TORONTO • BUFFALO • LANCASTER (U.K.)
2018

Michael Mirolla, general editor
Julie Roorda, editor
David Moratto, interior and cover design
Guernica Editions Inc.
1569 Heritage Way, Oakville, (ON), Canada L6M 2Z7
2250 Military Road, Tonawanda, N.Y. 14150-6000 U.S.A.
www.guernicaeditions.com

Distributors:
University of Toronto Press Distribution,
5201 Dufferin Street, Toronto (ON), Canada M3H 5T8
Gazelle Book Services, White Cross Mills
High Town, Lancaster LA1 4XS U.K.

First edition.
Printed in Canada.

Legal Deposit—First Quarter
Library of Congress Catalog Card Number: 2017960390
Library and Archives Canada Cataloguing in Publication

Yeh, David K. (David Kingston), 1966-, author
A boy at the edge of the world / David Kingston Yeh.

(Essential prose series ; 146)
Issued in print and electronic formats.
ISBN 978-1-77183-248-9 (softcover).--ISBN 978-1-77183-249-6
(EPUB).
--ISBN 978-1-77183-250-2 (Kindle)

I. Title. II. Series: Essential prose series ; 146

PS8647.E47B69 2018   C813'.6   C2017-907288-9   C2017-907289-7

for all the
Daniels of the world

CONTENTS

A BOY AT
THE EDGE OF
THE WORLD

CHAPTER ONE

The Hockey Song

Karen Fobister was the first person I ever came out to. I could remember that moment as easily as turning a page in a photo album. We'd agreed to be each other's dates to our high school senior Formal. Karen sat on her bed painting her nails, or trying to. It wasn't something she was terribly good at, but on this occasion she thought she'd give it a whirl. Her dress hung shimmering on the closet door. Her adoptive mom Mrs. Milton had made it herself. It really was beautiful.

"So, Daniel, my aunt says you're *agokwe*, two-spirited. Are you?"

I was nursing two black eyes. Just days earlier, I'd gotten myself kicked out of Midget AA. Grandpa was furious but I'd begged him not to talk to Kadlubek. Kadlubek was the head coach who'd suspended his own son Gary six games for smoking pot behind the rink. I heard rumours that he'd beaten Gary later at home with a belt. I didn't want anyone else to get in trouble, especially not Stephan.

Stephan Tondeur had moved to Sudbury that spring,

and just started volunteering with the league. He was a real estate agent with a beautiful wife and a brand new baby girl. It was all my fault. For months, I'd been sneaking away to meet Stephan. It was no secret I was being groomed for team captain come fall. But the other players began to suspect something more. Rumours started to go around. During a practice game, when things got ugly, my gloves finally hit the ice.

Stephan Tondeur and the first assistant coach escorted me out of the arena. I could never forget the look on Kadlubek's face watching me go. I could never forget the look on Stephan's face in the parking lot.

Now it was over. I told myself it was for the best. I remembered when they tacked the photo of his daughter up outside the shower room, along with a bunch of pink helium balloons and a giant card signed by the whole team. That baby was as beautiful as her dad.

I stood in front of Karen's dresser mirror. The rental shop had taken in too much around the waist of my tux. I could barely breathe. "What?"

Karen rolled over and sat up, blowing on her fingers. She was wearing only her bra and underwear, and the Thunderbird crest tattoo showed clearly on the back of her shoulder. Carefully, she plucked the cotton balls from between her toes. "*Agokwe*," she said.

"I'm white," I said. "I can't be two-spirited."

"You know what she means," said Karen.

She was serious. She wasn't teasing me. She brushed aside her blue-black bangs and sipped from our mickey of Crown Royale. On the stereo, Alanis Morissette belted out her undying gratitude to the world.

The first time Stephan met me in his office, he told me his nickname had been Rocket Man, given how he'd always been the biggest Ysebaert fan. He showed me a photo of himself when he was captain of his own AA team, not so long ago. Impulsively, I asked if I could have it. Up until that point in time, I'd never kissed another guy. He hesitated in surprise, searching my face, then took the photo out of its frame. I said thanks. He said keep it safe. Then the day came when he drove me home late one night. I gave him the wrong directions and we ended up lost out on Tilton Lake Road. After that, everything changed. I took to helping Stephan lock up after each practice. To this day, the smell of change rooms and sweaty hockey equipment still gives me an instant hard-on.

"Daniel?" Karen held out the mickey to me.

"Yes," I said. "Yes, I'm gay."

"Well, you always had really bad fashion sense. So I was never sure. You want a drink or not?"

I shook my head. "Don't joke."

Karen put the bottle down. She got up and stood next to me. I stared at her in the dresser mirror, framed by photos of family and friends. We'd been neighbours ten years. That was a lot of birthday cakes. "Do you think my tits are too small?" she asked.

"No, I think they're perfect."

Half my face was purple. I looked like a raccoon. "Daniel," Karen said, "you look like a raccoon."

"I know."

She wrapped her arms around me and squeezed as hard as she could. She held me this way for a long time. Part of me wanted her to stop, but she wouldn't stop.

Another part of me wanted her to never let go. After a while, I started to cry: silent, angry, gulping sobs. I couldn't help it.

I would've made a great team captain.

⌒ After high school, my brother Pat quit his garage band Krypton, and went backpacking overseas. Karen and I headed off to U of T. Only my brother Liam stayed in Sudbury. Karen and I were roommates our first three years in Toronto. The first time I walked into a gay bar was during the Halloween party on Church Street. I'd been in the city two months and was just learning how to navigate the Robarts Library stacks. I couldn't resist checking out the washroom up on the thirteenth floor where I'd heard a lot of cruising went down. I lasted a whole twenty minutes outside, pretending to read my textbook, watching faculty and students come and go.

It was Karen's idea to dress up as zombie hockey players. We planned it over Thanksgiving with the Miltons. Grandma only agreed to leave the nursing home after Grandpa showed her his ID. Thanksgiving with the Miltons had been our tradition since we were ten, but for the first time not everyone was there. A coffee-stained postcard of London's Big Ben had arrived bearing Pat's well-wishes. As usual, we set out a spirit plate for Mom and Dad.

The Miltons were college teachers who'd never had kids of their own. Pat was secretly convinced Mr. Milton had smoked too much pot back in the Sixties and killed off all his sperm. As usual, Mr. Milton carved the turkey and Grandpa served up his famous sugar pie. Mrs. Milton said grace, thanking the Great Spirit, Mother Earth and God. Karen's little sister Anne had turned fifteen earlier that fall. Her hair was cut spiky short, and she wore a tight black T-shirt over her boyish frame that said FIFTH COLUMN. She left the house right after dessert, saying she had friends to meet. It was in the silence that followed that Karen blurted out: "Zombies."

"I beg your pardon?" Mrs. Milton said.

"There's this big Halloween street party downtown in Toronto every year, and Daniel and I are going to be zombies."

"Weren't you zombies last year, dear?"

"Yeah, well, we were zombie Boy Scouts last year, and the year before that we were zombie Jehovah's Witnesses. But this time we're going to be zombie hockey players."

Then a big debate arose over whether we'd wear Maple Leafs or Habs jerseys. Even Liam got involved. Later that evening, Karen tried to convince him to come visit us in Toronto. I heard them arguing about it out on the front stoop. Karen and Liam went for a long walk after that, and I was left entertaining Grandma, fending off her flirtatious gropes and making sure she didn't hide mashed potato and gravy in her purse. I poured both of us some white wine when no one was looking, and let her eat all the cranberry sauce with a coffee spoon. She wasn't supposed to be drinking on her meds, but what the hell. It was Thanksgiving.

Of course, the party on Church Street was in the middle of Toronto's Gay Village. Halloween, I found out soon enough, was the gay version of Christmas. The street was cordoned off to traffic and the surging crowd was shoulder-to-shoulder at some points. With Grandpa's help, I'd fixed an old skate to make it look like it was stuck in my helmet, and Karen did an amazing job with our dollar-store make-up. People kept stopping us to take our pictures. We met the Queen of Hearts and her entire entourage, angels in eighteen-inch heels and leather harnesses, body-painted superheroes, and drag queens in full demonic, blood-soaked regalia. It was absolutely fantastical and awesome. After we emptied both our flasks, I wanted another drink, so we waited in line to get into a bar called Crews & Tango's. The line-up went half-way down the block and, by the time we got past the butch dyke bouncer, I was almost ready to pee my pants. I was at the urinal breathing the hugest sigh of relief when I noticed the guy next to me looking over. I don't know why it took me so off guard. It was what I'd fantasied would happen if I'd ever gotten up the courage to actually walk into the washroom in Robarts Library. He was wearing a football helmet, shoulder-pads, cleats and a jockstrap. That was it. He was also stroking himself. I was shocked and mortified and totally turned on. Before I knew it, I had a boner and could barely finish my business. Then he grinned and winked at me.

Football Guy was blowing me in the bathroom stall when I answered Karen's phone call. I'd been gone a long time. She wanted to know if I was having sex in a crowded public washroom and I said I was. She congratulated me and told me she was at the bar fending off lesbian vampires with our hockey sticks, and told me to take my sweet time. I was still trying to figure out whether she was being sarcastic or not when I felt myself start to climax. When I came, shuddering and spread-eagled, I almost dropped my phone in the toilet. He was deep-throating me and swallowed it all, which was something Stephan Tondeur had never done. After that, I barely managed to pull up my pants. Football Guy was putting his helmet back on and cinching his chin strap. Then I introduced myself, asked him his name and made to shake his hand. He gave me a look I'll never forget, shook his head, and turned and walked out without a backward glance. I still had my hand out when Freddy Krueger stuck his head in and demanded to know whether I was knitting a toque or if I was done with the stall.

When I finally found Karen, she handed me a pint. I drained half of it and thanked her. "How was it?" she asked.

"It was good." I wiped my chin on the back of my arm, scanning the crowd in a daze. I think I was still in shock at what had just happened.

"It was Mr. Quarterback, wasn't it?"

"What?"

"It was that football guy, the one with his ass hanging out. It was him, right?"

"How'd you guess?"

"Daniel, you've had this jockstrap fetish thing going ever since you got it on with that hockey coach of yours. Seriously, it wasn't a stretch. You could bounce a nickel off that tight end."

"I can't believe I just did that."

"I can't believe you asked him his name." I stared at her dumbly before fumbling out my phone. "Maybe," said

Karen, taking the pint glass from my hand, "we should have sex one day, you and me, just to see what it's like." I hung up my phone and put it away. "What do you think?"

"Karen, I'm like, really gay."

She searched my face. Gingerly, she plucked a piece of latex flesh dangling off my cheek. "Alright, I suppose this makes me a fag hag, doesn't it? God how I hate that term." She finished my beer, burped impressively and gave me back my hockey stick. "The next round's on you. We'll just eat Kraft Dinner for a week. Alright?"

"Alright."

⌒ Pat came home for Christmas, thinner, but tanned and healthy enough. He'd cut his hair and wore it now in a short ponytail. For the first time, Grandma refused to leave the nursing home when we went to pick her up Christmas Eve. She was angry at our intrusion and wouldn't calm down. She wanted to watch *Baywatch*. In the end, we settled ourselves in front of the big screen TV in the common room, and passed the time playing cards while David Hasselhoff cavorted in the surf. After Grandma dozed off, the head nurse Betty let us know nicely but firmly that it was time to go. Back home, Grandpa wished us well, patted each of us on the shoulder and retired early.

"Goodnight, Grandpa," I said.

"'Night, Grandpa!" Pat shouted.

"Bonne nuit, Pépère," Liam said.

After that, Pat insisted that Liam and I open his badly wrapped presents. As it turned out, he'd brought back scotch for everyone. I opened my bottle and Liam lit a joint which we smoked out back. After high school, Liam had gotten into construction full-time. Housing was booming and there was no shortage of work. Liam might've been just a kid, but he was Tom Garneau's kid and that was good enough for most. Grandpa himself had worked as a contractor in Sudbury for pretty much his whole life. It was all cash under the table and Liam had no complaints.

Close to midnight, Karen texted to let us know she was coming over. She tramped across the street and around the side of the house to meet us on the back deck. "Well, what do you know, it's the Garneau boys reunited." Liam handed her the scotch but she waved it away, pulling a bottle of Baby Duck out of her snow pants. "So when did you get back?"

"A couple days ago," Pat said. "It's good to see you, Karen Fobister. You're looking veritably rosy in the cheeks. Merry Christmas, Gitche Manitou and all that. How's your little sis?"

Karen took a drag off the joint I handed her. "Anne, she's fine. She just got her nose pierced."

"Seriously?" I asked. "How do your parents feel about that?"

Karen shrugged, tilted her head back and exhaled. "My mom was the one who took her. You shouldn't be smoking, Daniel. You get sick when you smoke pot."

"It's alright. I just had one puff."

"Anyone want a super?"

Pat threw up his arm. "Oh, yes, Miss Fobister, may I, please?"

"Good boy, Patrick. Now stand still and stop fidgeting."

She held the joint backwards between her teeth and blew out while Pat craned his neck sucking back.

"You're doing it wrong," Liam said.

"I don't think so," Pat said, grimacing.

"Look, you lost half the smoke. Give it to me. Daniel, come here."

"He's going to get sick."

Liam patted me on the cheek and turned his bill cap around. "It's just for medicinal purposes, Karen." He rested one hand on my shoulder and we leaned into each other. I jerked back and held my breath, trying not to cough. Expertly, Liam flipped the joint back around with his tongue. The ember crackled. "And that," he said out of the corner of his mouth, "is how it's done."

Pat plucked the joint from between his lips. "Amateurs." He sat up on the railing, took a nice hit into his mouth, and performed a perfect French Inhale.

"Show off," Karen said. Pat wiggled his eyebrows seductively. Karen poked me in the chest. "So, Daniel, did you tell them yet?" Ever since our Halloween outing in Toronto, she'd been pressuring me to come out to my brothers. In the end, I promised I would before Christmas. Tonight was the deadline. It was obvious from my expression that I hadn't. She took out her phone and held it up. "You have three minutes."

"Three minutes?"

"Three minutes to tell us what?"

"And counting."

"Okay, guys." There was no way this should be so difficult. I took another slug of scotch. "I have something to tell you."

The flash went off on Karen's phone. "What, that you're a queer?" Pat said. "That you're a limp-wristed fag? That you're a cock-sucking poof? We know that already. You have something else to tell us?"

The Christmas lights strung up in the pine trees and all around the back deck took on a sharper focus. My breath formed frosty clouds in the air. Karen raised both hands and backed away. "I didn't say anything."

"Dan, dude, we're your brothers," Pat said laughing. "We know. We've always known."

"I didn't know," Liam said.

"Of course you knew, Liam. We all know. Grandpa knows. Even Grandma knows! That's why you're her favourite."

"I'm not Grandma's favourite," I said. "She doesn't even remember my name half the time."

"Seriously, Dan, she doesn't remember our names most of the time. Why do you think she keeps groping your ass? Why do you think she keeps wanting to watch re-runs of *The Golden Girls* with you? She's spending quality time with her favourite gay grandson."

"I just thought she was crazy," I mumbled. But in that hazy moment, what Pat said made bizarre sense.

Liam looked sideways at me and then back at Pat. "Really, Pat, I didn't know."

"Liam," Karen said, taking his hand, "weren't you going to show me that moose skull you found?"

"Hold on, wait a minute," Pat said. "Before you two go off and shag like rabbits, I've got something to show everyone." He pulled off his coat, tossed me his toque, and pulled his T-shirt off over his head. "Check it out boys and girls," he exclaimed, turning his back. "Pretty nifty, eh?" Just below the base of his neck between his shoulder blades was a palm-sized tattoo of the Union Jack.

"Whoa."

"Impressive."

"I see you had a good time in London," Karen said.

"London, Glastonbury, Dover. I had a bloody brilliant time. Thanksgiving in Ibiza was sick. I missed you guys."

I'd thought the stamp on that Big Ben postcard had looked funny. I took another swig from the bottle. "Oh my god, what the fuck is that?"

Pat blinked. "Oh this? This. This is a nipple ring. I had it done in Amsterdam. The girls love it. What do you think? You can touch it if you want."

"No. No thanks. I can see it, plain as day."

"It's midnight, guys," Karen said. "Merry Christmas."

Pat slapped me on the back. "Merry Christmas. I'm glad you finally came out to us, dude. Props to you. You rock. You're tied in first place as my number one favourite bro." He grabbed my face and kissed me hard on the forehead. "We love you, man." He draped his arm over me and turned to Karen and Liam. "Go, forest children," he commanded, pointing straight-armed. "Go make beautiful love. I want to bond with my out-and-proud gay brother. And don't forget to use a johnny."

"Honestly," Liam whispered to Karen as they tramped back into the house, "I didn't know."

"Pat," I said, "put on your clothes. It's freezing out here." Obligingly, he put on his toque and lit a cigarette. He held out the pack, but I grimaced and backed away. I was starting to feel a little sick. "No thanks. What's a johnny?"

"A johnny's a rubber, a condom. Hey, if you're gonna banger, cover your wanger."

"Oh, right." I'd just come out to my brothers and it was like it was nothing. Maybe it was nothing, but I wasn't so sure. "So, like, when did you start smoking again?"

"Since I quit the band. Since I started hanging out in British pubs." (He pronounced the word *poobs*.) "Since I spent the last five months in Europe. Marlboro. Disgusting. But it's what everyone smokes out there. You'd love England, Dan. Very British, very proper. I actually bought that T-shirt for you, but I liked it so much I kept it for myself."

I held up his T-shirt which had a picture of Winston Churchill and the caption IF YOU'RE GOING THROUGH HELL, KEEP GOING. "You're kidding," I said.

"Why would I be kidding? See, Dan, you're like Churchill, you're our big brother. You always take charge. Grandpa did his best, but, well, you know Grandpa. You've gotten us through a lot since Mom and Dad died. Growing up wasn't easy. I'm grateful and proud to have had you leading the way."

I'd never heard Pat talk like this before. "Okay. Thanks for at least thinking of me."

"Naw, I'm just pulling your leg. Someone at a party gave me that shirt after I lost mine. But it does suit you, Dan. You can have it if you want. In fact, I'm giving it to you. Merry Christmas."

"Thanks."

Pat fiddled with his nipple ring. "Look, let me tell you something, just between you and me. I kissed a guy once.

It was nice. Scratchy but nice. We were playing Truth or Dare. I'd do it again you know. Not with you though. That would be wrong."

"I'm glad you feel that way."

"But sex and love, really, it's all fluid. Its all in here." Pat rapped the side of his head. "Biggest sex organ in the body. In Camden Market, I met this guy and two girls. They made these rockin' belts and purses. They told me they were poly. I thought that was the name of their band. Here I was this ignorant hick Canadian straight out of high school, eh, from northern Ontario. What did I know? Let's just say poly did not want a cracker."

"So what's poly?"

"Poly. Polyamorous. Having multiple, equally-loving partners."

"You mean they were a threesome."

"Better than that. They were an open threesome."

"You slept with them?"

"We played Truth or Dare. Yah, I slept with them. It was hot. I've been thinking a lot since then. With dudes, I figure anything above the waist is fair game, you know what I mean? I loved making out with that dude. It was such a turn on. The truth is, no one's really straight. No one is. I thought I was, and look at me. Who's that Green Day guy who said that, Billie Joe Armstrong. Think Morrissey and Molko, and all the greats, Bowie and Jagger. I figure it's all good, man."

Pat finished his cigarette in silence. It was starting to snow, but he didn't seem to be feeling the cold at all. I hated to admit it, but his nipple ring looked good, it suited him. His tattoo also looked good. I had a hunch it was the first of many. Karen was right, I shouldn't have smoked that joint. I was definitely feeling nauseous.

"So," Pat said, tossing his butt into the barbecue, "how many guys have you done it with?"

"A few."

"Have you gotten it up the ass?"

"I don't want to talk about this."

"You have a boyfriend?"

"No."

'You'll tell us if you did?"

"Sure." I leaned against the railing, feeling dizzy. "Why did you say Grandpa knows?"

Pat snorted. "Oh, I don't know if he knows. I was just messing with you. Everyone thinks you and Karen are an item."

"Karen's with Liam."

"You know that. I know that. Although I'm not sure Liam knows that."

"Liam's a little freaked out, isn't he?"

"You want me to talk to him? I'll talk to him if you want me to. Let me talk to him."

I put down the scotch bottle. "Okay. Thanks."

"Hey. What are brothers for?"

"What are brothers for." I gave Pat a high five, grateful for having pretty much the coolest brother in the world. Then I threw up all over him.

⌒ On New Years Eve in Toronto, I got raped. Technically, that was what happened. I woke up on my stomach, and someone was on top of me, and inside me. It took me a few seconds to figure out what was actually going on. I must've yelled something awful, because the guy jumped up and staggered back halfway across the room. By that time, I'd rolled over and grabbed the first thing I laid my hands on which was a huge, black, double-headed dildo. I blurted something which must've been incomprehensible, because the guy kept saying, "What? What? What?" over and over. Then I noticed he wasn't wearing a condom and I started to freak out. I recognized him as the guy I'd been flirting with all night at Fly Nightclub. He was a nice guy, really cute. I'd just forgotten his name. It took a while before I registered what he was saying. Then I reached around with one arm, felt with my fingers and pulled the condom out of my ass, slick with lube. It must have slipped off when he jumped off of me. He'd been fucking me. I'd never been fucked in my life. I shouted something and threw the dildo at him as hard as I could. I was so terrified and angry. The dildo bounced off the wall and hit him in the shoulder. You'd think I'd just whipped a crowbar at him. He crouched, cowering, with his hands over his head and actually started to cry. That changed everything. My anger cracked in half and crumbled off me. I was left breathless and dishevelled, standing naked on some bed with Star Wars sheets. A model of the Enterprise NCC-1701 hung from the ceiling next to a Tardis propping up some psych and computer textbooks. I was dizzy and sweaty-drunk, covered in sparkles in some fanboy's bachelor apartment. I stepped off the bed and set the condom down on the night table where my wallet, phone and keys were neatly placed. I'd done that. I'd put them there. The time on my phone read 2:46 a.m. I'd left Karen at Fly and gone home with this guy. "Brent," I said. "Your name's Brent."

"No. It's Brett."

"Sorry."

"Can you please leave?"

"Wait."

"Leave." He couldn't look me in the eye. "Just leave."

I put on my clothes, gathered my stuff and left. It was snowing hard outside and I had absolutely no idea where I was. I started to panic. Then a cab rounded the corner and I ran in front of it, waving like a crazy person. It was 3 a.m. on New Year's Day. What were the chances a cab would cross my path when I needed one the most? Someone was watching over me. Suddenly I skidded, slipped and fell in the salty slush. It was like something straight out of a Buster Keaton movie. It was a miracle I didn't get run over. I leaned on the bumper, hauled myself to my feet, felt my way around the vehicle and got into the back. As it turned out, I was a five minute drive from home. Karen was still up, listening to Sarah McLachlan and eating cold pizza, when I limped in through the door. "Hey," she said, "didn't you hook up with that Brent guy?"

"Brett. His name's Brett."

"What happened? You okay?"

"Yes, no. I'm not sure."

"Shit, Daniel, have you been smoking pot again?"

"No. I think I just drank too much."

"Okay. Oh, sweetheart, Daniel, what's wrong?"

I'd started to cry. "I went home with him and it was really great. We made out on his couch, then we started playing with these toys. Then he offered me something called poppers. And then he asked me if I could top him and I said yes but then I couldn't get it up, so and then he asked me if he could top me and I said yes, but then I must've passed out for a few seconds and then when I woke up I didn't know where I was except there I was and I panicked and I kind of went all psycho crazy and threw this really big dildo at him and totally freaked out. Oh, I am such an idiot. Fuck me fuck me fuck me."

Karen knew when to joke and when to be serious. She stood in front of me. "Did you hurt him?"

"No, I didn't hurt him." I wiped the snot running from my nose.

"Okay, just asking. Did he use protection?"

"Yes."

"Are you sure?"

"Yes, I'm sure."

"You're *sure* sure?"

"I'm sure!"

"Okay. You're all wet. You need a shower."

"Help."

Karen led me by the hand to the washroom where she undressed me as I stood leaning back against the sink. We'd seen each other naked lots of times over the years, during sleepovers and camping in Killarney. I'd never felt this way before in my entire life. "Daniel, where's your underwear?"

"Aww."

"Don't worry about it."

"Those were brand new. They were Calvin Klein."

"Okay, out of those pants. The truth is, you were never a Calvin Klein kind of guy." Karen ran a hot shower and drew back the curtain. "More Fruit of the Loom. Now get in. Oh my god, look at your leg."

The side of one knee was red and purple. "I slipped on the street. It looks worse than it feels."

"Tell me that in the morning. You're not going to fall down and hit your head and have me call 911 are you?"

"Maybe." I clambered into the shower. "Karen, don't leave me."

"I'm not going anywhere."

"Come in here with me."

The steam was filling the room. Karen opened her mouth, her hands on her hips, then closed it again.

"Okay," she said. "Okay. Hold on."

She left and came back with a bottle of Diet Pepsi and the pizza box which she set on the toilet seat. She took off her PJs and got into the shower with me. The hot water felt good. I let her wash my hair and then my back.

"You want some pizza?" she asked.

"Okay," I said. I was starting to feel better. She got us both a slice and we took our time eating in the shower, passing the big plastic Pepsi bottle between us. "Thank you, Karen Fobister."

"You're welcome, Daniel Garneau."

Afterwards we both got into our PJs and put on the Season Three of *The Golden Girls* DVD, which was our favourite season. We fell asleep on the couch before the first episode was over, and as the snow kept falling all the while, silently and gently, blanketing the city.

CHAPTER TWO

Working for the Weekend

That spring, I applied for a position with Community Living Toronto, an organization that supported people with intellectual disabilities. In the interview, they asked about my experience living with my grandmother who had dementia. "It was hard at first," I reflected, sitting straight-backed in my chair. "But structure and routine are key. And patience, a lot of patience. It was important we got the homecare staff to see her as a human being." The three interviewers just nodded, heads bowed, checking boxes on their clipboards and scribbling notes.

Later, when I told Karen they'd offered me the job, she laughed in my face. "You guys never had homecare. Your grandma's lived in a nursing home since you were ten. You'd visit her, what, like once a week?"

We sat on a concrete bench in front of City Hall, wearing our shorts for the first time that season, soaking up the sunshine, and sharing a carton of sweet potato fries. "I know," I said, "but they don't know that. And it's not like I was lying, not really, not about what really counts. Right?"

"Fine, whatever it takes to pay the rent. Congratulations

on your summer job. I'm sure you'll be great at it. I still think you should come back to Sudbury."

I dipped a fry into a side of spicy mayonnaise, and observed the flow of human traffic all around us: businessmen in their suits, scruffy skateboarders, tourists boarding their buses, homeless people with their entire lives in their bags. Toronto was almost twenty times bigger than Sudbury. White clouds reflected in the gleaming curved towers of City Hall rising over Nathan Phillips Square. "We'll visit each other," I said. "You're coming back down for Pride Week, right?"

"Definitely. I wouldn't miss it for the world."

"You're sure about this Derrick guy?"

Derrick McNeil-Tsao was a senior classmate of Karen's who'd sublet her room for the summer. He sported a military haircut, had calves like softballs, and was studying to be a math and Phys-Ed teacher. He was also engaged to his high school sweetheart back home in North Bay. He showed me pictures of her within minutes of meeting. She looked like a cheerleader. "Captain of her squad, Garneau," McNeil-Tsao announced proudly.

"Don't worry," said Karen, "He's a good guy. I told you, his little brother's gay, or at least the family thinks he's gay. The kid's five years old. He might be transgender. The parents let him play with Barbie dolls. They're really progressive. The point is, Derrick's an ally. He's just like me."

Alright. I'm going to miss you."

Karen tossed a fry at a seagull strutting nearby. "Just promise me one thing."

"What's that?"

"Don't contract anything horrible."

"Oh, that's nice, Karen. Really nice."

She took off her sunglasses and squinted at me. "I'm serious, Daniel. Be careful."

"Okay, I'll be careful."

One week after her last exam, I saw Karen off at the bus station. I told her to pass on my regards to her parents and little sister. Karen and Anne had been invited to spend the summer on their aunt's farm on Manitoulin. Pat was gone up north planting trees. Liam was still living at home with Grandpa. The bus pulled out in a puff of grey exhaust. I was on my own.

As it turned out, Derrick McNeil-Tsao was businesslike, tidy, and an amazing cook. He paid for his sublet in advance with four post-dated cheques and left me smoothies in the fridge every morning. He also got me a discounted membership at his gym and introduced me to squash. I was an athletic person, but McNeil-Tsao ran circles around me. For such a big guy, I couldn't believe how fast he was on his feet. That summer it became our Sunday afternoon ritual: chasing that little black bouncing squash ball like it was a puck on the ice. "It all has to do with spatial orientation and geometry, Garneau," he declared, which was why he was convinced men would always make better squash players, architects and fighter pilots than women. With his coaching, I quickly lost the extra weight I'd gained over the school year. He also announced he liked to be thorough with his hygiene and preferred waiting until he got home to shower. Secretly, I wondered if this was for his benefit or really for mine.

His fiancée's name was Rachel, and the first time she

visited, she brought me a loaf of home-made banana bread and a big pop-up thank-you card for allowing her to stay the weekend. She missed her Der-Der so much. The pictures on McNeil-Tsao's phone hadn't prepared me for the size of her breasts. They were enormous. She told me she was a youth leader at her church which fully supported LGBTQ people and same-sex marriage. I thanked her for her loaves and told her to make herself at home.

That Saturday, I worked a double-shift at the group home and came home exhausted just before midnight. The door to Karen's bedroom was closed, and at first I thought McNeil-Tsao and Rachel were having a hushed, angry argument. Then I realized they were talking dirty to each other. Rachel would yelp and giggle, and McNeil-Tsao would grunt like he was doing heavy weights. After half an hour, I heard the faint whine of an electric motor and Rachel squealing and some weird, irregular slapping sounds. After another hour, I put in my ear plugs, but I could still hear the thump-thump-thump-thumping coming through the bedroom wall. It was like trying to sleep next to a construction site. *Thump thump thump.* After a while, I took out my ear plugs and pressed a glass up against the wall. "Deeper," grunted McNeil-Tsao, "push it deeper, awwww, Jesus Christ, harder, fuck me sweet." Then Rachel would say: "You like that, motherfucker? You like that? You like getting rammed, you gawddamn pussy-licking mama's boy?" *Slap slappity slap.* Then I put the glass away and put my earplugs back in. *Thump thump thump.* As quickly as I could, I jerked off, and finally managed to doze off.

The next morning I kept expecting them to apologize for being so loud, but they didn't mention anything. Rachel was as chatty as ever and McNeil-Tsao insisted he make breakfast for all three of us. Blueberry pancakes with soy milk, and free-trade organic coffee from Nicaragua, because it was so important to help out the little guy, Garneau. Didn't I agree? Absolutely. I finished the banana smoothie he'd prepared for me, doing my best not to stare at Rachel's chest. When I asked Rachel if they'd visited much of Toronto yesterday, they exchanged looks and McNeil-Tsao replied: "We didn't really go out Saturday. We stayed in." Rachel squeezed his arm and added: "We had a lot to catch up on."

That summer, McNeil-Tsao and Rachel caught up in Toronto practically every other weekend. On those occasions, I made a point of picking up the unpopular Saturday nightshift at the group home. I'd bring my DVD box set of all seven seasons of *The Golden Girls*, make buttered popcorn in the microwave for the residents, and serve up frothy glasses of caffeine-free root beer to wash down their meds. I taught everyone the theme song, even Bill who was partially deaf (and who had a mole on his face the size of a beer coaster). They loved it. "Tank you bor bing a fand!" sang Bill at the top of his lungs. The sugar crash put them all to bed afterwards. They voted me their favourite staff, and let my housing supervisor know as much. After that summer, I stayed on as an on-call shift worker during my next two years at school. In the end, everything worked out for everyone.

It was great.

⌒ That June, Karen came down to Toronto for Pride Weekend. She'd coordinated her visit with McNeil-Tsao who was spending the weekend in North Bay. She arrived early, catching a morning bus just to surprise me. She keyed in the door while I was vacuuming and dancing in my underwear to Bryan Adams. When she snuck up behind me and slapped my ass, I must've jumped halfway across the living room, crashing into our bookshelf, knocking board games and DVDs all over the floor. Karen nearly doubled-over laughing. By the time I pulled on some pants, Karen was rummaging through the kitchen. "Whoa," she said, peering into the fridge, "what's with all this fruit?"

"We've been making a lot of smoothies."

"Oh right. Derrick's kind of a health nut."

"More like a full-blown junkie. You know he's pescetarian and doesn't drink at all?"

"Is that like Presbyterian?"

"No, Karen. He only eats fish."

"Sounds healthy."

I pinched my stomach. "Compared to him, my body's a toxic waste dump."

"You're body's not a toxic waste dump, Daniel."

"Well, not anymore."

"Don't sound so excited. Where are all your Creamsicles?"

"Gone. I stopped buying them."

"But you always have Creamsicles. You love your Creamsicles! C'mon, Daniel, it's the one thing gay about you." Karen narrowed her eyes. "Derrick?"

"What's gay," I asked, "about Creamsicles?"

"Do I need to spell it out?"

"What's that supposed to mean?"

"The next time you have a Creamsicle, Daniel, I'll show you."

I did my best to change the subject. "So how was your aunt's farm?"

"Awesome. Anne hated it. My parents had to come pick her up early. I got to drive a tractor. They have four horses. I've been learning how to ride. I can't believe you don't have any Creamsicles. Liam came up to visit."

"Liam?"

"He's still there. He and my aunt totally hit it off. He says he might try to find work on Manitoulin. He might even move out there." I thought about Grandpa in Sudbury living on his own. "We're taking a break, by the way. It's not really working out."

"Who's taking a break?"

"Liam and me."

"Oh, I'm sorry to hear that."

"It's just a break. Fuck, who am I kidding? I don't think Liam ever even thought we were together. How pathetic is that? I feel so stupid."

"Aw, Karen." Tears had welled up in her eyes. I hugged her long enough for my shoulder to get damp. "Liam's a complicated guy."

She sniffed and wiped her nose on my sleeve. "Yeah, right. He's a regular Henry David Thoreau."

"Who?"

"This guy. Never mind. Christ, look at you." She poked my chest and squeezed my arm. "You getting ready for the Ironman or something?"

"I've been working out with M.T. It's like having my own personal trainer."

"I told you, Derrick's a good guy. So he hasn't given you any problems?"

I filled up a watering can at the kitchen sink, and told Karen about Derrick's fiancée and Thump Night. "Oh my god, Daniel," said Karen, "I am so sorry. Why didn't you say something?"

"What was I supposed to say: 'Hey kids, keep it down'? It's okay. He alphabetized our CD collection by the way. He also scrubs down the washroom at least twice a week. I think he's a little OCD. Anyway, after that first night, I've been pulling Saturday nightshifts at the group home. The pay is good. They like me there."

"You're in your element, aren't you?"

"At the group home?"

"Yeah. You get to be in charge and take care of everyone."

"I suppose so. Except the sheets all have cum stains all over them, all the time."

"Really? And you're not used to this?"

"Ha-ha. Funny, Karen." I misted the giant fern Karen and I had bought our first week in Toronto. "You know, Pat once said I was like Winston Churchill. Pat's always been this huge goof-off, right? But last Christmas, he actually thanked me for taking charge and keeping us in line. I never thought he noticed."

"Of course he noticed, we all did. You were always kind of like an uptight parent around Liam and Pat."

"What do you mean, 'uptight'?"

"That's why I'm so good for you. We complement each other. We balance each other out."

"I'm not uptight."

"Okay. If you say so."

I spritzed her with the mister. "Don't do that. You're doing it again."

"What?"

"Patronizing me."

"I'm not patronizing you. I just said you were uptight, and you don't think you were. And that's that. It wasn't an insult. Uptight is good, sometimes. It's being responsible. Taking charge, like you said. Mist me again, it feels good."

I spritzed her again. "'Uptight' and 'responsible' are not synonyms."

"Fine. Daniel, whatever you say. So are you going to make me a drink or what?"

"It's three in the afternoon."

"It's Friday. It's Pride Weekend. I just got off a five-hour bus ride. I've been living on a farm on a rez on an island these last six weeks. I'm here to party."

"Next summer you're staying in Toronto."

"We'll see. First things first. There's still this summer." Karen rummaged in her suitcase and pulled out a box of Vachon cakes and a 60 oz. bottle of vodka. "Happy Pride, sexy guy." She threw the box at me. "That's for you. This is for me. You ready to rock 'n' roll?"

"I was born ready."

"Bring it."

⌒ In Toronto, people would regularly ask if Karen was my girlfriend. When I said no, sometimes they'd ask if I had a boyfriend. Then I'd also say no. When girls flirted with me, I was friendly but never flirted back. When boys hit on me, sometimes I'd sleep with them. But it was never the same as it'd been with Stephan Tondeur.

Pride that summer with Karen was fun but a little underwhelming. I realized I wasn't into crowds of a million people decked out in Speedos and feather boas, water-guns and ear-piercing whistles. That Sunday after the Yonge Street Parade, we ended up in a beer garden in Cawthra Park next to the AIDS Memorial, with a bunch of straight friends Karen had made during her first year of school. Like McNeil-Tsao, they were all students at OISE studying to become teachers. When I went to line up for more drink tickets, a stocky bleached blond named Chris chased after me. "This is fuckin' crazy, eh?" he whooped. His face was all sunburnt, and he was wearing rainbow tattoos on his forehead and cheeks.

"Yeah. Definitely."

"So, how long have you two known each other?"

"Karen and me? Since we were seven."

"Wow. It's like you're soul-mates."

"Sure."

"Did the two of you, like, play with Barbies together when you were kids?"

"Well. Let's just say I started surfing gay porn around the same time you guys starting surfing straight porn."

"You don't look gay. I mean, you know, like gay. I mean, you know what I mean, right?"

"No, Chris, I don't know what you mean."

"Sure you do."

"No, I don't."

"Aw, come on, buddy. You know what I mean."

"No, really, I don't know what you mean. Unless, you're talking about those flaming faggots over there." I pointed out two topless twinks decked-out in pink leotards and faux-fur leg-warmers. "I suppose I'm not that into the glitter. Did you say you're going to be a teacher?"

"Yep," Chris said nodding, "that's the plan. I'll have the children of the future in the palm of my hand." I'd paid for my tickets and now he was following me towards the bar like a big, blond St. Bernard. "That DJ's the bomb." He snapped his fingers and thumped his chest. "He's amazing! I can feel it right here. It's kinda like tribal what he's spinning, you know what I mean?"

I paused and watched the DJ for a moment. About a hundred people were dancing around the raised booth and speakers set up beneath the trees. "That's a woman."

"Oh shit, right. You're right. Wow. She's pretty cool."

"Yes. She is."

"Hey, so like, I've seen some gay porn too, you know."

"What?"

"You were talking about surfing porn, straight porn gay porn popcorn." He laughed at his own pun. "I've seen some gay porn."

"You mean lesbian porn."

"No, I mean, like, gay porn. Guy-on-guy stuff."

"Okay."

"It's hot."

"Alright. I'm glad you think so."

"You're pretty hot."

"Thanks." I pretended to puzzle over this for a moment. "So, are you into the glitter?"

"No." Chris blinked. "I'm not into the glitter."

"Oh, well. I guess that's settled, then."

"Well, hold on. Just cause I'm not into the glitter doesn't mean twat."

"Doesn't mean what?"

Chris hiccoughed, looking confused. Abruptly he burst into laughter and clapped me on the shoulder. "You are so fucking with me, man!"

"No. You're fucking with yourself."

"Hey, look, did I just offend you? If I did, Daniel, I apologize. I've a few drinks. I also dropped some E. I'm sorry. Honest. Really, I am."

"And what are you apologizing for?"

He stared at the DJ, and then back at me. "I don't know. Is that really a woman? Here, let me get that for you." He slapped three drink tickets on the counter. "Seriously, buddy, it's on me. Let me make it up to you."

"No, it's okay."

"C'mon, man."

"No, really."

"I absolutely positively insist."

"Okay. Thanks."

"No problem. It's all Happy Pride, right?"

"It's all Happy Pride."

"Happy gawddamn fuckin' Pride!" Chris stuck out his elbow, almost hitting me in the face, and downed half his plastic beer cup in one long quaff. I picked up my two drinks and started back towards the others. "So Daniel, how come a guy like you doesn't have a boyfriend?"

"I guess I haven't met him yet."

"Hey, how would you know him if you did meet him?"

"I guess I might not know right away."

"So you might really have met him already, and you just haven't realized it yet."

"Maybe."

"What do you look for in a guy?"

I stopped and turned to face Chris. I imagined punching him hard in the head and songbirds circling as he went down. Instead, I shrugged. "The same thing straight guys look for in girls, Chris."

"Fuck off," Chris grinned. "A big ass and big tits?"

"That's right. And don't forget nice teeth. And really nice toes."

"Nice teeth. Right. Nice toes, I never thought about that."

Someone bumped into me and beer sloshed over both my wrists. I closed my eyes momentarily and drew a breath. "Chris, you seem like a nice guy."

"Thanks. Look, can I kiss you?"

"What?"

"Can I kiss you?"

"I'd rather not."

"Okay, just asking. I really. Wow. I can't believe I just said that."

"Don't worry. I'm not offended. As I was saying, Chris, you seem like a nice guy."

"I am a nice guy."

"I believe you."

"I'm not an asshole."

"You're not an asshole."

"I'm not."

"I never said you were. You're a friend of Karen's."

"Kind of. I'm actually with her friend Megan. That's my girlfriend. I don't think Karen actually likes me very much. I think it was something I said about Indians in class once. But I love the Indians. They're the First Peoples, right? Rock on, First Peoples. Number One People."

"Right. Look, Chris, I need you to focus. Look at me. I need to tell you something."

"What?"

"I have a brother who'd love to meet you. Karen knows him. His name's Pat. I think the two of you would hit it off."

"Does he look like you?"

"He's my triplet brother. I have two brothers. We're fraternal triplets."

"No shit! I didn't know that. Are you all gay? That's freaky."

"No, Chris, just me. Karen's dating my other brother."

"Pat?"

"No, my youngest brother Liam. Or she used to. I'm the oldest."

"You're the oldest. Fuck, buddy, that's funny."

"Fuckbuddy, I'm glad you think so."

"Fuckin' A!"

"Fuckin' A. Happy Pride, Chris. Cheers."

"Cheers!"

He leaned in to kiss me and I barely sidestepped in time. As it happened, we knocked heads. At that moment, Karen appeared. "Hi!" she said brightly. "Is that my beer? Thanks. Chris, Megan wants to talk with you. She's over there. Go. Bye-bye. Go."

Chris stumbled off through he crowd. Karen peered

at me over the rim of her cup. I shaded my eyes, taking in the mass of half-naked people drinking and dancing and having a good time. Nearby, the two twinks in leg-warmers were blowing whistles as loudly as they could, pumping their fists and bouncing up and down like they were on invisible trampolines.

"I'm sorry about him," Karen said.

"So am I. What took you so long?"

"You seemed to be doing fine."

"Right."

"You wanna get out of here?" I just stared at her. Karen nodded. "Let's get out of here."

And so we did.

∽ On a Saturday early in September, I sat in the waiting room of the Hassle Free Clinic. I'd known about this place for a while, but this was my first visit. Other guys were sitting around reading magazines and trying to look casual, checking each other out without making it look like they were checking each other out. I was one of them. I kept worrying I might recognize someone or someone would recognize me. But that didn't happen. Thirty minutes later, someone called out my first name and I was escorted down a hall into an examining room. A male nurse sat me down and closed the door. He glanced up at me soberly. "So, Daniel, it says here you're nineteen years old." His name-tag said FRANCISCO.

"Yes, I am."

"You look older." He set aside my chart. "You can call me Frank. I'm a nurse here at the clinic."

"Hi Frank."

"You've scheduled an HIV test with us. You've also indicated you think you might have an STI?"

"I've been having these symptoms. It hurts every time I urinate. It's like a burning sensation. It's been going on for about three days now. I think I have chlamydia."

"How long have you been sexually active?"

"Since I was seventeen."

"And this is your first visit to a sexual health clinic?"

"That's right."

"I see your family doctor's back in Sudbury. Okay. Well, this should be no problem. We can open a file for you. We'll test you for all the STIs today. We'll just need to take a blood and a urine sample. We can also treat you for your symptoms. You're likely right about an STI. It could be either gonorrhoea or chlamydia. It sounds like you've done your homework, so you'll know both are treatable with antibiotics. Was there a particular reason you've requested an HIV test?"

"No. I mean, I don't think I've been exposed. But I've never been tested, and I thought I should. Just to be on the safe side. I hope that's okay."

"That's fine. In fact, if you're sexually active, you should be getting tested regularly."

"I hear you have the rapid testing here."

"We have the rapid HIV test, that's right. You can get your results within a few minutes. There are a few points I'd like to go over with you first, Daniel, just to make sure you understand what's involved."

"Okay."

By the time I was done at Hassle Free, it was still early

in the afternoon. I walked out of the building not really thinking about where I was going. I cut through the Ryerson Community Park. Fall classes were starting up Monday and the campus was crowded with students, professors and shirtless joggers. I got myself a large Tim Hortons coffee, wandered across Yonge-Dundas Square and ended up in the Eaton Centre where I bought a burger in the food court and put on my headphones.

A few tables away, a young couple was trying to feed a one-year-old baby. The kid had food all over its face and wouldn't stop crying. The father was wearing a Raptors tank top, a gold chain, and studs in his ears. He was also sporting a wedding ring. I wondered what sex was like between him and his wife. As I watched, the girl unbuttoned her blouse and started breastfeeding the baby who quieted down right away. The young father looked embarrassed and turned his back. Then I think he caught me watching. I pretended to text on my phone. After a minute, I noticed him checking out some school girls strutting past in high heels with their shopping bags. Unselfconsciously, he spread his legs, grabbed his crotch and adjusted himself. This time, I was sure he caught me watching. Then I wondered if he'd ever fantasized about another guy going down on him. His mouth looked beautiful. I pictured him in the shower after a game of pick-up, soaping himself up and fingering himself. I imagined coming up behind him, my hands gripping his hips, and the expression on his face as I pushed him up against the tiled wall and fucked him up the ass, slowly and deeply for the first time in his life. Maybe, like McNeil-Tsao, this guy got fucked all the time by his wife who happily strapped on a dildo every weekend after they put the baby to sleep. I figured there were a lot of people like McNeil-Tsao, or Chris, or even my brother Pat. But most guys just didn't talk about it.

When I got home, Karen was still unpacking her suitcase and the boxes in her closet where she'd stored her stuff over the summer. "How was shopping?" she asked.

I kicked off my sneakers. "Alright. The Eaton Centre was a three-ring circus. All these kids and their moms getting ready for school. I bought you something. It's a welcome-back present."

"Let me see," Karen said eagerly. I handed her a plastic Old Navy bag. I'd already taken off the price tag. It was a black-and-white knit toque with a giant pom-pom and a skull-and-crossbones pattern. "I love it!" She put it on in front of the closet mirror. "Thank you." She kissed me on the cheek.

"I got tested today."

"You what?"

"I made an appointment at a sexual health clinic. I thought I'd get tested. You know."

"And?"

I remembered waiting for Frank to come back with the results, sure I was okay, my palms sweating. "I'm negative," I said. "I'm good. The STI results will take a few more days."

Karen rested her hands on my shoulders at arms length. "Good boy." She studied my face. "Was there a reason you got tested?"

"No, not really. I just wanted to be sure."

"You've always used protection, right?"

I nodded. Karen ran her fingers through my hair. "You need a haircut. Are you seeing anyone?"

"Seeing anyone?"

"Sure. Is there any special boy in your life I should know about?"

I considered all the guys I'd met in bars and on-line. I'd gone out on dates with a few of them. At the start of the summer, McNeil-Tsao had even said if there was someone I wanted to bring home, he'd clear out and give me space. "No," I said, "there's no special boy."

"Liam and I, we're going to give it another try."

"What do you mean?"

"I'm saying we're together again."

"You sure about this?"

"Daniel." Karen sighed, and tossed the hat aside. "Of course I'm not sure." She started sorting bras and underwear in her dresser drawers. "But it's what we've decided, alright? He found a job out on Manitoulin, by the way. I thought you'd be happy for me."

"I am happy for you, the both of you. You're good for him. What's he doing on Manitoulin?"

"Working on my aunt's farm. They were needing a farmhand. He really loves it out there. He's still going to live at home. Your grandfather's loaned him his truck."

"That's a long commute."

"He plans on buying his own Jeep."

"And how was your summer?"

"It was interesting. I met a lot of good people. I think next summer I might work out there too. They might be able to secure some grant money and create a position for me at the Ojibwe Cultural Foundation. My aunt sits on their council."

"You're going to leave me again?"

"You're a big boy, Daniel. I trust you. Anyway, hello, I just got back. We've still got eight months ahead of us."

"I'm glad you're back. M.T.'s a nice guy, but he's a little intense. I don't think I want to see another smoothie the rest of my life."

"You want to go hit a patio? Grab a cheeseburger and a pitcher? Do a few shooters and cap off the summer?"

"Can we also get Creamsicles and sweet potato fries with spicy mayonnaise?"

"Yes," Karen said, her dimples showing, "we can also get Creamsicles, and sweet potato fries with spicy mayonnaise. I think I'll wear this too. What do you think?" She put the hat I'd bought her back on. She was wearing cut-off jeans and a tank top with a screen print of Leonard Cohen on the front.

"Perfect. Very hipster. I missed you."

"Me too." She leaned over, took my face between her hands and kissed me on the nose. "Me too."

CHAPTER THREE

Constant Craving

Our apartment was the first floor of a house just north of Little Italy in the downtown west end. It was a fifteen minute bike ride to campus, twenty minutes by streetcar in the winter. Little Italy and Queen Street West had become our regular haunts, a funky mash-up of indie outlets and galleries, bars and cafés. The Centre for Addiction and Mental Health at Ossington and Queen attracted a colourful array of personalities. Sometimes Karen and I would cycle all the way out past Roncesvalles and spend a whole afternoon lounging and wandering the trails in High Park. I figured if Liam ever visited us, High Park's four hundred acres could be his home away from home.

That September I started seeing a guy named Sean, a part-time DJ at the Drake Hotel. Over the summer, we kept spotting each other in the neighbourhood at random events and locations. He finally remarked on the coincidence one day while we waited side by side for our orders at Smoke's Poutinerie. He was thin, bordering on skinny, but had the most beautiful big brown eyes. He'd spent his childhood in Dublin before moving to Canada, and the lilt in his speech hadn't entirely gone away. I thought it was the sexiest thing in the world.

On our first date, we went to a matinée and spent the afternoon at Little Nicky's Coffee. We talked about how polite Canadians were, the defunct rave scene (which I knew nothing about), David Bowie and Eighties rock (which we both knew a little bit about), and hockey (which he knew nothing about). On our second date, we saw his friend play at the Poetry Jazz Café in Kensington Market, got drunk on gin and tonics, went back to his place and had sex. On our third date, Sean let me into his inner sanctum: he took me shopping for LPs. Our first stop was Sonic Boom, a warehouse record store up in the Annex. I observed him from a distance as he flipped through the jazz section, sporting his silver rings and bell-bottoms, tapping his foot to some invisible beat only he could hear. I'd never met anyone quite like him in my life. Standing in line at the check-out, he asked if I was seeing other guys. When I told him I wasn't, he nodded thoughtfully.

"Are you seeing other guys?" I asked.

"I don't know, Danny. Should I still? What do you think?"

In that moment, I wanted to fall to one knee and burst into song, professing my crush on this boy who poured music out of his soul like a mountain spring in May. Instead, I fumbled and dropped my change purse and coins scattered underfoot, rolling everywhere.

After we left the store, Sean slung his jean jacket over his shoulder and looked me squarely in the eye. "You didn't answer my question," he said.

"I know," I said. "No. I don't think you should be seeing other guys."

His eyes sparkled. I felt like I was in a Disney movie. "Alright, Danny. So it is." He reached out and gently pinched my ear. He liked playing with my ears. A week earlier, after an evening of Oscar Peterson tributes, when he was on his back and I was gripping his ankles, he'd reached out with one hand and held onto my ear while furiously jacking off with the other. Then I leaned over and kissed him open-mouthed, tasting gin and lime. When he came, ribbons of cum splayed across his chest hitting him in the face. The gesture was a little bit strange and my ear was sore afterwards, but I didn't complain. To each their own. For such a small guy, he certainly shot the hugest loads. Maybe one day, I figured, I might ask him to wear a jockstrap.

Sean and I had been seeing each other over a month when one morning I spotted him having pancakes with another boy. I was about to tap on the window when I noticed Sean smile, reach out and stroke the boy's ear. Their hands rested on each other's knees. Then I walked into the diner and introduced myself. Sean immediately turned bright red, but it was his boyfriend who had the meltdown. Apparently they'd been together over a year. He started in on Sean, and was still ranting when I turned my back and walked out. I never was one to make a scene. Part of me hoped Sean would chase after me, but that never happened. If he had texted or called, I would've sat down and talked with him. But that never happened either. Sean had almost a thousand friends on Facebook. That evening, I was scrolling through, trying to find out who exactly this other boy was when, without warning, I found myself cut off from his Facebook page. I'd never been blown off before, not like this, and I was stunned.

"What the hell?" Karen, sitting next to me at the time, exclaimed. "Did he just unfriend you?"

"I think he just unfriended me."

"No way."

"Wow."

"What a total douchebag."

I set aside the tub of Häagen-Dazs ice cream we'd been sharing, and flopped back on my bed. I felt dazed.

Karen knelt beside me. "When's he spinning next?" she demanded.

"What?"

"When is he DJing next at the Drake?"

"Why do you ask?"

"We should go. You and I, we should go. We'll dress ourselves up and sit cozy close. We won't talk to him. We'll just have a drink. What do you think?"

"No, Karen. I'm not really into that kind of drama."

"Who said anything about drama?"

"It's drama. It's fucking gay drama. I don't want to have anything to do with it. I'm tired of it. It's juvenile and stupid and there's no way, okay?"

Karen sat back. I'd never spoken to her this way before. "Sorry."

I held her hand and closed my eyes.

"You really liked this boy, didn't you?"

I sighed. "I suppose." I listened to the clock ticking on the wall. "The next time we were going to do it," I confessed, "I was planning to have him wear a jockstrap."

"Sweetheart."

I pointed at a bag on the dresser. Karen pulled out the jockstrap in its unopened box. "You still have the receipt here. You want me to return it?"

I nodded, then shook my head. "No. Thanks. It doesn't matter." I sat up. "I'm over it."

"Here." Karen scooped up a spoonful of Rocky Road and fed me. "He's obviously got issues. Good riddance, right? You're too good for him, Daniel. You can do so much better than a scene-ster like him. He didn't deserve you. There's plenty more in the sea."

By the time Karen finished feeding me all the rest of the ice cream, I actually was feeling better.

I never did like jazz music anyway.

⌒ Late in October, I found myself out in High Park. It was unseasonably warm, what people called an Indian summer. The black oaks and maples had begun to turn fiery yellow and red, but the sun was blazing hot and the grass still lush beneath the carpet of fallen leaves. I'd brought my collapsible MEC camping chair and was working on a school assignment on my laptop. I'd set myself up on a slope overlooking Grenadier Pond; maybe a dozen others like myself were out enjoying the rare weather. I'd taken off my shirt and pulled my baseball cap low over my face. I noticed two men sunbathing close by. They were older, maybe in their early thirties, clearly a couple. I watched one massage sunblock into the other's back. If passers-by noticed, nobody seemed to care. Now I put on my sunglasses, mainly so I could spy on them more closely while I worked. After a while, one of them got up and walked barefoot over to me and asked for a light.

"Sorry." I squinted up at him. "I don't smoke."

"Okay." He smiled and returned to his companion, tucking the cigarette behind his ear. They exchanged a few words and he lay back down again. I was acutely conscious of the fact that he hadn't approached any of the others on the hillside. I wasn't sure what to think. I did know that the moment he'd approached me, I'd gotten an uncomfortable hard-on inside my cargo shorts. They were both put together in a lean and coiffed, metrosexual kind of way. Not the usual kind of person I'd be attracted to. I shifted in my duct-taped chair and adjusted myself as discreetly as I could. Thirty minutes later the two got up and left. The first man nodded pleasantly in my direction. Then he retrieved his cigarette and his companion lit it for him. They disappeared, strolling through the luminous trees along the path by the pond.

A Chinese family arrived and settled noisily in their place. Mom and grandma unpacked the cooler while dad and uncle set up beach umbrellas and lawn chairs. Grandpa bounced a baby on his knee, grinning toothlessly. When the older kids started tossing a bright neon Frisbee back and forth, I gathered my belongings and left.

The path by the pond led northward along the secluded edge of the park. I strolled with the sun at my back, encountering the occasional jogger or dog-walker. The truth was, I'd never deliberately gone cruising in a public place before in my life. The closest I'd come was the Robarts Library stacks a year ago, and I hadn't even ventured into the washroom then. Karen would regularly point out cute boys while grocery shopping or at the laundromat, but I simply wasn't confident at meeting people on my own. On a few occasions, when Karen was away during the summer, I'd go into the Village close to last call, and let some usually older guy pick me up. But most of the time, when I was feeling particularly horny, I'd watch porn at home and jack off in a peremptory fashion like regular people did.

This afternoon, the pond was full of geese and ducks. Black squirrels roamed through the underbrush and on the boughs overhead. I followed a narrow trail branching off the wide path, which led me deeper into the heavily wooded interior. The sunshine through the leaves cast everything in a golden, flickering light. I deliberately kept my shirt off and tugged my shorts lower over my hips. I felt exposed and vulnerable, and subtly thrilled. Furtively, I smelled my armpits to make sure my deodorant was still working. I kept my eye out for any sign of the two men. I'd never hooked up with a couple before, and I wondered if I was getting myself into any kind of danger. I thought of *American Psycho*'s Patrick Bateman with his perfect physique and bone-coloured business card. I imagined Karen reporting me missing and the police finding my body weeks later, decomposing and covered in frost, stuffed into the hollow of some fallen log. Utter ignominy.

Eventually, the trail led out of the woods onto a paved road near a baseball diamond. My little adventure was over, I was back in civilization. I had to admit, I felt disappointed. There'd been no sign of anyone looking for sex, much less the two men. For years, I'd heard about cruising in parks, but it remained as mysterious to me as ever. I drank from my water bottle, put my shirt back on and headed up the road to the parking lot where I'd locked up my bike. I was securing my helmet when a red BMW rolled up next to me. Cigarette Guy leaned his head out the passenger window and asked mildly: "You sure you don't have a light?" His teeth were perfectly white and straight.

I swallowed and let my hands fall to my side. "I might," I said without thinking.

He looked at his companion and back at me. "Okay." He nodded. The trunk hood popped open. "Why don't you throw your bike in the back?"

Then I realized this man looked exactly like Bateman from *American Psycho*. The thought flashed through my mind that I'd stow my $80 Kijiji bike in the trunk of their $80,000 BMW only to have them drive off in a cloud of exhaust. I imagined a storage unit in the basement of their penthouse where they kept dozens of bikes and skateboards like trophies. Maybe it was some weird fetish of theirs, and these two would have sex down there with young guys covered in bicycle grease, tying each other up in makeshift slings fashioned from inner tubes. When I didn't move, he glanced at the obvious bulge in my shorts and back up at my face. "We haven't got all day."

"Aah," I mumbled. "I've got to go." I started riding away. Even though I wasn't pedalling so hard, I could feel my heart thumping. The red BMW pulled back up alongside and slowed. I kept pedalling and forced myself to keep looking straight ahead. I was prepared to be sideswiped or to be cursed out or to have a handful of money waved at me. But the car accelerated past and disappeared ahead around the bend, scattering a flock of seagulls. I braked and pulled over onto the grass. "Holy shit," I muttered under my breath. "Holy shit." I felt dizzy. Something wet hit the side of my helmet. When I touched it, my fingertips came away sticky and white. A bird had crapped on me.

Later that evening, when I told Karen everything that had happened, she said it was good luck.

"Good luck?"

"When a bird poops on you, it's good luck. Didn't you know that?"

"Is that like some native superstition thing?"

"No, Daniel, it's just some thing. Everyone knows that."

"Oh, gee, well then." I sat back on the couch and folded my arms. "Is that all you can say?"

"What I'm saying, is that maybe you were lucky today. Those two could have kidnapped you, drugged you and had their way with you. Daniel, you have to be careful. Something awful could've happened."

"You really think so?"

"I have no idea. They also could've been really nice, normal guys who just wanted to pick up a cute boy. They might've served you champagne in their roof-top hot tub and driven you home with a swag bag."

"Normal people don't drive BMWs," I mumbled. I didn't tell her I thought Christian Bale was on the down low in Toronto with his secret male lover.

"Normal people actually do a lot of things, Daniel, believe it or not."

"What's that supposed to mean?"

"It means who are we or anyone to say what's normal?

Everyone and everything's normal at some point in time and place. What's not normal is simply whatever the people in power at the time happen to say is not normal."

"I think Christian Bale is on the down low in Toronto with his secret male lover."

"What?"

"Never mind."

That evening, I fantasized I was Dick Grayson on a date with Bruce Wayne, wantonly seduced in the underground chambers of his secret lair. My life was so boring, I could hardly believe myself. I wished I could be more like my brother Pat, fronting a rock band, backpacking around the world, having wild sex and getting tattooed. Even Liam was following his passion, building fences and smoking salmon out on a native reservation close to nature, away from all the mendacity and mundaneness of human civilization.

Karen had said I was uptight, and the truth was she was right. I'd spent half my life working to keep our family together and safe. Growing up, I don't think Pat or Liam had any idea how close we came to being taken away by child welfare. I played by the book, toed the line and did what I was told. Our social worker was a burnt-out bitch who had it in for Grandpa, watching our family like a hawk for any reason she could use to have us three boys removed. The day we turned sixteen, that danger was over. Except, I still kept following the rules. It was like that with hockey, with school and work, and it was still like that with life. I was tired of playing by the rules. I promised myself: the next time someone invited me for a ride in their BMW, I would get in.

⌒ That winter in Toronto, I discovered bathhouses. I'd never heard of them before, and after doing some research, I was shocked that I'd never heard of them before. Most of them were clustered around the Gay Village, and in early December, I found myself walking through the front doors of one shortly after midnight. Earlier that night, at a bar called Woody's, I'd met a young guy named John from out of town. He told me he'd rented a room just a couple blocks away. He was sweet and wholesome looking, with a scruffy beard and the nicest laugh. Even after we passed through the big oak doors with their brass handles, I had no idea where we were. Only when John flashed his pass at the caged booth and slid a bill over, did it slowly begin to dawn on me we weren't in the Holiday Inn. Some transaction was conducted, a buzzer sounded and John opened a second set of doors. "You coming?" Men were lining up behind us and giving me looks. I followed him in.

I found myself in what appeared, at first glance, to be a typical downtown lounge. Couches were arranged comfortably in front of a big screen TV. Guys were standing around chatting, reading the paper, even playing pool. Everyone was nude except for white towels around their waists. Baskets of condoms lined the bar. In my winter jacket, I started to sweat. I took off my toque. The bartender handed John a neatly folded towel and a numbered key, both of which he passed on to me. "Here," he said. "C'mon." He led the way out another door into a confusing array of dimly-lit stairwells and hallways. I could hear showers running and the interactions of other patrons. The place was labyrinthine, with a seemingly endless series of identical doors. Eventually, John keyed open one door, revealing what looked like a miniature dorm room, just large enough to hold a bed and a dresser closet. He hung up his coat. "You okay?" he asked, reaching out and patting my arm.

I was still standing in the doorway, clutching my toque. "We're in a bathhouse."

"We are."

"I've never been in a bathhouse."

"Oh shit." John squeezed my shoulder. "I am so embarrassed. I. I just thought you knew."

"Why would I know?"

"I told you I'd rented a room."

"I thought you meant a hotel room."

"Look, Daniel. Look, I'm not wanting to get it on with random guys. I stay here when I'm in Toronto because it's more convenient and cheaper than a hotel. I like you. I liked you the first moment I set eyes on you. I just want to be with you tonight." He caressed the side of my neck.

I thought to myself, if he touched my ear I was leaving. But he didn't. Instead, he pulled me in and kissed me gently. Then he kissed me again. By the time he kissed me a third time, I was inside and he'd closed the door behind us. It was warm, but we took our time taking off our clothes. He had the softest skin, and he smelled nice. By the time we were finally naked, I felt I knew every part of his body. We didn't have anal sex, but we jacked each other off. After that, he spent ten minutes playing with my cum, spreading it over my nipples, tracing it along my collar bones and jaw, and my lips. He had me suck it off his thumb, which was something I'd never done before. That got me hard again. Then he lay between my legs, cradling my hips, stroking and kissing me, using his fingertips and the tip of his tongue, until I finally came a second time. Afterwards, he asked if I wanted to go into the hot tub with him and I said I would.

By now, the place was practically crowded. There were men of all body-types, young and old, roaming the darkened hallways. Some would brush up against me in passing, but the overall ambiance was respectful and discreet. John and I washed ourselves first in a communal shower. The stinging water roused me from my drowsiness. The hot tub room was surprisingly tasteful, all marble and mirrors. We hung our towels on chrome hooks and gingerly waded in through the steam. Two other men were already in the tub. I wasn't sure if I should make eye contact with them or not, so I didn't. The water felt luxurious and we reclined side by side, savouring the penetrating heat of the jets at our backs. After a moment, John squeezed my hand and said he had to go pee and that he'd be right back. He wrapped himself in his towel and stepped out of the room.

One of the men across the tub had been staring at me for some time. Now I returned his gaze. My heart skipped a beat. I recognized his face. It'd been two years since we last saw each other. It was my old assistant hockey coach from Sudbury, Stephan Tondeur. "Daniel," he said in greeting. For one terrifying moment, I expected him to tell me that I'd ruined his life, that I'd broken up his marriage and left him destitute and alone, shunned by family and community. But he was smiling shyly, stunningly handsome as ever. "How have you been?"

"I ...," I said. "This is my first time here."

"That's okay, you don't have to explain. Was that your boyfriend?"

"Who? Oh, him, no. No, I just met him tonight." I mentally swore. That just made me sound like a slut. Then I asked: "Do you come here often?" and mentally cringed. That just made me sound like an idiot.

Stephan nodded. "Whenever I'm in Toronto. It's clean, the staff are friendly here. The bartender makes a terrific Caesar."

"Great."

"You're in school?"

"U of T."

"Good for you. How are you enjoying school?"

"It's good."

"What are you studying?"

"Arts and sciences right now. I'm not sure where I want to go with it yet."

Stephan raised his eyebrows. "Are you still playing hockey?"

"No."

"That's too bad."

"Are you still coaching AA?"

"In Sudbury? No. I've been too busy. The real estate market is booming. You might consider getting into it."

"How's your daughter?"

"She's two." Then I thought he might show me photos of her, but we were naked in a hot tub in a bathhouse. "We're getting her ready for pre-school. You have to understand, my wife doesn't know I come here."

"Okay."

"I better get going. It's really good to see you, Daniel.

I'm glad you're doing well." As he climbed out, I couldn't help but stare at his pendulous genitals, his muscular legs and enormous hands. All I wanted was for him to have reached out and touched me. I was aching to feel his hands on me. But he'd made no such gesture.

"Hey," I called out. At the entranceway, between two plaster urns containing fake plastic trees, he turned. "I still have it. The picture. Rocket Man. I've still kept it."

Stephan drew a breath. "I'm glad. Take care." He smiled sadly and waved in an oddly effeminate manner. Then he was gone.

After a few moments, an elderly gentleman across from me cleared his throat. "Old boyfriend?"

His watery eyes were sympathetic. I looked at him, and looked through him. "Yes," I finally said. "Yes."

John hadn't come back yet. I got out and went looking for him. There were open doorways and shadowy chambers full of half-naked men coming and going. I recognized the smell of poppers. Someone groped my ass. I got lost and found myself circling back. I kept my eyes on the floor, and shrank back against the walls so I didn't have to touch anyone. Eventually, I returned to our room. The door was open, a bright light was on and a cleaner was briskly remaking the bed. "Where's my stuff?" I asked.

"I beg your pardon?"

"This is my room. Where's all my stuff? Where's John?"

The cleaner pulled off his gloves and tossed them into a plastic bin on his cart. He shrugged. "I don't know who John is."

"I was here with a guy, his name was John. This is our room. Where's all my fucking stuff?"

"Sir, please lower your voice. The last person who rented this room checked out. I suggest you talk to someone at front desk."

Downstairs by the exit, there was a line-up of people leaving, turning in their keys. Everyone had their jackets and coats on. My hair was still wet. The towel kept slipping from my waist and I had to clutch it in one fist. Across the narrow hallway, laundry tumbled in half-a-dozen industrial-sized washing machines. The linoleum felt clammy and sticky beneath my bare feet. I had to wait five minutes before I could speak to a staff person with a mohawk. By that time, I was so upset, I was shaking.

Apparently I'd been given a key to my own locker. I kept trying to explain that I hadn't used any locker, and that all my stuff had been stored in John's room and now everything was gone, including all my clothes and shoes, my phone and wallet. I had nothing. Couldn't they understand that? I had nothing.

Mohawk Guy conferred with another staff person. "Look," he said, "do you want to make a phone call?"

"A phone call? It's like fucking four in the morning!"

"Sir, as I've pointed out already, we can't be responsible for lost or stolen items. We can let you use our phone. Is there someone you can call?"

I refused to cry. "Okay," I said as calmly as I could. "Okay. Let me make a phone call."

Mohawk Guy had someone replace him at the checkout counter, and escorted me into a small office space. I called Karen's cell and immediately got her voice mail. I tried again with the same result. I didn't leave a message. "Is there anyone else you can call?" Mohawk Guy asked.

Impulsively, I called my own phone and after five rings, got my own voice mail. I hung up.

"No," I said.

"Here." He rummaged out a T-shirt from a cardboard box. "You can wear this." I tore open the flimsy clear plastic and put it on. The desk phone rang and he picked it up. After a moment, he glanced at me sidelong. "What did you say your name was?"

"It's Daniel."

He handed me the phone. "It's for you."

It was John's voice on the line. "Daniel, where the hell are you?"

"Where the hell am I?" I shouted. "Where the fucking hell are you?"

A three second pause. "I'm in our room, where do you think I am? I couldn't find you anywhere. Your phone was ringing. I just pressed call-return."

"The room's empty, asshole. It's empty. I want my fucking stuff back."

"What room's empty? What are you talking about?"

"Room 303. It's empty."

"Our room is 305, Daniel. I'm sitting in room 305. Look, you're at front desk, right? Come on up. I'll wait here for you."

He hung up.

I put the phone down in its cradle.

Mohawk Guy held out a box of Kleenex. "You find your friend?"

"He's upstairs. I'd gone to the wrong room. He's in room 305."

"305." He folded his tattooed arms. "Well, I'm glad

that's worked out." He opened the door. "S'okay, you can keep the shirt. Cheers. Have a good night." I shuffled out of the office. I went up two flights of stairs and down a corridor where John was waiting in our room. 305.

"Where'd you get that T-shirt?" he asked.

"The staff gave it to me. Look, I thought you'd bailed on me. I thought you'd stolen all my stuff."

"Your things are right here where you left them. I'm not a thief, okay?"

"You didn't come back from the washroom."

"Yeah, well, it took a little longer than expected. All the washrooms were being used. When I came back, you were gone. This guy said you'd hooked up with someone else."

"I didn't hook up with anyone."

"According to him, you took off after your old boyfriend. You told him it was your boyfriend."

"What? No. What does he, no. I mean, yes, I met someone I used to know a long time ago. But I didn't take off after him. He left. I went looking for you."

"Right."

"You have to believe me."

"I'm tired. I think you should go."

"Wait, no. Not this time." I drew a deep breath and let it out again. "I fucked up. I am so sorry I called you an asshole. I'm sorry. What more do you want me to say? I don't want to leave. I really like you, John. I really like you. This is all a big misunderstanding."

"Daniel, I believe you. But what I really need right now is some sleep. I have a bus to catch tomorrow. I had a good time with you tonight, okay?"

"I'm sorry about what happened."

"Don't worry about it. Why don't you get dressed?" I dressed while he sat on the bed watching me. When I was ready to leave, in my snow coat and shoes, I went to kiss him, but he handed me my toque, stood back and held the door open. "Take care."

"Bye."

He closed the door in my face. I rested my forehead against the number 305. Two young guys in towels walked past, staring at me. I held out my arm and gave them the finger.

On my way out, I kept looking for Stephan Tondeur, but he was nowhere to be seen. Outside, a thin, drizzling rain was turning the snow to slush. I thought Stephan might be waiting for me, but there was no one but the cold and empty city.

I hailed a cab and went home.

CHAPTER FOUR

Underwhelmed

McNeil-Tsao was destroying me. Ever since he'd moved out at the end of summer, we'd continued to meet every Sunday afternoon for squash. He used to give me a five point advantage. I'd worked him down to two. But today I was throwing every game. "Move your feet," he kept shouting. "Keep your eye on the ball!" Eventually, he caught the ball mid-game, walked up to me and barked in my face: "Garneau, you're playing like a gawddamn school girl. You're better than this. What's up?"

I was dripping with sweat and it took me a moment to catch my breath. "Nothing," I mumbled. "Sorry. I didn't sleep much last night. I've got a lot on my mind."

"Alright. Well, tell me about it."

"You don't want to play?"

He opened his arms wide. "It's a mental game, Garneau. It's all up here. If you want to get better, you've got to work through what's up here. So what's up?"

"You wouldn't understand."

"Try me." He drank from his water bottle.

"It's about boys."

"Go on."

"Like I said, you wouldn't understand."

"You think just because I'm engaged to Rachel, I wouldn't understand the dating game? I've been dating, breaking hearts and getting my heart broken since I was nine years old. Don't insult me."

"Look, M.T., no offense, but it's a gay thing."

"So what? You think you gays are so different from everybody else? When my grandparents harass me to marry a nice Chinese girl, would I say to you, you wouldn't understand just cause it's a racial thing? You insult me and you're hurting my feelings, Garneau."

"M.T., c'mon."

"Fine. We're done here." He threw me a towel. "You hit the showers, I'm going to work on my core. I'll meet you at fifteen-thirty at the bar. I'm buying you a smoothie. We'll throw in some wheatgrass, and you are going to tell me all about it."

That afternoon, to my utter amazement, I found myself telling McNeill-Tsao everything, at least everything that mattered. Karen had always been my confidante, but it was different talking to another guy. It was also different talking to someone who had no investment whatsoever in my life. By the time we finished our smoothies, I felt lighter, like I'd gotten a huge weight off my chest.

"So," McNeil-Tsao said, "how come you didn't tell Karen about meeting this old hockey coach of yours?"

"I didn't want her to know I went to a bathhouse. I dunno. I suppose I'll tell her eventually. She'll probably want me to sneak her in, just so she could see for herself."

"That's the problem, Garneau. She's too involved. Sometimes a man's got to walk alone."

"What's that supposed to mean?"

"You're a mama's boy, Garneau. You let these guys walk all over you. You do that because you know whatever happens, no matter how shitty things get, you can always run back to Karen."

"That's not true."

"Fine. Prove it."

"I don't have to prove anything. Karen's my best friend. We tell each other everything."

"Did she tell you she was thinking of quitting school and moving to M'Chigeeng?"

"What?"

"Don't worry. I convinced her to finish her degree first. The point is, you don't tell each other everything. You tell her everything. She probably sits you down and feeds you ice cream while you tell her every single detail of every single date you've ever gone on."

"That's an exaggeration."

"She tells you what you want to hear. I'm telling you what you need to hear. Man it up, Garneau. Forget the cheerleading squad, and focus on your game. Things will get better when you do."

I thought of McNeil-Tsao's fiancée with her enormous tits, and how he liked to get it up the ass. There was a comeback in there somewhere. There had to be. But the truth was, it was all irrelevant. A week later, as Karen and I were packing, getting ready to catch a bus back to Sudbury for the holidays, she stopped and turned to me.

"Daniel, last Saturday, I got two missed-calls at three-thirty in the morning. You want to tell me about it?"

I froze. Her tone was mild, but I realized she'd been waiting all week for me to mention this. But she hadn't said anything until now.

"No," I said. I looked at her. "No."

To my surprise, Karen didn't press the issue. "Okay." She handed me a tiny parcel wrapped in Christmas paper. "Here. This came for you in the mail."

When I opened it, I discovered a single, brand-new squash ball in its box. A folded-up note read KEEP YOUR EYE ON THE BALL.

"What's that all about?"

"It's just a squash thing," I said, "between M.T. and me." And that's all I said.

⌒ That holiday season, Grandpa made arrangements to spend Christmas Eve overnight at the nursing home. He said he wanted to wake up Christmas Day next to Grandma. Apparently, last year was the first time he hadn't done that in fifty-five years. He wasn't about to let it happen again. Grandma's health was stable, but she simply refused now to leave the home. Traffic frightened her. I used to let her kiss me on the mouth whenever we hugged, until one day she grabbed my crotch and tried to slip me the tongue. Since then, I made sure to hold both her hands and offer my cheek whenever we said good-bye.

After dropping Grandpa off, Liam drove us home in the pickup truck. He'd bought his own used Jeep some months back, but had left it parked at the house. The house seemed different without Grandpa in it. Three days earlier, as was our tradition, all four of us had driven out past the airport, tramped into the woods and cut down our own tree. Now it scraped the ceiling of our living room, covered in gaudy ornaments, tinsel and strings of popcorn, and the same tiny, colourful lights we'd untangled every year when Mom and Dad used to be around. Liam had gotten himself a golden Lab that fall, a one-year-old rescue dog they'd found half-starved on Manitoulin. He told us the dog's name was Jackson, and warned us not to make any sudden movements around him and never to approach him from behind. As it was, Jackson stayed under Liam's bed almost the entire time Pat and I were there.

When we got home, Pat put on an old Loverboy album and prepared us all flaming sambuca shots with whiskey chasers. Pat had enrolled in Cambrian College that fall and was living downtown now with his new girlfriend.

"So where'd you meet this girl?" I asked.

"Blonde Dawn? Met her at the Battle of the Bands this summer. I was one of the judges."

"What? You were one of the judges? How the hell did you get to be one of the judges?"

Pat opened the back door and tossed Liam and me cold beers from the case we'd left outside. "You know someone who knows someone who knows someone." He kicked the door shut behind him. "Anyway, so this chick turns up playing drums for this all-boy band. The band sucks big time. She's awesome. We get to talking. She needs a roommate for September, so I move in."

"Just like that?"

"Totally. Check this out." He modelled the red, white and blue scarf he was wearing. "She knit this herself. She knew I was a Habs fan." Pat flicked his beer cap into the garbage bin. "She also makes this mean matzah ball and bakes the best rugelach you've ever tasted. She's the one who got me into the Paramedic program."

"So is she your roommate or is she your girlfriend?"

"Or your chef?" Liam asked.

"She's like my agent," Pat said, laughing. "How about that? She's my roommate with benefits. She's local, went to Lasalle. Blonde Dawn Singer. Two years ahead of us. Apparently, she knew who I was."

"Everyone in Sudbury," I said, "knows who you are, Pat."

Liam propped his feet up on the kitchen table. "'Blonde Dawn'?"

"She's blonde. At least up top. What can I say? All her friends call her Blonde Dawn."

The doorbell rang and we all answered it. Karen entered, stamping the snow from her boots. "Merry Christmas, yada yada yada. So are the Garneau boys playing nice? I hear there's no adult supervision in the house." She tossed her jacket onto the coatrack Grandpa had made from deer antlers, and helped herself to my beer.

Pat cranked up the stereo. "Now that you're here, Karen Fobister, we're feeling nicer than nice." He started swaying his hips. "You're looking spicy nice." He put on a Santa hat and held out a box of rum-filled chocolates. "Rumbly-filled chocolata, little girl?"

I followed Liam into the kitchen. "So how is Grandpa doing?" I asked.

"Fine." He handed me a fresh beer. "He's been spending more time up at the Good Medicine Cabin."

The Good Medicine Cabin was our nickname for the family cottage. It sat on forty acres, an hour north of Sudbury, land our great-great-grandfather had won on a dare back in the day (or at least that's how the family legend went). "On his own? How much time?"

"He'll go up on weekends. Sometimes, he'll go up for a week at a stretch, maybe longer."

"A week? Liam, are you sure that's safe?"

"What's not safe?"

"He's in the deep bush all by himself."

"Better not talk like that in front of him, Daniel. He's been going up to that cabin his whole life. He's two clicks from the highway. I'd hardly call that deep bush."

"There's no electricity or hot water. What if something happens to him? What if he has a heart attack or runs into a bear or the truck breaks down? I don't think he should be up there by himself."

Liam folded his arms. "You going to tell him that?"

"The least we can do is get him a cell phone."

"He won't use it. The cabin's his retreat. That's the whole point. Sometimes a man's got to walk alone." He sipped from his beer. "What is it?"

"Nothing," I said.

"A cell phone won't work up there anyway."

I picked tinsel and pine needles off my sweater. "Remember when we used to spend Christmases up at that cottage with Mom and Dad?"

"Of course I do."

"Us kids would camp out in our sleeping bags in front of the fireplace."

"Pépère would dress up like Santa Claus."

"That's right."

Liam cracked his neck and stretched. "Daniel, you should come up sometime."

"Naw. No thanks."

"You sure?"

"Yeah, I'm sure. How are the two of you doing anyway?"

"Pépère and me? It's all good. The garage roof was leaking, I fixed it. We got the furnace cleaned. Pat drops in now and then, mainly to do his laundry. Look, Daniel, I think I might move out to Manitoulin come spring."

"So I've heard. You talk to Grandpa about this?"

"He's the one who suggested it. I think he's actually looking forward to having some space on his own."

"Really?"

"Ask him tomorrow."

"What does he do up at the cottage anyway?"

"What he's always done. He takes the canoe out, shoots partridge, goes for walks around the property. Now that he's retired, he's got all sorts of renovation ideas for the place. I've been helping him out here and there. When the weather's warm, he goes naked."

"What?"

"Last September, I went up to visit. I was a day early. I spotted him from across the lake chopping wood in the buff."

"What did you do?"

"I pulled over, took off all my clothes, then drove up the rest of the way to meet him."

"You're kidding."

"I parked the Jeep a little ways away. Then I walked up the drive and said: 'Hey, Pépère, how's the fishing?'

We had a laugh over that. We never did put our clothes back on. We spent the whole weekend naked together."

"You're pulling my leg. This is something Pat would make up. You are so pulling my leg."

Liam shrugged. "You can think that if you want. But it's true."

"Grandpa." I shook my head in disbelief. "Grandpa's a nudist?"

"Daniel, he's the same grandpa we've always had. I'm thinking he's probably been doing this nudist thing since we were kids. For all we know, both he and Mémère might've been doing it together all their lives, before she got sick. You should try it sometime."

"Thanks, but no thanks. Ask Pat."

"Okay."

"Liam." I rubbed my temples. "You and Grandpa, you don't go around this house naked, do you?"

When Liam was drunk or high, it was almost impossible to tell. He'd just get quieter with a more focused look on his face. He regarded me intently. "Sometimes. Since that weekend, sure, why not?"

"You mean to tell me the two of you sit around, in this house, on our couch in our living room watching TV stark naked?"

"I don't watch TV, Daniel. Haven't watched TV in years."

"Aw, c'mon, Liam. You know what I mean."

"Maybe, like I said. Sometimes we might."

"Tell me you're joking."

"Were you joking when you told us you suck cock?"

My hands went numb. I remembered dropping my

gloves on the ice and punching Gary Kadlubek, the head coach's son, in the face.

"I didn't say I suck cock."

"You're right. In fact, the way I remember it, you didn't say anything. You just let Pat and Karen do all the talking. It's okay. I got over it. I'm okay with it. You're my brother. Pépère's Pépère. He's not hurting anyone, is he?"

"No," I said after a minute. "He's not hurting anyone."

"Pépère can take care of himself. We've all got our own lives to live. He's got the Good Medicine Cabin. What's important is that he's happy."

"What about Grandma?" .

"He's with her now, isn't he?"

I scraped my fingers through my hair. "Liam." I finished my beer and dropped the bottle in the recycling bin. "Liam. I'm sorry I never talked to you about this."

"Just don't get AIDS."

"Fuck, Liam! It's not like I'm some faggot whoring myself out to every shithead I meet."

"I never said that. It's just that Karen's father has AIDS."

"What?"

"In prison, They found out he's got full-blown AIDS. Probably from sharing needles."

"She never told me this."

"Don't tell her I told you. Let her tell you. She hasn't seen him in thirteen years. But she's been talking with him for a while. She just found out this fall."

"Since the fall? She's known for months?" I paced the kitchen. "Do the Miltons know?"

"Of course they do. They've been really supportive."

"And what about Anne?"

"Anne doesn't want to have anything to do with it. Look, don't tell Karen I told you, okay?"

"Fine."

Screaming and laughter erupted in the living room. The music was blasting, and Karen and Pat both had their pants off and were jumping up and down on the furniture, throwing pillows at each other. The curtains were wide open and I hurried to close them. A pillow hit me in the back of the head, knocking me to the floor.

Long after midnight, when Karen and Liam had retired, and Pat had gone to his room to text with his matzah ball girlfriend, I stayed downstairs on the couch, in the dark, by the blinking Christmas tree.

A shadow moved in the hallway. I was too drunk by now to be startled. Jackson peered around the corner and whined. I held out a pretzel. He crept forward, tail wagging tentatively. His nose was cool and damp against my palm. He ate the pretzel, lay down at my feet and sighed. On the stereo, Gordon Downie sang about Bobcaygeon and the stars in the sky.

I fell asleep. When I woke up just before dawn, the room was grey and cold. The timer had turned off the Christmas lights. Jackson had crawled up onto the couch and was curled up between my legs. He was twitching in his sleep, dreaming. I'd been dreaming too, but the dream was fading away like the aurora borealis. I held onto a fleeting image of Grandma as a young woman again and Grandpa as a boy, Josette and Tom, both of them stark naked and beautiful, laughing and running and catching snowflakes on their tongues. And it was joyful and it was golden. And it was Christmas Day forever.

⌒ From January to March, I dated a man named Charles Ondaatje. We'd met at a friend's New Year's Eve party. He was five years older than me, working on his PhD in psychology. At no point did we ever call each other boyfriends, but we spent every other weekend together and some weekday evenings too. We never argued. Sex was comfortable. He was clean and tidy, and rarely complained. He was tall, with limbs like pasta. When I explained this to Karen, she asked: "What kind of pasta?"

I thought about this for a while and said: "The kind that's round tubes."

"You mean penne?"

"No, I mean the bigger kind, the kind that you stuff."

"Cannelloni?"

"Yeah, that's it. Charles, he's like cannelloni."

"That," said Karen, perched up on the kitchen counter, "doesn't sound sexy." She was using nail polish to paint the cupboards with tiny, multi-coloured flowers. Outside, the snow fell thick in the bare trees and on the crowded sloping rooftops.

"I never said he was sexy. But cannelloni's like comfort food, it fills you up. It's nice. He's nice. I like it when he holds me. He lets me keep a toothbrush at his place."

"And what, pray tell, is this Charles stuffed with?"

"David Cronenberg."

"I beg your pardon?"

"He's the hugest David Cronenberg fan. There's a whole section in his research proposal where he talks about him."

"This is that horror director guy who made all those movies like *The Fly*, right?"

"Right."

"Okay. Well, some people would think that's a little creepy, but it's always good to keep an open mind. Does this Charles have any other interests?"

"Um, besides watching Cronenberg movies? No, not really."

"What do you do together?"

"Anything I want to do. Watch a game, go out to the movies, make a meal. He's a walking encyclopaedia. He knows his wines. I forgot to mention that. He can tell you all about beers and wines. He doesn't really drink though. He just likes talking about it. He's really caught up in his work."

Karen hopped off the counter, tightened the caps on the nail polish, and tossed the bottles back into a shoebox full of make-up. "And what is that?"

"Like I said, he's working on his PhD. His thesis is all about the breakdown of the human body and cybernetics, and, well, I'm not so sure."

"And you like this guy?"

I thought a moment before answering. "He's comfortable. He's safe."

"Daniel. Is that so important to you?"

"I can depend on him. Yeah, at this point in my life, that's important to me. You of all people should understand that."

"Okay," Karen said. "Okay." She stood back and appraised her work. "What do you think?"

Flowers framed the cupboard doors. Over the stove, a red-breasted robin perched on a ivy branch. "Nice."

"Check it out."

By the baseboards, she'd painted mushrooms which I hadn't noticed. "Whoa. Trippy."

"It's my secret garden."

"You want to meet him?"

"Oh, it's finally come to that?"

"Don't give me a hard time. So do you want to meet him or not?"

"Sure, look, why don't you have him over? I'll make dinner for the three of us. I'll make cannelloni."

"Be nice."

"I am nice. I'm spicy nice."

In the end, we decided to invite three additional guests. This was our first time hosting a dinner party and we spent a whole day shopping in Kensington Market for just the right ingredients. We got three different kinds of cheese and a liver pâté, fancy olive bread, and two magnums of Bordeaux. We even bought wine glasses and a tablecloth. I felt like we were kids playing at being adults.

Mike and Melissa, who were a couple living in the apartment above us, were the first to arrive. Melissa was a tall blonde, and a technician with CBC Radio. She was also five months pregnant. Mike was a supervisor in a youth shelter. When Charles came over, he brought a bottle of wine with an unpronounceable name which he took three minutes to explain standing in the doorway, before handing it over to Karen. Then he presented her with a vase of mixed flowers.

"Look at that," Melissa said, draped over Mike on the couch. "He brought a vase. That's so thoughtful. Don't you think that's thoughtful, Michael? When you're a host and people just bring cut flowers, and you're up to here in the kitchen, it's nice not to have to scramble to find a vase. It's nice." Mike nodded brightly and gave Charles a thumbs-up sign.

Charles gave me a sideways hug, appraising the apartment which I'd spent the afternoon tidying. He held up his arm and checked his watch. "Am I late?"

"No, you're right on time." As I hung up his overcoat, Karen's classmate Megan appeared. Charles sidestepped and stood at attention while Karen introduced her to the rest of us. "We've met before," Megan said, shaking my hand. "At Pride last year."

She was a short, mousy-looking girl with bright red lipstick and bright red mittens. "Of course," I said. "That's right." Then we gave each other an awkward hug. Silently, like a well-trained butler, Charles took her jacket.

"I'm sorry," she said, "about what happened."

"What happened?"

"Chris, last summer, he was acting like such a jerk. Karen, he's such a jerk. Don't you think he's such a big dumbass?"

Karen made a face. "Chris has issues." She served a glass of sparkling water to Melissa and a beer to Mike. "Classmate of ours. Megan and Chris used to date."

That evening, when the conversation turned to dating and relationships, Charles remained unusually quiet. Eventually, Melissa leaned across the table and squeezed his arm. "So Charles, you're the PhD psychology candidate. What do you think of all of this?"

Charles finished chewing and swallowing, and put down his knife and fork. "Well, as you've noted," he said carefully, "much of it is hormonal and biological. In many ways, we are slaves to our bodies. Take your pregnancy, for example. Your breasts are getting bigger and more sensitive, your vulva is becoming engorged from extra blood flow. With all that increased sensitivity, your sex drive could be fired up just about all of the time. This is not a choice, but a physiological state of affairs every pregnant woman has to cope with."

"Oh my god," said Melissa, sitting back in her chair. Michael's expression had gone blank. Karen cleared her throat. Megan let our a nervous twitter. Melissa looked from one of us to the other. "It's true," she declared. "My sex drive these last few months has shot through the fucking roof, pardon my French. Michael here can barely keep up. Isn't that right, Michael? It's like I've regressed to when I was a slutty teenager ready to sleep with the entire senior boys rugby team. And the senior girls rugby team, for that matter. Thank you, Charles." She gripped Mike's arm. "I'm pregnant, see, honey? I'm pregnant. I'm not crazy. This is normal."

Mike smiled in a tight-lipped fashion, and gave her a thumbs-up sign.

Charles sipped his wine. "This is a very nice wine, Karen."

"Why, thank you, Charles."

Charles set down his glass. "Have you tried a cock ring?" Mike's eyebrows rose. Megan choked on a piece of bread. Charles rested both palms on the tabletop. "If you're having a difficult time performing, Michael, certain drugs can help, but a cock ring might be a simple solution."

"Charles," I said, "I don't think anyone wants to hear about cock rings right now."

"Hold on," Melissa said, "I want to hear about this. What exactly is this?"

"Chris uses a cock ring," Megan declared breathlessly. "He's always had a hard time keeping it up. I always thought it was me, but then I heard his ex say the same thing."

"Oh honey, it's not you," Melissa said. "It's not you. You're beautiful, you're a sexy girl. If that boy of yours has a problem keeping it up, then that's a problem that boy's needing to work out. Of course, this doesn't apply to you, Michael, honey. I'm pregnant. This is an extraordinary circumstance you and I are dealing with. Now this cock ring device, you slip it on over the penis, isn't that right, to keep it erect?"

"You can do that," Charles said. "Although I'd recommend securing it around the base of the penis and the scrotum. Here let me show you." He wiped his mouth on a napkin and reached into his pants.

"Daniel," Karen said.

"Charles," I said.

Charles withdrew his smart phone and spent a moment surfing the Internet. "Here, like this." He handed the phone to Melissa. Her eyes widened and she started scrolling down. Charles glanced at me. "Wikipedia."

"Have you actually tried one of these?" Melissa asked.

"I've never needed to use one myself. My erections have always been quite healthy. Although, Michael, at your age, I'm sure yours are too. It's just that—"

"I'm pregnant," Melissa said. "That's what it comes down to. People don't talk about it, do they? But pregnant women become like whores. Honestly, I can't get enough. Look at this. We're getting one of these. Either that or a dildo. I used to own a dildo, back in college. It even had a vibrator built into it, and this thing that curled around."

"Oh," Megan said perkily, "I have one of those."

"Michael, what do you think? Look at this, it says here sometimes cock rings are even worn as genital jewellery." She handed the phone across the table to Megan. "Genital jewellery, who would've known? Well, Michael doesn't wear jewellery of any kind, but we'll make an exception in this case, won't we, honey?"

I counted to three, and Michael made his thumbs-up sign.

Later that evening, as the guests were leaving, everyone gave everyone big, long hugs. Dinner had been delicious. Charles offered to stay behind and help with the dishes, but I assured him Karen and I were fine to manage on our own. He kissed me on the cheek, and announced he was going to walk Megan to her streetcar stop. They left holding hands. I closed the door behind him.

"Well, for a first effort, I'd say that was a success," Karen said, pouring two large glasses of wine. She handed one to me and flopped down on the couch. "I'm exhausted. We're doing the dishes tomorrow." I lay down with my head in her lap. After a moment, Karen remarked: "He's nice."

"I'm breaking up with him."

"You're breaking up with him? Daniel, I just met him. I just cooked an entire three course meal for him."

"I'll do the dishes."

"He's nice."

"Then you date him."

"Or Megan can date him."

"He is bi, you know."

"Is he? I didn't know that. I'm not sure Megan knows that. He seemed kind of asexual to me." Karen wiped the pale lipstick from the rim of her glass. "He could use a different haircut. Does he have a big dick? He looks like he has a big dick."

"Yes, he has a big dick."

"He brought a vase."

"That's nice."

"You're really going to break up with him?"

"I've got you to be comfortable with, Karen, haven't I?"

"That's true."

"He'll be fine. He won't argue, he never does. I figure we can stay friends."

"Or friends with benefits."

"With Charles? I doubt it."

"If you say so."

The next time I met Charles, he told me he was breaking up with me. He and Megan had ended up sleeping together the night of the dinner party, and they were in love. He couldn't, in good conscience, continue to see me when he was in love with somebody else. He apologized for hurting me, and asked me if we might possibly stay friends, but if I needed time to think about it, that I should take all the time I needed. I let him know my feelings weren't hurt and congratulated him on being in love. I told him I thought Megan was a nice girl and wished them the best. Then Charles did something completely and utterly unexpected. He broke into tears and draped his big cannelloni arms around me. "I love you, man," he said. "I love you." Then he said: "Thank you" over and over again. I never would've guessed he had it in him. I patted him on the back, and told him he was a good guy and that he was probably the best thing that ever happened to Megan.

And I meant it.

CHAPTER FIVE

High For This

A fter school ended that year, I started working full-time again at Toronto Community Living. Karen moved back to Manitoulin where she'd gotten an internship at the Ojibwe Cultural Foundation. Both she and Liam were living on her aunt's farm. Pat moved in with me for the summer. He and his matzah ball girl-friend were apparently on a break. He said he needed to get out of Sudbury, and practically begged me to let him sublet Karen's room. He arrived on my doorstep in his battered backpacking gear, with his guitar in one hand and a case of Moosehead in the other.

That first weekend I figured I'd show Pat around town, and we made plans to go out Saturday night for a drink. I came home from work to find *Ricky Martin's Greatest Hits* cranked on the stereo. Two girls were dancing in my apartment, slicing avocados and going through my DVD collection.

"Who are you?" I asked, standing in the doorway holding my keys.

They immediately turned down the music and introduced themselves as Carolina and Yuko from Colombia and Osaka (respectively) and friends of Pat, and I must be his homosexual brother Dan. They were to have an extravaganza bonanza movie night and wanted to know if I would join them.

"Where's Pat?"

As if on cue, Pat arrived hefting two grocery bags, accompanied by a statuesque brunette balancing a two-four of Corona on her shoulder. "Hey big brother! I see you've met Yuko and Carolina. This is Sindija. She's from Latvia. Girls, meet my brother Dan."

I waved. "Hi."

Pat dumped the groceries on the counter. "When I spotted these beautiful ladies, I just had to help them out. I ran across Dundas Street and practically got creamed by a streetcar, isn't that right?"

"Creamy by streetcar." Yuko nodded emphatically.

"Help them out?"

"They were lost downtown looking for the Eaton Centre. And get this." Pat clapped me on the shoulder. "They all go to U of T."

"We are international students," Yuko explained, "in summer intensive at University of Toronto English Language Program."

Pat flung open his arms. "Dude, they're your classmates!"

"Pat, seventy thousand students go to U of T."

"Dan, Pat tells to us," Sindija said, handing me the two-four, "you are very good ice hockey player."

"Um, I used to play hockey, that's right."

"Sindija played goaltender two years," Pat said, "at the Latvian women's national level. Dan here was almost captain of his team. Isn't that right?"

"Sure."

The truth was, Sindija looked more like a fashion model than a goaltender. When I set down the beer case, she reached out and ran her painted nails through my hair. "I love to play," she said, "good ice hockey."

"Well." I blinked and swallowed. "Welcome to Canada."

"Thank you, Dan," Carolina exclaimed, washing her hands at the kitchen sink.

"Thank you so very much, Dan." Yuko giggled. I noticed she had a red streak in her hair, and a tiny skull tattoo on the side of her neck.

Pat tossed limes and salsa chips onto the counter. "We're having an extravaganza bonanza movie night. Their instructor wants them to watch English-language films so I told them about your famous movie collection and here we are about to taste the best, kick-ass guacamole in the entire mundo, because that, big brother, is what Carolina has promised us."

"Hola," I said. "Gracias."

"De nada." Carolina smiled sidelong at me, sorting through her ingredients. "That is very good. Do you speak Spanish?"

I shook my head. "No."

Carolina winked. "I will teach you. I am very good teacher."

"Did you know," Pat said, "that 'avocado' comes from the Aztec word for 'testicle'?"

"No, Pat," I said, "I did not know that."

Carolina crushed a garlic clove with the flat of a knife. "This guacamole, it is very special recipe by my mother. She teach us how to make with love."

Sindija dabbed on some honey-coloured lip gloss with her pinkie finger. "Yuko, Carolina and I, we meet one week ago. Now we are best girlfriends, jā?"

"Sí!"

"Hai!"

The girls high-fived each other. I half-expected them to break out pom-poms, but instead they just group-hugged and kissed. "We," Carolina declared, "are the Three Amigas!"

That evening, Pat and I squeezed onto our couch with the Three Amigas and watched *Charlie's Angels* and then the sequel *Charlie's Angels: Full Throttle* back-to-back. The girls fed Pat and me Carolina's mother's guacamole, and it was the best, kick-ass guacamole I'd ever had in my life. Matt LeBlanc was cute, but I'd forgotten just how hot Justin Theroux was as Drew Barrymore's evil ex-boyfriend. When Yuko told us she actually had her brown belt in jujitsu, Pat insisted on pausing the DVD and moving the furniture just so she could teach us all exactly how to immobilize a larger assailant in real life. The girls enthusiastically practised their moves on Pat and me. After each take-down (resulting in one broken lamp and more than one rug burn), Yuko and the others would shout: "And that's kicking your ass!" By the time we were done, we'd polished off all the beer and the girls were feeling festive and wanting to go out. Like Pat, they'd just arrived in town, so by default, I was their point man. Then I figured I'd take them all down to Little Italy to check out El Convento Rico.

My ex, Sean the DJ, had introduced me to El Convento which, he explained, always offered up a worthwhile mix of Top 40's, hip-hop and Salsa, Merengue and Chacha with a bit of Bachata. I really had no idea what he was talking about, but the drunken bachelorette ensembles that night were amusing, as was the midnight drag show. Half the guys in the club were straight Latinos, but the other half were gays. Something for everyone. Since then, I'd never thought to go back on my own. But I figured at least Carolina would feel at home, and the club was a five minute cab ride away.

When we finally got in, it was getting on towards 1 a.m. and the venue was packed. All three girls were delighted. As it turned out, Carolina was an excellent dancer, and immediately attracted a colourful entourage. She took it upon herself to teach us the Merengue. She had both her hands on my hips, helping me move to the rhythm, which the girls thought was hysterical. I did my best to be a good sport, but balked when she tried to take off my shirt. Then Pat cut in and cheerfully whipped off his own shirt, and soon there was a small cluster of dancers grinding, at which point I bowed out and headed outside to get some fresh air.

Because of hockey, I never did get into social smoking, but tonight, on an impulse, I bummed a cigarette from a passer-by. I was puffing away, enjoying the cool breeze, when I observed a man in a Second City tank top give the bouncer a fist bump. When he noticed me looking,

he strolled over and asked if I was looking for any favours. I asked what he had and he rattled off an impressive list. Apart from pot and poppers (and acid once at a
bush party), I'd never tried recreational drugs in my life.
I told him thanks I'd think about it, and he told me
where I could find him. I tossed aside my cigarette butt,
headed down the block, took some money out of an ATM,
returned, showed the bouncer the stamp on my hand,
and went back inside. If at all possible, the venue seemed
even more packed than before. I found Pat and the girls
on a leather couch in the back doing tequila body shots.
"Pat," I said, "I need to talk with you." In the alcove to the
washroom, I told him I wanted him to buy some drugs. I
described the dealer, and gave Pat the cash I'd taken out.

"You sure about this?" he shouted in my ear.

"No, but fuck it. There's a first time for everything,
right?"

Pat laughed in my face. "Alright. What do you want?"

"I don't know. Surprise me."

Fifteen minutes later, Pat shouldered his way back
through the crowd and pressed up next to me. He palmed
into my hand a tiny plastic Ziploc bag. The girls waved
to us from the dance floor. "What is it?" I asked, scanning the mass of patrons.

"I got us MDMA, five caps."

"You swallow it?"

"Yes, you swallow it. Here." He handed me a beer.

"I can't do this here. Let me go to the washroom."

"Yes, you can. Give me the bag."

I gave him the bag and after a minute, I felt him press
a single capsule back into my palm. I felt subversive, ener-

gized and absolutely thrilled, like I was some covert operative in a spy thriller. "Where's yours?" I asked. Pat opened his mouth to reveal a capsule already on his tongue. He raised his bottle in salute and took a swig.

"Cheers." I followed suit. Down the hatch. There was no turning back now. All the bridges were burning, in flames. After a moment, I leaned into him. "How long is this going to take?"

"I dunno. I guess we'll find out."

"Well, what's this going to feel like?"

"I dunno. We'll find out."

"Look, Pat, what's this going to do to me?"

"It'll make you feel good. Just go with it."

"Well, how good?"

"Dan, freakin' chill. I don't know. I've never done MDMA before."

"What? Pat, I thought you had."

"Why would you think that?"

"I just assumed you had."

"Well, I haven't." Pat draped his arm over my shoulder and grinned. "But there's a first time for everything."

Sindija cha-chaed over to where we were standing. Smiling at both of us, without missing a beat, she reached into Pat's pants pocket and extracted the bag with the remaining three caps. She blew us a kiss and danced away. Dumbly, Pat and I stared after her, and then at each other.

"Latvians."

"Whoa."

That night, Yuko, Carolina and Sindija took turns giving us head on our living room couch. I'd never had sex in front of my brother Pat before. I'd never had sex in front of anyone before. I'd never had sex with a girl before. As it turned out, the girls had also acquired a quantity of coke, so while two of them were on their knees in front of us, the third one would be tap-tap-tapping with a credit card and assembling lines on the Ricky Martin CD case. As their heads bobbed up and down to "She Bangs" on the stereo, *Charlie's Angels* played on the TV in the background. At one point, Pat and I happened to glance over at each other at the same time. Our arms were splayed across the back of the couch, and I wondered if I looked as dishevelled and sweaty and crazy-eyed as he did. I'm sure I did. Our hands touched and we locked fingers. When I finally came, the girls cheered. But whether because he was too drunk or too high or a combination of both, Pat couldn't come. In the end, he did a line off my shoulder, pulled on his underwear, jumped up and simply danced with the girls until dawn.

⌒ "You woke up with what in your face?"

"Pat's underwear. Pat and Carolina had sex in the shower later. And Pat finally got off."

"And these girls," McNeil-Tsao asked, "you're planning to see them again?"

"Pat definitely is. I'm not so sure. They know I'm gay. They still want to hook up again. The next morning they all kept saying: 'The Chad was great.' They want to meet Liam, but that's not going to happen. They all go back home at the end of the summer."

"Did you enjoy it?"

"What?"

"Sex with these girls."

"It was, I don't know. It was weird. I don't want to lead them on, you know? One part of me thinks Pat orchestrated this whole night from the beginning. But that's not true. It really was just a random hook-up."

"Purchasing illicit street drugs isn't random, Garneau."

"I know."

McNeil-Tsao and I were taking a break, sitting against the wall of our squash court. He was beating me four games to two. He'd stopped giving me any advantages months ago. There was absolutely no way I was going to tell Karen about what had happened, but I had to tell someone.

"Your brother," McNeil-Tsao said, "Pat. You say he does this all the time?"

"Pat's been a Casanova ever since I can remember. In middle school, he'd spy on the girl's change room and jerk off in the broom closet. He started a garage band in grade ten just so he could attract groupies. He gets around."

"So really, all things relative, this was nothing out of the ordinary for him."

"All things relative, I guess you could say that. Although he keeps insisting he's never done party drugs before, besides pot and acid."

"Acid?"

"There was this bush party back in our senior year. You ever heard of a bush party?"

"I'm from North Bay. I know what a bush party is."

"Okay, well all three of us, my two brothers and I, decided we'd drop acid. It was towards the end of our final year in school."

"And?"

"It didn't do much for me. It wasn't even that psychedelic. It was some cheap-ass batch some local kid cooked up in his bathtub. But practically the whole graduating class dropped that night. Someone made a speech. It was a memorable moment. There was also a lot of rum and whiskey going around. Out there in the forest under the stars, we felt like pirate kings and queens. We all bonded over it." I balanced the squash ball on my racquet. "The point is, I don't do drugs. I haven't done drugs since. I can't believe I let some strangers blow me in front of my brother."

"Maybe the point is the bonding. And everything else is just a means to an end."

"What do you mean?"

"I mean, every human being is wired to connect. We all crave intimacy in one form or another."

I closed my eyes and thought of Grandpa taking a hacksaw to my old pair of skates for Halloween. I thought of Liam's excitement at showing me a moose skull he'd found. I thought of the time Karen and I shared pizza together in the shower. I remembered clasping Pat's sweaty hand in my own as I climaxed from a blow job by Carolina Sanchez. "In one form or another."

"You ready for another game?"

"You ready to finally get your ass kicked?"

"Don't make me bury you, Garneau." McNeil-Tsao drew himself to his feet and then helped me up. "Because I will bury you."

"You just try, old man." I spun my racquet, and tossed him the ball. "You just try."

⌒ That summer, living with Pat never got as crazy again as it had that first weekend, but it was memorable. We got into the habit of shooting pool at Sneaky Dee's and checking out live music at Rancho Relaxo and The Free Times Café. Pat made friends as easily as someone else might take out library books. At the Christie Pits drum circle, he met a bunch of musicians, and by mid-summer was spending most of his time hanging out with them on the Toronto Islands.

Around this time, at the group home, I started working shifts with a new staff member named Parker Kapoor. Although we were both gay and about the same age, there was never any weirdness or tension between us. Instead, we hit it off almost instantly. Parker Kapoor thought my encounter with the Three Amigas was the funniest story he'd ever heard in his life. Parker laughed at pretty much everything I said, even when I wasn't trying to be funny. Somebody else might have thought he was permanently stoned, but he was Hindu and didn't even drink or smoke. He was the youngest of five siblings, and had come out to his parents (both doctors) when he was twelve. Ever since, they'd been enthusiastically on the lookout for a nice Canadian boy to match him with.

One Saturday we were sitting on a Church Street patio when his eyes grew big and he said: "Don't look around don't look around don't look around."

Of course, when someone says something like that, a person looks around. Although the patio was full, I didn't see anything unusual. It was a pleasant evening in June, and the Village community was out in numbers, like Serengeti fauna at the watering hole. The tables were crowded with pitchers of beer and sangria, frosted martini glasses and baskets of pita and calamari. Parker, who was wearing Birkenstocks, low-rise jeans and a loose-fitting tee, leaned forward, pretending to sip on his virgin mojito, and mumbled something without moving his lips.

"What?" I asked.

He mumbled again, his large eyes swivelling in his head like semaphore.

"Parker, I can't understand a single word you're saying."

Then Parker picked up his over-sized aviator sunglasses and placed them on me, turned in his chair, crossing his legs, and studied the high tree canopies intently. "Now look," he instructed. "But don't look like you're looking."

I pretended to reach for my wallet in my back pocket and glanced over my shoulder again. This time, I spotted a distinguished-looking gentleman three tables away in the company of a woman in an eggshell dress. I didn't place him at first, since he was dressed casually in a polo shirt, but I recognized his face from the media. He was a well-known politician based in Ottawa who had come out publicly some years ago.

I asked Parker if that was who I thought it was. He indicated frantically with one finger that I should return his glasses. I did so, and he immediately put them on and moved his chair to better conceal himself.

I'd become accustomed to Parker's dramatics, and waited patiently for him to compose himself. To his credit, it was an aspect of his personality he kept in check at work. Parker was a boy who had played with Barbies when he was young, and was the hugest Bollywood fan I knew.

"Daniel," he said, "I have had sex with him." He enunciated each syllable like he was speaking to Bill, our group home client who was partially deaf.

"Really? When did this happen?"

"Six years ago. He picked me up at Goodhandy's." Although he didn't drink alcohol, Parker Kapoor was the quintessential barfly. Early on in the summer, Parker had taken me to a burlesque show fundraiser at Goodhandy's benefitting a friend's sex reassignment surgery. Goodhandy's was billed as a pansexual playground, notorious for its live porn-tapings and rent boys with questionable hygiene.

"What on earth were you doing at Goodhandy's?"

"I was going through my neo-Depeche Mode phase back then," Parker explained. "And I was wearing eight thousand dollars worth of braces. It was not a pretty time in my life."

"Okay." I thought of when I was seventeen, high on acid at drunken bush parties, secretly jacking off to a cum-stained photograph of my assistant hockey coach, my hair cut in a style frighteningly reminiscent of a mullet. I certainly wasn't one to judge anyone.

"He offered to buy me a drink. I had no idea who he was. Older guys hit on me all the time."

"They do?"

"Look at me, Daniel. I'm jailbait. I look like I'm twelve years old."

Parker was regularly prone to exaggeration. He looked at least sixteen. "So what happened?"

"What happened? What's more to say? We went to one of the back rooms upstairs. I never saw him again."

"So what did you do?"

"You mean what sexual perversions did this older man get up to with that seventeen-year-old brown boy? Not much. To tell the truth, it was a little boring. He made me show him my ID, can you believe it? Although I will tell you," Parker whispered, "his penis goes like this." He manoeuvred his fingers into a painful-looking position.

"Parker, do your parents know their son is having sex with high-ranking Canadian politicians?"

"It happened once, Daniel. Once. This girl has class. Mind you, if that man over there and I publicly professed our undying love for one other, I think my parents would be thrilled. We already have doctors, two lawyers, a physics professor and a microbiologist in my family. No politicians though. Although, by the way, he was only a mid-ranking official back then. You do realize his ministry funds our employer?"

"I never thought of that."

Parker peered around me and over the rim of his glasses. "I should hit him up for a raise."

"Didn't he marry his accountant last year? It was all in the news. I hear they're planning to adopt."

"They are. A little brown baby."

"Really?"

"From Florida. That's probably his adoption agent he's talking to right now."

"How do you know these things?"

Parker tapped the side of his large and perfectly straight nose. Holding his straw with his pinkie extended, he sat back and slurped down the slushy remains of his virgin mojito.

I found out later that Parker had skipped two grades in elementary school and was a freshman at university at the age of fifteen. It was Parker's idea to take me shopping one Sunday afternoon. We met in a part of town called Yorkville, a high-end district of art galleries, boutiques, chic cafés and fashionable eateries. We strolled from store to store, admiring the architecture, the elaborate window displays and various passers-by. I felt conspicuously underdressed, but Parker reminded me that the neighbourhood had been the epicentre of the Canadian hippie movement back in the 1960s.

Parker had an opinion on almost every brand name. I eventually bought a T-shirt off a 50% sales rack. It was by far the single most expensive shirt I'd ever owned in my life. I usually wore a size large or extra-large, but Parker insisted I get the medium. He had the staff snip the tags, and I wore it out of the store sipping on a Dixie cup of complimentary espresso. Then Parker bought himself a pair of skinny jeans and a pair of Ray-Bans and gave me his old sunglasses, since they framed my bone structure so much better than his. After that, he took me to the MAC store. He seemed to be on intimate terms with the staff and I stood by self-consciously as he underwent a makeover.

"He's not my boyfriend," Parker said, waving in my direction, "although my parents would be absolutely thrilled if he was. He's going to be a doctor."

One of the girls asked if this was true and I told them I was considering applying to med school. Her smile was whiter than Wite-Out. None of the MAC staff appeared to have pores. When they were done with Parker, neither did he. Apart from that, he actually didn't look that much different, which made me wonder if he wore make-up more often and I just never noticed. Then the staff insisted it was my turn; I adamantly refused, but eventually let them test swatches of foundation on my wrist. That opened a floodgate. One thing led to another and, under Parker's incessant cajoling, I caved and found myself perched up on the high stool.

I'd been at the MAC counter ten minutes when I heard someone call out my name. Melissa poked her head in the store. "Oh my god! It *is* Daniel. Michael, look, it's Daniel." Mike peered around Melissa and gave me a cheerful thumbs-up sign. Apparently, they'd been shopping at the babyGap around the corner. As my MAC girl massaged a hypoallergenic moisturizing foundation into my forehead, Melissa and Mike introduced themselves to Parker who offered a civil, if somewhat chilly, response. Melissa gingerly settled herself on a stool next to mine. She looked like she was ready to deliver yesterday.

"One more month, can you believe it?" she huffed. "Someone should build strollers for expectant mothers to ride in. My back is killing me, I feel absolutely bloated and disgusting. Look at me, I am a cow. I am a whorish, crippled cow. But Michael here has been simply wonderful, haven't you been, Michael? He's been patient, compassionate and attentive in every way a woman might possibly want or need." She silently mouthed for my benefit, "Cock ring," and squeezed my knee.

The MAC girl leaned on my shoulder, brow knit in concentration, her breasts pressed firmly into the side of my arm, and applied some kind of lip gloss with a brush.

I mumbled something unintelligible and gave Melissa a thumbs-up sign.

After that day, I politely declined Parker Kapoor's eager invitations to go shopping again. A few weeks later, Pat did the laundry and shrank my Yorkville T-shirt so that it barely covered my ribcage. When I took it to work and offered it to Parker, it fit him perfectly. I liked the sunglasses he'd given me though, and wore them for the rest of the summer, at least until Pat sat on them one day. When I went to buy a similar pair, I discovered they cost a whole lot more than my Yorkville T-shirt had. Then I figured I'd spend the money instead on a baby gift for Melissa and Mike. In the end, she'd given birth to a beautiful healthy boy whom they'd named Benjamin. In all their Facebook postings from the maternity ward, both parents appeared exhausted but ecstatic. Melissa looked luminous. The kid was tiny, pink-faced and more than cute. He seemed to be sticking out his hand in what strangely resembled an affirmative thumbs-up sign. Welcome to the world, little guy.

That fall, Karen's biological father died. He'd been in a federal prison in Kingston for fourteen years. The last time they saw him, Karen and her little sister Anne were seven and four. It was Karen who arranged for the body to be transported back to M'Chigeeng on Manitoulin. She took a bus home to oversee the paperwork. She insisted it was merely a formality and that I should stay in Toronto and hold the fort. School had started already, but she'd gotten an accommodation for a leave of absence.

Karen reminded me she had the Miltons and her extended family for support. She also had Liam. Later, I heard Anne had refused to attend the funeral. On the day Karen was to finally return to Toronto, I vacuumed and tidied, set flowers in a vase, and prepared her favourite foods: grilled cheese-and-steak sandwiches and tomato soup. When Karen stepped through the front door, she gave me a hug, shuffled into the kitchen and lifted the lid to the pot simmering on the stove. Then she opened the door to the oven where I was keeping a stack of sandwiches warm on a foil tray. I offered her a glass of red wine which she cradled mutely in both hands.

"Karen," I finally said. "You okay?"

She nodded and set the glass down. She looked past me. Liam was standing in the doorway. I hadn't seen him since I'd visited Sudbury during Toronto's Pride Weekend in June. He was unshaven and heavier than I remembered. His hair had grown out, framing his dark features.

"Liam," I exclaimed.

Liam set his backpack down on the doorstep. "Hey."

"Holy cow." During my two years in Toronto, he'd never visited once. "What are you doing here?"

He glanced at Karen and then back at me. "Karen and me, we thought I'd come visit, a week maybe. Sorry we didn't ask you sooner. Is that okay?"

"Sure. Sure, of course. As long as you want."

"Jackson's in the Jeep."

"Jackson?" For a second, I couldn't figure out who Jackson was. "Jackson, right. Okay, of course. Bring him in. Don't keep him out there." While Liam went to fetch Jackson, I grabbed his pack which was surprisingly light and compact. It smelled faintly of burnt sweetgrass and cedar. "Karen, you guys hungry?"

They were ravenous. Apparently, they'd driven from Sudbury through Parry Sound to Toronto non-stop. Liam fed Jackson before doing anything else. While we ate, Jackson settled himself on the couch, licking his chops, and curled his bushy tail up beneath his chin. His eyebrows individually rose and fell as he watched each one of us in turn. "How was he on the drive down?" I asked.

"Jackson? Great," Liam said. "He loves the Jeep. He's been riding with me all summer."

"So how are things on Manitoulin?"

"Great. Karen's whole family is great." Liam glanced again at Karen.

"This is really good soup, Daniel," Karen said.

"Thanks."

When Liam was in the washroom, I asked: "Look, is everything okay between us, you and me?"

She squeezed my shoulder. "I'll explain later. But everything's good. Trust me. We're good."

Later that night, I thought I heard Karen and Liam arguing. After a while, just as I was dozing off, I was sure I could hear them making love. I could tell they were trying to be quiet about it, but I could make out their exhalations and the rhythmic creaking of Karen's bed. I imagined their hands and their mouths, the position of their limbs. I imagined Liam inside of her. I resisted an impulse to sit up and press my ear against the wall. Jackson nosed open my bedroom door and tentatively crept up onto the mattress. I rolled over and let him curl up on top of my feet. After some time, the apartment and the whole house fell quiet. Directly above me, Melissa and Mike's newborn baby slept in his crib, breathing in and out through his tiny nostrils, with his miniature hands curling and uncurling. I fell asleep feeling the pulse of Jackson's heartbeat against my feet.

CHAPTER SIX

Lost Together

That fall, Liam went on what he called a walkabout. He said he wanted to see the Pacific Ocean, packed his Jeep and started driving west. Apparently, he'd told Karen his plans at her father's funeral. It was what they'd been fighting about. In hindsight, the week he'd spent in Toronto was a farewell of sorts. In Sudbury, Pat moved back in with his girlfriend Blonde Dawn. During Thanksgiving at the Miltons, he let everyone know he'd dropped out of his Paramedic program and started a course to teach ESL.

Around that time, I started seeing a man named Marcus Wittenbrink Jr. I'd actually been introduced to him six months earlier by Charles, who had interviewed him for his research. The first time I laid eyes on Marcus, he was naked (except for a pair of diapers), tarred and feathered from head to toe, and standing in a pile of pigs' intestines, alternating between reciting nursery rhymes in a little baby's voice and throat singing in the tradition of the Siberian Tuva people. He did this non-stop for twenty-four hours, cordoned off within a square of red velvet rope inside a warehouse art studio in the west-end. People paid money to see him, drank cheap wine out of plastic cups and exchanged discreet commentary in hushed, reverent whispers. It was a fundraiser for Tibet, and the overall effect was fantastical and disturbing. Charles had seen a lot of performance art in his time, but confessed this piece was particularly unusual. Incredibly, Marcus had won multiple grants and awards for similar avant-garde productions over the years. His vitae was more than impressive. After three wine spritzers, I signed a guest book that night, and within days found myself accepting a Facebook Friend Request from Mr. Diapers himself. I was shocked by his self-portraits. He was, in fact, a physically beautiful man, with the flawless and androgynous features of a Renaissance saint. I figured the images must have been seriously Photoshopped, until the day Marcus approached me while I waited at a streetcar stop.

"You're Daniel Garneau," the soft-spoken, pale-faced individual poised in front of me said. He was wearing cords and Doc Martens, a camel cashmere coat and a moss-coloured scarf. On this occasion, his neatly-trimmed hair was thick and glossy chestnut brown. Snowflakes settled on his eyelashes as we spoke. Even though I recognized him instantly from his Facebook images, it took me a moment before I could form a reply. Then he said his name and smiled at me, his hands resting at his side.

"I know who you are," I said.

"You were at my fundraiser for the Dalai Lama."

"You were wearing a diaper."

"That's right. You'd come with Charles Ondaatje. I never forget a face. Can I tell you a secret?"

"Sure."

"The diaper wasn't really meant to be part of the piece. I was simply wearing it so I could pee."

"I see."

"Mind you, I've staged other performances where I have urinated and defecated in front of an audience."

"Oh, okay." The streetcar was nowhere in sight.

"I'm kidding." He smiled at me sidelong.

"Right."

"How did you like the show?"

"That chanting you were doing ..."

"Overtone singing."

"That was really interesting. I've never heard anything like it. How'd you learn to do that?"

"I trained with a sheep herder from Siberia. It took over a year and a half before I was able to master the technique."

"You've been to Siberia?"

"Oh no, it was at the Kadampa Meditation Centre here in Toronto."

"Okay. Well, it was pretty cool."

"Thank you. Charles tells me you plan to be a physician?"

"I should stop telling people that. I haven't even applied to med school yet."

"The human body is truly a miracle of nature." He stood perfectly still when he spoke. I couldn't help but feel he was undressing me with his hazel eyes.

"I suppose it is."

"Capable of all sorts of things."

"No kidding."

"If you're interested in overtone singing, Daniel, let me know. I'd be happy to instruct you. It's all a matter of muscular control in the mouth, larynx and pharynx. It can be a very powerful experience."

I didn't know if he was flirting with me or if I was just chronically, pathetically horny. "Okay, I'll keep it in mind."

My streetcar had arrived. After I boarded, he stood waving as I pulled away. Later that night, I found a link to Marcus' official website. Apparently, while overtone singing was best known as a Tibetan Buddhist tradition, it spanned many world cultures, from Inuit to Irish to Indian. I looked up a tutorial on YouTube and was practicing when Karen walked into the apartment. "What on earth is that hideous noise?" she called out, unpacking groceries in the kitchen.

"Nothing." I cleared my throat and quickly closed the lid to my laptop.

After Charles broke up with me, I found myself continuing to follow Marcus' activities. That spring, I secretly attended a live reading at his book launch, a compilation of poems and short stories entitled, *Tales from the Bottom of My Sole*. I was sure he saw me in the back row. Afterwards, I slipped away as quickly as I could. Later that summer, I took Parker Kapoor to the Art Gallery of Ontario where Marcus was one of nine individuals featured in an exhibit of up-and-coming Toronto-based artists. I didn't tell Parker the real reason why I'd come. To my amazement, he'd actually heard of Marcus Wittenbrink Jr.

"He's a freak," Parker said. "He goes out of his way to be outrageous. He's all about shock value. Look at this, it says here he identifies as two-spirited. That's ridiculous. His parents are whitebread lawyers from Burlington."

"People think he's one of Canada's top young emerging playwrights."

"All I'm saying, is here we have this privileged white guy who goes native and everyone thinks he's hot shit. Woohoo. Look at this, the *Globe & Mail* writes: 'What Tom Thomson did for Canada's geographical landscape in the 20th century, Marcus Wittenbrink Jr. does for Canada's cultural landscape in the 21st century.' The *Toronto Star* calls him 'quintessentially Canadian.' What on earth is that supposed to mean? That his underarms smell like maple syrup? The truth is, if he wasn't so incredibly good-looking and prone to taking his clothes off half the time, he wouldn't be half as popular. All this postmodern neo-paganism is a little pathetic. You know I heard he performed naked once chanting in a pile of pig shit? How much Ontario Arts Council money is this guy getting?"

"It was pig intestines. And he was wearing diapers. And it was Tuvan throat singing. And it was a fundraiser for the Dalai Lama."

"Okay, Mr. Fanboy."

"Don't patronize me, Parker."

"Fine. I'm just jealous, alright? I admit it."

"You're jealous?"

"Of course I am. Look at him! He's gorgeous. Who has a body like that? I'm sure he's got groupies following him everywhere. I'm the same age as him, and what have I got to show for myself?"

"Um, you hold the high score on every pinball machine at Playdium?"

"I'm done with that." Parker collapsed on a bench. "That is so yesterday. I need a change."

"Why don't you try writing?"

"Writing? Are you kidding me? That would take discipline, that would take focus. I don't have either, I have ADHD. It takes me forty-five minutes just to decide what breakfast cereal I want to eat in the morning."

"You could write your memoirs."

"My memoirs?"

"You've been around the block, Parker. You're always making observations of the people around you. Think of all the craziness that happens at the group homes. You could write it all down. *The Adventures of Parker Kapoor.* I see a movie deal in there somewhere."

Parker's eyes swivelled wildly in his head. "I should, shouldn't I? Dinner conversation at the Kapoor household could fill up half a novel by itself. You have no idea what it's like being the youngest in this family. I should invite you over during Diwali just so you can witness the spectacle for yourself. *The Misanthropic Misadventures of Parker Kapoor.* Daniel, you are a genius."

"I try."

Parker pressed his nose up against a semi-nude image of Marcus tied to a tree and shot through with arrows. "You think I'd ever have a chance with this Wittenbrink guy? I could be a groupie. Do you think he hosts Bacchanalian orgies? I'll bet he does. What do you think?"

"Parker, I don't think you'd make a very good groupie. You should focus on your memoirs."

"You're probably right. When I'm famous I won't forget you, Daniel. I promise."

"I'm holding you to it."

A month later, I attended Marcus' one-man show *Philophobia* at the Tarragon Theatre and brought Karen along. During intermission, to our surprise and delight, we bumped into Charles and Megan.

"You were in the front row, weren't you?"

"How can you tell? Oh, of course, you can see we got splashed."

"Just a bit."

"Don't worry, its water-based and comes out. It says so here in the program."

"I totally wasn't expecting him to do that upside-down thing."

"Which upside-down thing?"

"That thing with the giant puppet."

"Oh, I thought you were talking about that thing with the gymnastic rings."

"I didn't know he could beatbox."

"I didn't know he was double-jointed."

"I knew he was double-jointed."

"When was he doing anything double-jointed?"

"When he was upside-down on the rings."

"Oh, I thought there was something weird about that. That last tableau was kind of like a Picasso."

"Holy shit! That's exactly what I was thinking."

"He's amazing."

"He's a genius."

"He's in my thesis."

Charles wanted to meet him backstage after the

performance. By the time Marcus had showered and cleaned off the body-paint and gotten dressed, all of the audience was gone except for the four of us. We greeted him in the green room where the walls were plastered with dozens of faded posters from past productions. He came out wearing a plain black dress shirt and jeans. The first thing he said was: "Daniel Garneau, you look well." He stood back appraisingly. "You must be Megan Calderon and you must be Karen Fobister. Charles, your friends here are even more beautiful in real life."

"Real life?" Megan squeaked.

"Facebook," Marcus said. "It is a new reality. I think my next project will be a deconstruction of Facebook."

"Marcus," Charles said, "has a photographic memory. Be careful what you put on Facebook."

"That one image, that expression on your face, Daniel, when you were just about to come," Marcus said thoughtfully, "out to your brothers, it is sacred."

"I beg your pardon?"

Karen scratched her nose. "Daniel, remember? I tagged you on that picture I took of you, on Christmas Eve, two years ago."

"Oh, right."

"Megan, you and Charles were truly meant for each other. Have you thanked Daniel and Karen for bringing you together?"

"Um, no," Megan stammered, clutching Charles' arm. "Not yet. Karen, thank you. Daniel, you too."

Karen and I glanced at each other. "You're welcome," we said in unison.

"Thank you for coming to my show," Marcus said. "It

is always humbling when people take time out of their lives to notice my work. Charles, you have been a constant support over the years. Daniel, I missed speaking with you after my book launch at Hart House. I wanted to ask your opinion of my title poem. My stage manager will close up here." He regarded each one of us. "Shall we go for a drink?"

At Charles' suggestion, we ended up cabbing across town to a bar on Queen West called The Beaver, an eccentric and packed little hole-in-the-wall. As it turned out, Marcus had no money on him. The rest of us took turns paying for rounds. At one point, the waiter served up five shots of Goldschläger, compliments of the house. Everywhere Marcus went, people's heads turned. He was even more beautiful in real life. When his hand came to rest on my knee beneath the table, I banged my teeth against the edge of my glass. He was speaking to Charles and Karen about the appropriation of aboriginal culture and the works of this well-known artist and that well-known artist. He didn't glance at me once. But his hand massaged the inside of my thigh as he spoke about the Woodland School of Art and the troubled life of Norval Morrisseau. Then he leaned back, removed his hand and took a sip from his pint. He nodded towards me politely. "What do you think, Daniel?"

Everyone's head turned. "I think," I said carefully, "there are some people who feel you're a privileged white guy gone native."

"I see," Marcus said. "Well, I am. That is clear. But what do you think of it?"

"I think," I said, "your work does for Canada's cultural

landscape what Tom Thomson's work did for Canada's geographical landscape."

"This is why," Charles said, laughing and tousling my hair, "I dated this guy." He draped his arm over Megan and hugged her close. I'd never seen Charles this relaxed or happy before.

Later that night, when Karen and I returned home, I asked her how her evening went. "It was interesting. I had a good time. Thank you for taking me out." She untied her hair knots, collecting pins in her mouth. "It was great to hang out with Megan and Charles like that. We should do it more often. Your friend Marcus seems to really like you."

"He's not my friend. He's Charles' friend."

"You're friends with him on Facebook."

"Yeah, and three thousand other people. It's like his professional Facebook page."

"Was it weird?"

"Was what weird?"

"Being at the Beaver. You know we were just a block down from the Drake Hotel. Your ex Sean was spinning there tonight."

"Oh, Karen, you know what? That wasn't even on my radar."

"Okay, Daniel. Just checking in. You and this Marcus guy, you've got some chemistry going there."

"What?" I threw my shirt in the hamper and went to brush my teeth. "Are you kidding? Marcus Wittenbrink Jr. is so out of my league."

"Daniel Garneau." Karen followed me to the washroom. "Do you know how pathetic you just sounded there?"

"No. Karen." I focused on squeezing the last bit of toothpaste of out the tube. "I'm just being realistic."

"His hand was on your knee half the night."

"Oh. I didn't think anyone noticed that."

"I noticed."

"I just don't want to be another groupie."

"A what?"

"He probably sleeps around with all of his fans. He probably hosts these Bacchanalian orgies."

"You're a fan?" Karen poked me in the butt.

"That"—I waved my toothbrush—"was just a figure of speech."

"Daniel, you like this guy."

"He's interesting."

"And so are you. You should go on a date."

"What would we have to talk about?" I was frothing at the mouth but I didn't care.

"Tom Thomson?"

"Oh, shit, Karen, I was just quoting a newspaper article. I'm Fruit of the Loom, remember? This guy's been featured at the AGO, he's been nominated twice for a Dora Award and who knows what else. He knows how to Tuvan throat sing, for chrissake." I rinsed and spat.

"This isn't like you."

"What do you mean?"

"You used to think more highly of yourself."

"This isn't Sudbury, Karen."

"No, this is Toronto. You and me, we have a right to be here just like anyone else."

I opened and closed my mouth. I raised and dropped my arms. Finally, I put my toothbrush back in its holder and just shook my head. "Fine. I'm just not so sure where here is."

"We're right here."

"I think." I sighed. "I think I'm just feeling a little lost."

"You're not lost. You're right here."

"I worry about Grandpa. I worry about Liam. I worry about Pat. Fuck, Karen, I worry about you."

"Don't worry about me. I'm serious. I'm doing okay. It was hard having Liam leave like that. The timing sucked. But I'm okay."

"Karen." I drew a breath. "I'm so sorry about your dad, I should've been there, I really should've been there." I was crying again. It was ridiculous how much I cried. But I couldn't help it. "Why didn't you tell me about him? You told Liam."

"That man wasn't my dad. He was my biological father, okay? I barely knew him. Look, Daniel, it's over now. Really, it's over."

"I'm so afraid I'm losing you."

"Daniel, you know I'm leaving Toronto after I finish this year." I nodded. "And you're applying to med school. I know we don't talk about everything. And after this year, we're going to go our separate ways. But listen to me. You're never going to lose me. Never. You and me, we're gum stuck to the bottom of each other's shoes, alright? We have one year left together here. We have this amazing apartment. We have friends who live right upstairs. We have us. Let's make the best of it, okay? Did you notice they had sweet potato burritos on the menu?" I shook my head. "Well, they did. You and I, we're going to go back to The Beaver and check it out. There's a million things in this ridiculous city we haven't done yet. We've barely scratched the surface." She gripped my shoulders. "I want you to promise me one thing."

"What's that?"

"I want you to ask this Marcus Wittenbrink guy out on a date."

"Oh, shit, Karen."

"Promise."

"Karen."

"I mean it."

"C'mon."

"I mean it."

"I promise."

"Good boy. Now make me a nightcap, and you're having one with me."

"I just brushed my teeth."

"I don't care."

"Alright. What do you want?"

"Surprise me."

∽ That Christmas season, I performed half-naked in Marcus Wittenbrink Jr.'s gala multimedia art production. We'd been seeing each other exclusively for almost three months. His parents were coming down from Burlington for the show, a one-off staging at a fundraiser for the Royal Ontario Museum. I was one of twelve actors he'd incorporated into the script which he'd written to be staged inside the Michael Lee-Chin Crystal accompanied by a string quintet and an all-female taiko drumming troupe. It was a black tie affair. As usual, there was nudity in the production. In my case, I had to show my ass. I was wearing a mask, so I didn't feel so bad about it. When it was over, we got a standing ovation.

Later, when I'd changed and slipped back into the crowd, I found Karen by the punch bowl. Glittering holiday garlands and lavish wreaths, emerald and gold, decorated the canted walls and cavernous space. The string quintet played by the stairwell. "These heels are killing me," Karen said. "You were great, by the way."

"Thanks. Have you seen Marcus?"

"I think he was talking to the Governor-General over by the cheese table. But that was ten minutes ago. You look good. Here, don't move." I stood still while Karen fixed my bow tie. "Remember the last time you wore a tuxedo?"

"No, when was that? Oh, right."

"Senior prom. You came out to me that night."

"I did, didn't I?"

"Yes, Daniel Garneau, you did."

Karen was wearing a red satin dress she'd bought in a Kensington Market thrift shop called Courage My Love. She'd had one small stain removed and restitched a loose seam. It fit her perfectly. She'd also had her hair done up in blue-black ringlets highlighting her cheekbones. "Karen, you look beautiful."

"Thank you."

"I mean it. You really look great."

"You know these pearls are fake, right?"

"I don't care."

"Well, mister, you're looking pretty darn fine there yourself. Mind you, that ivy leaf thong you were sporting earlier was pretty cute."

"We were animistic spirits."

"I'm sure you were. Speaking of which, let's grab a drink. It's an open bar."

"Thanks for waiting for me."

"Are you kidding? I've already had three glasses of wine. 'Tis the season. Oh my, and here come the cougars. Let me get us those drinks."

Two middle-aged women wearing what looked like barbed wire encrusted with semi-precious stones circled me hawkishly. "I'd recognize that jawline anywhere," the taller one said. "You, my young man, played the forest god."

"Um. I was an animistic spirit."

Her companion squinted. "Was he the one with the antlers?"

"Of course he was, dear. He was the Horned God, the personification of the life force energy of wild beasts and the primordial symbol of male virility. Can't you tell?"

I cleared my throat. "In the script, actually, it just said I was 'animistic spirit #6'."

"Didn't I see you on *Degrassi: The Next Generation* last season? I think my youngest daughter is your biggest fan."

"No! No, I'm not an actor. I just … the director just asked me to wear that costume and stand on stage. I was doing him a favour."

The shorter woman glanced archly at her taller companion. "The Horned God?"

"The Horned God is born in the winter, he impregnates the Goddess and dies in the autumn. Then he is reborn again by the Goddess at Yule."

"That is fascinating. Well, sir, your performance was excellent. The production was most engaging."

"Thank you."

"Most engaging."

"Indeed."

"Ah, here comes your lady friend. Let's leave these young lovers, shall we? It was a pleasure." The taller woman proffered her hand. On an impulse, I pressed her knuckles to my lips, and did the same with her companion.

Karen handed me a wine glass. "You little devil, you," she exclaimed in a low voice, watching the two women depart.

"I am the Horned God. I am the paragon of male virility."

"I thought you were fairy #6."

"I wasn't a fairy, Karen. I was an animistic spirit."

"Whatever."

We eventually found Marcus by the ice sculpture chatting with a woman in a dark pant suit and a man with silver sideburns. "Daniel," Marcus said. "I'd like you to meet my parents, Linda and Marcus Senior."

"Pleased to meet you."

"Daniel is my boyfriend."

Marcus Senior stiffened. "Let me freshen your drink." He took his wife's glass, said something in German to her and walked away.

Linda Wittenbrink adjusted her holly corsage. "And what do you do, Daniel?"

"I'm a student at U of T."

"He's going to be a physician," Marcus said.

"You're in medical school?"

"Um, no. I've just applied this year."

"I see."

"And this is our friend Karen."

"That is a beautiful dress, Karen."

"Thank you."

"Is it an Alfred Sung?"

Karen blinked. "Why, yes, it is."

"And how long have you known our Marcus?"

"Not long. We met through Daniel. This is the first show of his I've seen."

"And what did you think?"

"It was very special."

"He is quite the celebrated golden boy, isn't he?"

Marcus bowed his head. "Mother and Father both wanted me to study law. Join the Wittenbrink Firm. Carry on the family tradition."

"Your son, he's very talented, Mrs. Wittenbrink," Karen said.

"Obviously. Now where has your father gotten to? Marcus, we'll be heading back to our hotel. I know you must have many people who want to congratulate you." She handed him two tickets. "Fetch us our coats, and see us off. It was a pleasure meeting you, Daniel. Karen."

The string quintet had begun to play Pachelbel's *Canon*. "Your parents," I said, "they're very nice."

"My mother is an ice queen," Marcus said, "but she can be civil. My father's just a bastard. Period." He took my wine glass and drained it. "They have no understanding whatsoever of my work. They don't even try. My grandfather was a Nazi officer who collected and burned art in bonfires. Did I ever mention that to you?"

"No, you haven't."

"My life is a cliché," Marcus said, sighing. "Karen, those pearls aren't real, are they?"

"No, they're not."

"I didn't think so. The cellist was playing like shit tonight. You'd think he'd never rehearsed. I'll have to speak with his union. Let me get these coats. Daniel, go get us another drink?" He strode away.

After a moment, I said: "Don't take it personally."

"How often is he like this?"

"Rarely. Sometimes. He has his ups and downs. He's an artist."

"Then he is a cliché."

"Karen, please don't let him ruin our evening."

"It's his evening. It's your evening. It's not mine."

"It is yours. It's our evening."

"Is it? Are you here with me or him? Anyway, look at me. This isn't me. I don't belong here. And what the fuck is an Alfred Sung anyway?"

"Karen, c'mon. We were having fun ten minutes ago. We're here, we're right here. Right? You and me."

"Daniel, go be with your boyfriend. He needs you. I love you and you're my best friend. But I don't need you. Seriously. Go."

"No."

"Go."

"No, Karen. And you're not going either. C'mon. Look at this. How often do we get to do something like this? There's an open bar. You look beautiful. They're serving lobster bisque and fancy pâté. It's Christmas. I want to take a picture of us. Let's take a picture of us."

I stood next to Karen and rummaged out my phone. Reluctantly, Karen let me put my arm around her waist as I held it out at arm's length. The flash went off and Karen pulled away. "Okay, Daniel."

After that, I got three more drinks from the bar. Karen downed hers and set the empty glass aside. Finally, I said: "How are you getting home?"

"I'll walk."

"It's really far. I don't want you walking."

"I'm fine."

"In this weather? C'mon. Karen, take a cab. Your shoes are hurting you anyway."

"Fine. I'll take a cab."

I held her hand. "I can't leave."

"I know."

"Text me when you get in."

"Okay."

I leaned over and kissed her on the cheek. "You're amazing, you know that?"

"Are you coming home tonight?"

"I'm not sure. I don't think so."

"Okay. Be safe."

As it turned out, Marcus wanted to sleep alone that night. He had a lot on his mind and needed space for himself. By the time I arrived home, the apartment was dark and Karen's bedroom door was closed. When I got out of the shower, I stepped on something hard and round. It was a single pearl. Then I noticed Karen's pearl necklace in the waste can. I wrapped a towel around my waist and, for the longest time, stood at her door. But it was late and I didn't knock. Eventually, I changed into my PJs and went to bed.

⌒ On Christmas Eve in Sudbury, Pat told me that both he and his girlfriend were going to move back home to live with Grandpa. Apparently, Grandpa and Blonde Dawn had already met on a number of occasions. They'd gone bowling and cooked meals together. She'd visited Grandma more than once in the nursing home, and had even spent a weekend up at the Good Medicine Cabin.

"So when do I get to meet this Blonde Dawn?" I asked.

"She's vacationing in Disney World with her nephews and nieces right now," Pat said. "She'll be back in the New Year. You've seen pictures of her. She's great."

I had seen pictures of her. She was blonde and busty, covered in tattoos. Since returning from tree planting in the fall, she'd been working full-time in Sudbury as a paramedic. "Is she still in a band?"

"No, man, that fell apart. But we're thinking of forming our own band. Definitely."

"Well, I look forward to meeting her."

"She's awesome. She's crazy. She's crazy awesome. She's so totally dying to meet everyone."

Pat and I worked in the kitchen, our sleeves rolled up, preparing food for the next day. I had shortbread cookies cooling on the counter, and Pat was energetically mashing a big pot of potatoes on the stove. Tomorrow morning, I would put the turkey in the oven and make the gravy. Grandpa already had a dozen freshly-baked sugar pies in the freezer. Like last year, he was spending the night with Grandma. But this time around, the family plan was to bring Christmas dinner to the nursing home.

"Guys," Karen shouted from the living room, "he's here! Liam's back. He's here."

Liam's Jeep pulled into the driveway, headlights cutting through the falling snow. Karen ran outside in her T-shirt. He'd been gone just over two months. He stepped out of the Jeep wearing an enormous parka. When Jackson bounded into the house, I knelt in my kitchen apron and gave him a hug. He wriggled from my arms, raced through the living room and dining room, around the Christmas tree and out the front door again trailing silver tinsel. I vaulted a couch and caught the tree just as it was tipping over. Ornaments rolled everywhere. Liam staggered into the house carrying Karen in his arms, knocking over Grandpa's deer antler coat rack and tracking snow across the hardwood floors. Jackson wouldn't stop barking and jumping, his bushy tail whipping back and forth.

"Welcome home, little brother," Pat yelled. He emerged from the kitchen with two beer bottles dangling from each hand. "How was the Pacific Ocean?"

"I got to dip my toe in," Liam said, putting Karen down. He pulled off his gloves and drew back his fur-lined hood. "The heater's not working in the Jeep. It's good to be back." He wore an unkempt beard and his hair was longer than ever. He looked like Jesus. I hurried to stand up the coat rack and gather up the scattered jackets and scarves.

"You look like Jesus," Karen said.

"It's Christmas Eve," Liam said, laughing. "What do you expect?" He gave Pat a bear hug and then me. His eyes were red-rimmed and he smelled unwashed. An unpleasant odour of pot and whiskey clung to him. I wondered if he'd been drinking and driving.

Karen pulled out her phone. "Well, it'll be Christmas Day in eleven minutes. You're right on time."

"Smells good in here. Who's baking?"

Pat jabbed a thumb at me. "Who do you think? By the way, we're all volunteering tomorrow at the nursing home. Grandpa's already there."

"Alright. Looking forward to it." Pat handed out the beers. Liam raised his bottle. "Santé."

"Okay, wait, hold on," Karen exclaimed. "Hold on. Everyone, squeeze in. Hold on hold on hold on." She positioned her phone-camera on the edge of the stairs. Liam sat down cross-legged and hauled Jackson into his lap. Pat and I crouched and huddled close. Karen hit the timer and ran to join us, clambering up onto our shoulders. "Cheers, guys. Merry Christmas!"

We all held up our beers. "Cheers!" The flash went off. "Merry Christmas."

CHAPTER SEVEN

All the Things I Wasn't

After Christmas, I took a bus back to Toronto to attend Marcus' New Year's Eve party. Karen stayed in Sudbury with Liam. Pat asked if he could come and crash at my place for a couple days, as he had his own party to go to out on the Toronto Islands. When we got back into the city, I lent him his old set of keys, a sweater and a T-shirt of mine he said he liked. In the end, he also borrowed an extra pair of socks, a vest and a toque he'd rummaged out of my closet which I'd forgotten I owned. "I'll be gone overnight," he said at the door, his backpack full of beer.

"Alright. Don't get into too much trouble. Happy New Year, Pat." I gave him a hug.

"I borrowed some of your cologne."

"I noticed."

"And thanks again for the toothbrush. Hey, I don't suppose you could spot me a twenty?"

I gave Pat a twenty and sent him on his way. Marcus was throwing his party in his warehouse loft, in a building that had once been an east-end printing factory. He'd moved in just last September, so it was a combination housewarming and end-of-year event. In the main space, he had a gigantic framed reprint of a black-and-white photo of Andy Warhol and members of The Factory. The loft was otherwise undecorated and spare, all raw brick and concrete, accented with brushed metal and hardwood flooring, lit throughout with theatre lightning. It was the perfect, all-purpose party space.

My job was to answer the door and take people's coats. Over the last three months, I thought I'd met a number of Marcus' friends, but on this night I hardly recognized anyone who came in through the door. Marcus had someone named Marwa catering, and two others named Fang and Amanda DJing throughout the night. At one point, Marwa brought me a sample of her famous Egyptian meatballs. She was a small girl with huge, sparkly eyes like a Japanese anime character. She let me know that if there was anything I needed, she would be my go-to person. As promised, her meatballs were moist and delicious.

With Marcus' permission, I'd invited Parker Kapoor who, coincidentally, showed up at exactly the same time as Charles and Megan. I introduced them all and took their coats. By eleven p.m., most of the guests had arrived. A white-haired gentleman turned out to be one of Marcus' old university professors. A bald Asian woman was his yoga instructor. As I helped Marwa serve hors d'oeuvres on silver trays, I spotted Parker in the corner talking animatedly with an elegant, elderly drag queen named Michelle DuBarry, cradling her bejewelled hand like it was a Fabergé egg. He followed DuBarry around all night. I think if she'd had a train to carry, he would've

carried it. The countdown to midnight kicked off a cabaret performance of five acts set up on a low stage in front
of Andy Warhol. A trio of opera singers opened, followed
by a dreadlocked rapper, a burlesque contortionist, and a
drag king Elvis impersonator.

Finally, Marcus himself stepped up accompanied by a
didgeridoo player. He proceeded to cite fifty-two Defining
Moments, the highlights of each week of the last year of
his life. While most of the images were joyful or comical,
others were darker: traffic accidents or dead animals, con-
frontations with homophobes, physical ailments, or atroci-
ties in the news. But each encounter taught him a lesson
from which he had grown. I was Defining Moment No.
39: "The-First-Time-My-Boyfriend-Asked-Me-Out-On-
A-Date." Finally he proclaimed Defining Moment No. 52
as "Right-Here-And-Now-In-Front-of-All-of-You" at
which point he picked up a camcorder and panned slowly across the room. When he lowered the camcorder, the
didgeridoo fell silent. Two heartbeats. You could have heard
a pin drop. Then the room exploded into raucous applause,
and Fang the DJ dropped a killer beat. Right on cue.

An hour later, Parker found me helping Marwa packing away cutlery, dirty plates and wine glasses. While a
few guests had left, even more had arrived and the party
was in full swing. Furniture had been pushed back and a
dozen people were dancing. Others were clustered doing
lines of coke. People stumbled in and out of the bathroom
in twos and threes. Parker found me to say good-bye. He
was going to accompany Michelle DuBarry home. "Daniel,
thank you," he said. "Thank you thank you thank you.
You are the best friend I've ever had."

"You think this might make it into your memoirs?"

Parker rolled his eyes, laughing, and wagged a finger at me. "No. 39, you are a good man."

"Happy New Year, Parker," I said, and gave him a hug.

I hadn't seen Charles and Megan in some time. I eventually found them making out in the bedroom on the pile of coats. "We're leaving, Daniel," Charles said.

"You don't have to leave."

"No, I mean we're leaving."

"We've been trying to leave for twenty minutes," Megan said, fixing her hair and buttoning her blouse. She wiped the lipstick from Charles' mouth. "It's an urgent matter. Can't wait. Tell Marwa thanks for us, okay?"

"Marwa?" I recognized the sweaty look on both their faces. "Okay, be safe. You want me to call you a cab?"

"We already have." Charles grabbed my face and kissed me. "I love you, man." Megan did the same. "Oh, and say bye to Marcus, will you. Bye!"

I found Marcus on the rooftop, with a large number of the remaining guests, setting off fireworks. Roman candles and bottle rockets whistled and burst overhead. Gold crackling crosettes illuminated everyone's upturned face. A hand slipped into mine. "Thanks," Marwa said, "for all your help tonight. You're really sweet."

"You're welcome." Showers of sparks fountained across the sky. Our breath formed frosty clouds. Someone handed out sparklers. "Charles and Megan just left," I said. "They told me to tell you thanks."

"Charles and Megan? Was that the big guy with the funny haircut and that girl with the red lipstick?"

"That's them."

"Oh, they were such a cute couple. Is he her sub?"

"What?"

"Is Charles her sub?"

"I don't even known what that means."

"They're in a dom/sub relationship, aren't they?"

"Oh, um. I don't think so."

"Really? I'm surprised."

"What makes you think that?"

"Oh, just something about their energies. I can read people's energies, you know. If they're not, they should be." Marwa squeezed my hand. "They'll figure it out. How do you know Charles and Megan?"

"Charles and I used to date. Megan's my best friend's best friend. Well, second best friend."

"And where's your best friend?"

"Karen? Not here. She's with my brother Liam. They've been an item since high school. Kind of."

"Kind of?"

"It's complicated."

"Interesting."

Now people were lighting sparklers and flinging them off the rooftop. "This keeps up, someone's going to call the cops."

"Lighten up, Daniel. It's New Year's. No one's going to call the cops. You want to smoke a joint?"

"I can't. It makes me sick."

"Coke? E? K? Shrooms?"

"What are you, a dealer?"

Marwa smiled up at me and nodded. "Mm-hm."

"Oh. Um, no thanks. Marcus doesn't do drugs."

"I wasn't asking if Marcus wanted drugs. I was asking

if you did. It's on the house, anything you want. He has me cater all his parties. You can trust me."

"I trust you."

"How about a beer, can I get you one of those?"

"Okay."

I followed Marwa back downstairs, careful to grip the railing. The fire escape was slick with ice. "He does, you know," she said over her shoulder.

"What?"

"Marcus. He does do drugs. Or he used to. He went through rehab a couple years ago."

"I didn't know that."

"Don't tell him I told you."

Back inside, someone had lit candles, lots of them. Pillows were strewn across the floor and people were making out. Boys with girls. Girls with girls. Boys with boys. DJ Fang had taken his shirt off, the sweat glistening on his torso under the hot theatre lights. Most of the remaining guests dancing were also topless.

"And he's okay with all of this?"

"You're a funny guy," Marwa said. She handed me a cold beer from a silver tub filled with half-melted ice. She wiped her hand on my chest. Swaying her hips, she untied her blouse and pulled it off over her head. Her bra was frosty white. A crystal jewel nestled in her navel. She placed a pink pill on her tongue. "Here." She held up another pill. "Stay with me." An image of a red BMW pulling away flashed through my mind. I opened my mouth and let her place it between my teeth. She took a sip from my beer and handed it back. I also took a sip and swallowed. "There you go. Now that wasn't complicated at all, was it? Happy New Year, Daniel the Doorman."

"Happy New Year. Marwa the Meatball Queen."

"I like that," she murmured. "I really like that."

"I made that up myself."

"You're funny. I can see why he likes you."

"Who?"

"Marcus. He really likes you. I've met all his boyfriends. We go back years, Marcus and me."

"You're from Burlington?"

"Don't sound so surprised. Everyone in Toronto is from somewhere. Burlington hosts Canada's largest ribfest, did you know? Actually, there's Millcroft, South Burlington and Lakeshore. Marcus and I grew up in Millcroft. Us Millcrofters along with Orchard kids are sheltered cunts and assholes shat out by rich people, although we'll take on any pussy from Oakville."

"Okay."

"Am I boring you? You want an Egyptian meatball? I am the Meatball Queen, I'll have you know."

"No. No thanks, and no, you're not boring me. I was just. I was just thinking. Marcus, he never talks about his exes."

"Who does? Who wants to hear that?"

"What were they like?"

"Marcus' boyfriends?"

"Yeah."

"Well, not like you. You know he dated his semiotics professor once?"

"You mean that old guy who was here?"

"Mm-hm. Oh, now that's going to get me in trouble. Don't tell Marcus I told you. Although, the truth is ..."

"What?"

"This is really going to get me in trouble."

"What?"

Marwa leaned in conspiratorially. "Well, the last time I looked, four, no, five of his exes were here, I think? That's not counting Professor Dumbledore."

"What, tonight? Here?"

"Marcus stays friends with all of his old boyfriends."

"Okay. He never mentioned this. Which ones were they? Are any of them still here? What is it?"

Marwa was biting her lower lip, staring up at me with her big Sally Bowles eyes. "I'm sorry. I shouldn't have said anything. That's why I cook and bake. When I cook and bake, I don't get into trouble. I should stick to cooking and baking."

"You're not in trouble."

"You're not one of those jealous types, are you? Marcus can't stand jealous types. A lot of his boyfriends couldn't handle the attention he gets."

"I have no problem with the attention he gets, Marwa."

"I am in trouble."

"No, you're not in trouble. I'm good. Really. Honestly. Here, cheers." I grabbed an open bottle of whiskey on the counter. "Happy New Year." I took a swig.

"Slow down there, Daniel. That pill I gave you is pretty strong."

"I'm happy, okay?"

"Okay. I can see that." She took the bottle from my hand and set it aside. "You're sweet."

"So are you."

"You want to dance?"

"Definitely."

I was still dancing when Marcus found me an hour later. "I see you've been consorting with Marwa." He nuzzled my neck. Then I took his face between my sweaty hands and kissed him. He smelled so good, like Egyptian meatballs, patchouli and sulphur. I couldn't stop smelling him. Amanda had taken over DJ duties from Fang. "I'm sorry," Marcus said, "I haven't been more attentive."

"That's okay." I couldn't stop dancing while I was smelling him. "This is an amazing party."

"Thank you." He was the only person on the crowded dance floor with his shirt still on. "You're one of a kind, Daniel Garneau."

"People loved that spoken word piece you did. They loved it. They just loved it. I loved it. It was great."

"Thank you."

"It was amazing. Marwa tells me you used to date Fang."

"I did."

"He's really cute."

"He is."

"You should introduce us."

Marcus glanced at Fang across the room. He regarded me sidelong. "Are you sure?"

"Of course, I'm sure."

"Alright." Marcus rested a hand on my shoulder. "Walk with me."

He led me over to Fang who was sucking on a slice of lime while mixing himself a drink. "Hey Fang, you've met my boyfriend, Daniel."

"Yeah, man, we met earlier. Happy New Year, Dan-the-Man."

"Daniel thinks you're cute."

"Alright. Tell him I think he's pretty rockin' too."

"Fang think's your cute too."

"Well, tell him I think he's fucking hot."

"My boyfriend here thinks you're fucking hot."

Fang smiled and held out a wedge of lime, bopping to the music. When I bit into it, the juices ran down my chin and his hairy wrist. He ate the rest of the slice and threw the peel into the sink. "Tell him," he said, licking his fingers, "he should take off his pants."

"Fang wants you to take off your pants."

I realized to my amazement I was the only person left in the loft, apart from Marcus, who was still wearing pants. I unbuckled my belt and pulled off my pants. Marcus folded it for me and set it on top of the microwave.

"Tell him," I said. "Tell him I've never danced in my underwear before. Wow."

"Daniel wants you to know he's never danced in his underwear before. Wow."

Fang laughed, showing dimples like Karen's. When he exchanged glances with Marcus, I looked down and discovered to my horror I had an enormous, unmistakable erection. My embarrassment ended when Marcus knelt in front of me, pulled down my underwear and took me into his mouth. The three of us were behind the kitchen island separating us from the rest of the loft. But it was still pretty obvious what was going on to anyone who might look our way. Fang leaned in and started kissing me. He wasn't gentle. He kept biting my lips. I held him by the back of his head and pressed his mouth hard against mine. After a minute, I realized Marcus was alternating between Fang and me. This was a whole lot better than the Three Amigas. If anyone on the dance floor noticed, they just kept dancing. When Marcus took both of us into his mouth, I felt dizzy and for a second felt like I was going to pass out.

"Daniel, you okay?" It was Marwa, leaning on the opposite side of the island. She had her bra off and I noticed both her nipples were pierced with studs that matched the jewel in her navel.

"Yeah," I gasped. "I'm okay."

"You want some water?"

"No," I grimaced.

"You sure you're okay?"

"Marwa," Fang said, "fuck off."

Marwa gave Fang the finger, smiled benignly and strolled away. At least she was still wearing her panties.

"Holy shit," I said, my eyes rolling back. After another minute, Marcus stood and gestured with his head. He walked away towards the bedroom without a backward glance. Fang and I both pulled off of our underwear and followed. I couldn't help but think Parker Kapoor had missed out. Marwa was making out now with Amanda the DJ. The whole room was turning, in fact, into one Bacchanalian orgy. I wondered if this was what the *Toronto Star* meant by "quintessentially Canadian."

I didn't think so.

⌒ Two days later, I called Parker and had him come over to my apartment. When he arrived, I told him, in bits and pieces, everything that had happened. "OMG, Daniel," said Parker, "there is no such thing as TMI, JFYI. Here." He handed me a steaming bowl of Mr. Noodles. I was huddled on my couch wrapped in a blanket. "You look awful." Parker stared at me. "How do you feel?"

I closed my eyes. "Like shit." I concentrated on picking up the spoon. "Like I've been run over by a posse of dykes-on-bikes and tarred and feathered from the inside-out."

"Oooh, throw in a marching band and there's a Marcus show in there somewhere."

"He's already done the tar-and-feather thing."

"Has he?" Parker folded his hands on his knees. "Why am I not surprised? Eat your noodles."

I sipped on the broth. I had no appetite whatsoever. Karen had left a message saying she'd be staying an extra few days in Sudbury. There'd been no word or sign of Pat. I'd called Parker because I couldn't stand being alone in the apartment anymore. "I think I overdid it."

Parker pursed his lips. He could've said a lot of things in that moment, but what he did say was simply: "I'm sorry you're not feeling well, Daniel."

I hadn't slept at all the night of New Year's Eve. Come morning, the small group of us remaining took two cabs across town to an after-hours called Comfort Zone where we continued to party into the next day. The Zone was a claustrophobic cave, barely illuminated and packed with sweaty bodies from all walks of life: ginos with their bleached-blonde girlfriends, glowstick-twirling club kids, middle-aged men in suits. By evening, I finally made the decision to go home. The venue hadn't thinned out at all, but I was done. At the Zone, I'd lost my shirt and left wearing only my winter jacket. Back home, I fell asleep huddled in the shower. I woke up, dried off and crawled naked into bed. Marwa texted to see if I'd gotten home okay, and I let her know I was going to sleep. I woke up the next day feeling as though the inside of my mouth and head had been carved out like a watermelon and filled with sawdust. That was when I called Parker.

"Thanks for coming over, Parker."

"Well, I had planned to go shopping today." He pulled his chair closer. "All the good sales happen after the New Year, you know. Every year I stroll along Bloor Street in my Burberry scarf with a venti Caramel Brûlé Latte and a Danish, and feel just like Audrey Hepburn in *Breakfast at Tiffany's.*"

"And here you are."

"Daniel Garneau, listen to me." He rested his hands on mine. "There is no place in this world I'd rather be. I'm glad you called."

"Thanks."

"Besides, shopping alone isn't all it's cracked up to be. You should come out again, Daniel. We had a fun time together."

"Maybe."

"Is it okay," he asked, "if I make myself a tea? Do you want one?" I shook my head. "Finish up. You'll feel better after you eat." I did feel better after I ate. A lot better. But I was also starting to worry about Pat. A text came through on my phone. Parker handed me a steaming mug of Earl Grey. "Who was that?"

"It's my brother Pat."

"He's alive."

"He's in Montreal."

"I thought he was on the Toronto Islands."

"He was. Now he's in Montreal."

"Is he okay?"

I nodded and tossed my phone aside. I lay back down again. "How was your night, Parker? You left with that drag queen."

"I had the most wonderful time. I saw Michelle DuBarry back home. A lady of her quality should not travel unaccompanied. Daniel, she is the most extraordinary human being I have ever met in my entire life. We have a luncheon-date coming up."

"You sound like a groupie."

"She is a living legend, Daniel. She's Toronto's oldest drag queen. She was born in 1931. At the rate she's going, she'll probably live to be a hundred."

"I'll be happy if I get through to next week."

"Well, Miss DuBarry told me her motto's always been: 'If you're going through hell, just keep going.'"

"I have a T-shirt that says that."

"Very apropos. Has your boyfriend called?"

"No."

"Isn't that a little odd?"

"Well, I haven't called Marcus either, have I?"

"Is everything okay between the two of you?"

"As far as I can tell. He was acting kind of funny at Comfort Zone. I think he fell off the wagon."

"What do you mean?"

"He kept going to the washroom with Fang. Then he was acting all sketchy, like he owned the place. I dunno.

When I told him I wanted to leave, all he asked was whether or not I had cab money."

"You should call him, Daniel."

"I don't want to."

"What's wrong?"

"I'm embarrassed. I did a shitload of drugs. I had sex in front of a dozen people I barely know. This isn't the first time, right? What if someone took a picture? What if this gets all over Facebook? Parker, I'm planning to be a doctor. What if five or ten years from now some photo turns up on the Internet? My career is ruined. I'm fucked, this is so fucked!" I whipped a pillow across the room. Parker flinched. "I'm sorry. I'm sorry. This isn't me. This is so not me. I'm not into open relationships. I really, really don't like this. I'm scared."

"Look, Daniel, it's going to be okay. These things happen. You'll feel better about it tomorrow. And then next week you'll feel a whole lot better about it."

"You think?"

"I promise."

I massaged my temples with the heels of my hands. "Okay. Okay." I sighed. "Alright."

"Alright?"

"Alright."

"Do you want to watch a movie?"

"Sure."

"What are you in the mood for?"

"You pick one."

"Happy or sad?"

"Happy. No, sad. No, happy. I dunno. You pick."

I fell asleep on the couch while Parker was still browsing

through my movie collection. When I woke up, the curtains had been drawn, and someone had covered me with a blanket. I found Chinese take-out on the dining table, still warm in its white cardboard boxes, with extra plum sauce and soy sauce in little plastic packets, along with a handful of cellophane-wrapped fortune cookies. Parker had set out my Collector's Edition copy of *The Wizard of Oz* on the DVD player. The towels and dirty clothes had all been picked up in the washroom, and my bed had been made. There was a single text on my phone: GONE SHOPPING. ENJOY JUDY. KEEP GOING. AUDREY.

⌒ Marcus and I broke up on Valentine's Day. Marcus wanted to keep our relationship open and experiment with a threesome with Fang. After New Year's Eve, I sure as hell wasn't about to call the kettle black. For a while, I tried my best, but I couldn't get on board. Pat had introduced the word polyamory to me, but it always remained just a word. You don't pick and choose the people you love. Fang was friendly enough, but I think deep down he found me boring. Then I started to wonder if Marcus did too. The last straw came when we were having Valentine's dinner at the 360 Restaurant in the CN Tower. During appetizers, Marcus remarked that he'd invited Fang to join us for drinks afterwards. He'd made arrangements for the three of us to sample ice wines in the restaurant's Cellar in the Sky which, at 351 metres above sea level, was apparently the highest in the world.

To my own surprise, we got into a fight over it and I walked away before the main course was served. The restaurant revolved slowly, offering a panoramic view of the city in the wintry dark 351 metres below. Sex with Marcus and Fang had been exciting, at first. Maybe, in the end, I was the jealous type. I took off my tie and flung it aside. I walked along the LookOut level, unfastening the top buttons of my shirt. My hands were trembling.

Marcus caught up to me standing on the Glass Floor. At night, it was difficult to gauge the distance to the ground. But I could sense the vast, windy emptiness falling away beneath our feet. He stood next to me, arms clasped behind his back, gazing down below.

"I'm sorry, Daniel," he finally said. "I should've asked you first. I thought you'd be pleased."

"Well, I'm not."

"I can see that."

"It's Valentine's Day, for chrissake."

"Like I said, I thought you'd be pleased."

If the glass broke now we'd both plummet to our deaths. "I guess I'm just old-fashioned that way."

"Yes, you are. It's what I love about you the most. It's been unfair of me to have imposed Fang on us the way I have."

"Well, I opened that door, didn't I?"

"No. That door was open long ago. You just walked us through it."

"Are you still in love with him? Is that what it is?"

"I never stop loving my lovers, no matter what difficulties end my relationships. I always remember what I loved about them the most."

"That's not what I asked."

"It's the best answer I have."

"Marwa says you stay friends with all of them."

"I do. I try. My friends are my family. They're all that I have. You've met my parents."

"Sure."

"Do you remember the first time you asked me out?"

"Yes."

"No one's ever asked me out on a date. Ever. When you asked me, Daniel, it was momentous."

"What do you mean?"

"I mean just that. I know what effect I have on people. I awe people. I intimidate people. I sometimes do it on purpose. But most times, it just happens. People think I'm out of their league. If they only knew how starved I am for attention of any kind. I'd have coffee with a street person if they asked me to."

"That's why you accepted my invitation?"

"Also because you're handsome and shy, and you seemed interested in my work. And because you quoted the *Globe & Mail* article about me when we were at The Beaver. And because you have the most beautiful, genuine smile in the world, when you do smile. And because you're simple."

"Simple?"

"Simple, Daniel. Like a glass of water. Or a pane of glass."

I pondered this for a moment. "Marcus, look, I can't keep seeing you when Fang's in the picture. I regret what I did New Year's Eve. I regret it a lot. I knew exactly what I was doing, and I did it anyway."

"Daniel, what happened happened. If it didn't happen that way, it still would've happened."

"Marwa says she caters all your parties. She's a drug dealer. Were you expecting it to turn out the way it did?"

"My friends, they're artists, they're free spirits."

"Marcus, cut the bullshit, please. Just tell me, were you expecting things to end up as a sex party?"

"Yes," he said. "I was."

"You could've warned me."

"I didn't think something like that needed warning. I treat my friends as adults."

"It'd be nice to be treated as a boyfriend too."

"That," Marcus said, his brow creasing, "is such a quaint and old-fashioned label."

"You didn't tell me you'd invited all your old boy-friends to the party."

"They're my friends, alright? You took off your pants first, Daniel. Not me."

My hands felt numb. Beneath us, I felt the glass crack. "So are you going to keep seeing him?"

"He's special, like you. I'd really like the three of us to work."

"Well, that's not happening."

"Fang and I go back a long way."

"Okay." My throat felt constricted. I struggled to breathe. "Then we're done here, aren't we?"

"That's one option."

"There are no options here!"

"This kind of black-and-white thinking saddens me."

I wanted to say, "Fuck you, Marcus," but I didn't. He hadn't done anything wrong. I just wanted him to fight more for me. I wanted him to sacrifice more for me. I was shocked and unnerved how easy this appeared to be for him. I was freefalling again, and it was familiar, and it was cold and it was awful. When he handed me my tie, looking like an angel, like a martyr, I wanted to choke him with it. But I didn't. Instead, I just thanked him and folded it carefully and placed it in the pocket of my blazer. I even let him take my hand as he walked me to the elevator. He embraced me until the elevator doors opened. He waved goodbye. It was a long, long way down. He was still waving when the elevator doors closed.

CHAPTER EIGHT

Brother Down

"**M**arcus Wittenbrink Jr.," said Karen, "is a narcissistic prick. You really need to forget about him, Daniel." We watched as a butcher expertly dismembered a side of beef, his white smock stained with blood. It was a bright Saturday afternoon in April and we were browsing through St. Lawrence Market in Old Town Toronto. Even though we were indoors, I kept my sunglasses on. Final exams were a week away, but I'd barely even started studying. "Have you had sex with anyone," Karen asked, "since the two of you broke up?"

"No."

"Well, you should at least go on a date. It'll help take your mind off things."

"Who says I want to take my mind off things?"

"You want to get back together with him, is that it?"

"No. He treated me badly."

"Then what is it, Daniel? You've been moping around for months. This isn't like you."

The butcher worked confidently and methodically. He was young and stocky, with chest hair poking up over the collar of his shirt. Briefly, he glanced up at Karen and me, nodded and smiled. Karen waved back. I imagined myself lying on his block, naked and pale, neatly eviscerated, my internal organs in a bloody pile set to one side.

"Whatever happened to the Horned God, paragon of male virility?"

"What?"

Karen made an exasperated sound and grabbed my elbow. "C'mon." We made our way through the cavernous South Market crowded with fruit and vegetable stalls, fish and meats, racks of marinades, preserves and cheeses. We stopped in front of a glass display lined with pies and cakes where Karen bought half a dozen Portuguese tarts. She also bought an extra-large tea and coffee before leading the way outside. We crossed the busy avenue and sat by a fountain facing the sunshine. Distant skyscrapers dwarfed the red wedge of Toronto's Flatiron building down Front Street. "You're subletting the apartment to Pat this summer?" Karen handed me the coffee.

"Yeah, Pat and his girlfriend Blonde Dawn. They might take over the lease in the fall if things work out."

"I'm going to miss that place."

"Me too."

Karen passed me a tart. "We had a lot of good times in that apartment."

"We did."

"Mike and Melissa and baby Benjamin are moving into their condo next month."

"Well, they've got a family to raise now." I observed the pigeons milling underfoot, the sidewalk vendors, the green buds speckling the branches of the trees. "So I've lined up a few bachelor apartments."

"I thought you and Parker were going to find a place together."

"That was his idea. We still might this fall."

"Why don't you just stay with Pat and his girlfriend for the summer? It's only four months."

"I think I'm just needing my own space for a while."

"Daniel, am I going to have to worry about you?"

"I'll be fine."

"When does med school get back to you?"

"Next month."

"Well, I'm sure you're going to get in."

"Thanks."

"You'll let me know when you hear from them?"

"Okay."

"Here. I got you something."

"Karen."

She brushed the crumbs from her hands and rummaged out a small box from her back pack. "To commemorate our three years in Toronto, and the future." She sat back. "Open it."

I opened the lid. It was a man's ring, silver and gold, etched with a quartered circle inlaid with four different coloured stones. I took off my sunglasses. "Oh wow, Karen."

"That's onyx, opal, coral and jasper. It's a medicine wheel. Each colour has a different meaning: resilience and calm, courage and clarity."

"I don't know what to say."

"Put it on." Karen sipped from her tea. "I got it custom-made. How does it feel?"

"It feels good. It's perfect. Thank you." It did fit perfectly. "This really means a lot to me. Thank you. I love it." I gave her a hug. "I got you something too."

"Fuck off. What is it?"

"A graduation present. Close your eyes."

"What for?"

"Close your eyes."

"What it is?"

"Will you just close your eyes?"

Karen squeezed shut her eyes. I took out her gift, opened it and sat close next to her. Today, Karen had pulled her hair up into an unruly bun, so it wasn't hard to reach around and clasp the thin chain around her neck. "Okay, you can open your eyes now."

She looked down and held the pendant in her hands. When she didn't say anything, I cleared my throat. "I have matching earrings too. Here." I held out the thin box.

Karen brushed back a wisp of hair from her face. "They're beautiful," she whispered.

"You deserve it."

When she looked up, her eyes were bright. "These are really expensive, Daniel."

"Well, like I said, you're amazing. You deserve it."

Karen wiped away a tear. "Thanks."

"You okay?"

"I've just never owned a real pearl necklace before."

It was a single teardrop freshwater pearl mounted in sterling silver. I'd gotten the set at The Bay months ago. New green tulip leaves were pushing up through the thawed earth. The breeze blowing in from the lake raised goosebumps on my arms, but the sunshine was warm.

"Well, now you do. We've come a long way, Karen Fobister, you and me. I'm going to miss you."

"Daniel Garneau, I'm going to miss you too."

That summer, Karen moved back to Manitoulin where she'd been offered a full-time job at the Ojibwe Cultural Foundation. I found myself a bachelor apartment in the basement of a townhouse by Dundas and Sherbourne. It was close to downtown and the best I could afford. The apartment itself was spacious enough, with two deadbolts on the front door, and bars on all the windows. I was blocks from a strip club / hotel called Filmores, as well as Toronto's largest homeless shelter. Fights and drug deals in the streets were common. I made sure to carry my bike inside every day, and took to wearing my headphones just so no one would bother me. Pat and his girlfriend Blonde Dawn helped me move, and had me over for dinner that first weekend. Blonde Dawn made matzah balls and a chicken casserole. I brought flowers in a vase, and a magnum of Chardonnay. After three years, it was strange to think the apartment wasn't mine anymore. Blonde Dawn wasn't what I expected. She was smart, no-nonsense and more than direct.

"Here, Dan," she said over dinner, "I'm giving this to you, just in case." She rummaged in her gym bag and handed me a small black canister. "It's pepper spray. Keep it on you. Dundas and Sherbourne is not a pretty part of town." She wasn't drinking that night as she had to work that same evening. It was her first shift as a Toronto EMS ambulance worker. At the door, she grabbed Pat by the jaw, kissed him on the mouth, slapped him on the ass and pointed at the sink. "Dishes." Then she rapped his belt buckle with her keys. "And don't jack off. Bye, Dan. And thanks again for the vase."

"Wow," I said, after she was gone. "Is she always like that?"

Pat refilled both our glasses, emptying the bottle. "Her mom and dad divorced years ago. She's the oldest of five kids. Yeah, she's always like that."

"What's with the tattoos?"

"She loves her ink, what can I say? Here, check it out." Pat lifted his shirt. Over his heart in bold black script were the words: BLONDE DAWN.

"Oh man. Pat, that's pretty serious."

"I got it done for Valentine's Day. We are serious, man. We're in love."

"Okay. Okay, good for you guys. I'm happy for you guys."

"I know what you're thinking. But if we ever break up, she'll still always be my first." Pat sprawled in the love seat. "And if I ever do end up with someone else, well, then they're just going to have to be open-minded enough to understand and appreciate that."

"Did you tell her about the Three Amigas?"

"Look, last summer we agreed we'd see other people, so I wasn't cheating on her, if that's what you're thinking. It was her idea. She was heading up north to go tree planting. How many girls do you think go tree planting up north?"

"Very few, I take it."

"Well as it turns out, there was this other chick but she like breaks a nail and drops out the first day, so Blonde Dawn ends up the only girl on a crew with eleven guys out in the middle of butt-fuck nowhere. Ten weeks, man, ten weeks out in the bush. You have to be realistic about these kinds of things."

"So did you tell her or not?"

"We have a kind of don't-ask-don't-tell policy."

"So you didn't tell her."

"We're not always super strict about it."

"Super strict about what?"

"Don't-ask-don't-tell. I mean sometimes we do talk about it, you know? Sometimes it's hot."

"Really?"

"Sure, really. We're open that way. It can be a turn-on to hear how other guys find your girlfriend hot. Or your boyfriend or whatever. You just have to both be down with it. It's all about trust, man. Blonde Dawn and I, we trust each other."

I thought of the times Marcus and I got together with Trevor Fang since the New Year. Marcus had wanted the three of us to fuck without condoms, but I hadn't been down with that. I hadn't been down with a lot of things.

"To answer your question, Dan, no I haven't told her about the Three Amigas. But one day maybe I will."

"I'd rather you didn't."

"Alright, whatever. It's cool. Carolina says hola, by the way."

I realized I'd started washing the dishes piled in the sink. I put down the casserole pot, dried my hands, and walked away from the kitchen. I'd washed enough of Pat's dirty dishes during my lifetime. I wasn't about to start up again. "Who?"

"Carolina. I'm on Facebook with her, sometimes we Skype. She's back in Colombia."

"And what about the others?"

"Yuka and Sindija? I'm on Facebook with them too, they're all good. But I message with Carolina the most. You never replied to their Friend Requests."

"I'm not really into the Facebook thing anymore these days."

"Alright, Dan, what's going on? You've been acting like a zombie all week."

"Well, Karen's gone. I dunno. I didn't get into med school."

"What does that mean?"

"I mean my application was rejected."

"What. Aw, shit. I'm sorry to hear that. That sucks big time. So, like, are you kicked out?"

"What? No, Pat. No. It just means I didn't get in. I'll be going into my fourth year undergrad. I can apply again next year."

"Definitely. You do that. Don't give up." Pat jabbed a finger at me. "Don't ever give up."

"Did I mention I broke up with my boyfriend?"

"When did that happen?"

"A couple months ago."

"A couple months ago?" Pat rolled his eyes. "Okay, well, sorry to hear that. You were dating that actor guy, right?"

"Marcus."

"How long were you seeing each other?"

"Five months."

"Five months."

"It was intense."

"Were you in love with him?"

"What? I dunno."

Pat slapped his knees and jumped up. "Dude, we need to get you out! I'm taking you out. Come on, finish your drink. We're heading out."

"What, right now?"

"Yeah, right now. It's Saturday. Did you think we were just gonna sit on our butts all night? This is my first official weekend in the big T.O.! We're going out to celebrate. We're going to have a good time. We are going to a gay bar. You want to go back to El Convento?"

"No, I don't want to go back to El Convento. And no, we're not going to a gay bar."

"Sure you are. I'm taking my gay brother to a gay bar."

"No, I'm not going to a gay bar. I'm not, Pat. You can't make me. I'm not going to any fucking gay bar."

"Okay, okay. Don't blow a gasket. So we're not going to a gay bar. How about Sneaky Dee's then? Is that un-gay enough for you? We'll shoot some pool, have a few beers, just like old times." He picked up my shoes and threw them at me one after the other. "We are not staying in."

"Alright." I caught my shoes. "Alright, fine."

We ended up walking to Sneaky Dee's so Pat could have a smoke. As usual, when we got there, the place was packed with student-types and the tables were loaded with platters of nachos and pitchers of beer. Layers of graffiti covered practically every visible surface. Pat shouted out the name of one of the bartenders, acquired two pints, and found us a corner in the back. I was a decent bar pool player. Pat was a shark. Last summer, between the two of us, sometimes we'd hold a table for hours taking on all challengers. Tonight, we chalked up our names and found ourselves facing off against two girls named Nadia and Sam. They were good but we were better. I could tell Pat was holding back. I was taking my time lining up the eight ball when I overheard Pat comment how they could stare at my ass all they wanted, and that while it was a great ass, they should know I was gay, which was a pity since gay guys always had the best asses, didn't they agree? I missed my shot. When we finally won, Pat offered to buy the girls a round. Inexplicably, the conversation turned to how Nadia and Sam had never actually been to a gay club. By then, I was feeling my buzz and, even though I saw it coming a mile away, I went along with the eventual plan to take the girls out.

The four of us took a cab to Fly Nightclub, which was the biggest gay club in the city. Karen had come here once with me on New Year's Eve. Since then, I'd gone back a few times only because Parker insisted on it. As usual, the house music was pounding, and the go-go boys were gyrating up on their pedestals beneath the blazing disco balls. A catwalk circling the dance floor offered a kaleidoscopic view. We were at Fly about an hour before I began to notice how guys kept coming up and chatting with me. Eventually I asked one of them flat out if my brother had set him up to it and he said maybe. After that, I found Pat at the bar, and let him know I was done and calling it a night. When he started to protest, I just gave him a hug, told him to tell the girls bye, and left.

After the chaos of the club, the night was eerily quiet. Stars glimmered overhead, and I could hear the leaves rustling in the trees. I was strolling down the street wishing I'd bummed a cigarette off Pat when someone said: "Hey, 305." I was on a residential block just outside the Village. At first I couldn't make out who it was. Then I saw it was some skinhead sitting on his front stoop smoking a cigarette. When I kept walking, he jumped up and started following me. "Hey," he called out. The street was poorly lit and my fist in my pocket gripped Blonde Dawn's pepper spray. I would've preferred a roll of quarters, but I figured it'd have to do. When he called out a third time. I stopped and turned.

The guy approached me. He was wearing a sleeveless hoodie and his arms were covered in tattoos. "You don't remember me, do you?" He flicked his butt aside. "You were Room 305. I used to have a mohawk?"

Then I remembered him. It was the staff from the bathhouse. Room 305. Right. "You gave me a T-shirt."

"Yeah, I did."

I blushed and looked away, suddenly grateful for the dark. "Sorry about that."

"No worries, man."

"I was having a bad day."

"I was glad I could help."

"I can't believe you remember me."

"You were memorable."

"Fuck."

"S'okay. We all have those days. You were having yours."

"So, what happened to the mohawk?"

"Shaved it off."

"It was a good look. Why'd you do that?"

"Chemo."

"Chemo. Oh. Chemo. I'm sorry."

"Don't be, it's all good. I'm in remission. I did it just last month. It still feels fucking weird."

"Being in remission?"

"No, man. Losing my hair."

"I'll bet." I reached out and felt his head. "It feels nice." My hand came to rest on his shoulder.

"Look, buddy, I'm actually straight, okay? I just wanted to say hi."

I let my hand fall to my side. "Sorry."

"No worries."

"Alright."

"Except now," he said, laughing, "I look like some piss ass skinhead."

"No. No you don't."

"You heading out somewhere?"

"I'm not sure. I think I was just going home."

"It's a nice night."

"Yeah, it is."

"You want a beer?"

"I dunno."

He shrugged. "I'm offering."

"Okay."

I followed him back to his house, a dilapidated semi-detached set back from the street. I sat and waited for him on the front steps. After a minute, he came back out with two beers. "Here." He opened a bottle and handed it to me. "I'd invite you in except my nephew's sleeping."

"Your nephew?"

"My sister's kid. She's working tonight."

"What does your sister do?"

"Bartender down at the ACC."

"That'd be the Leafs playing the Flyers tonight."

"If you say so."

"The game should be over by now."

"Then she's out drinking with her girlfriends. Girls Night Out, y'know. Woohoo."

"You're not working?"

"Naw, not tonight. It's my night off."

"And you're baby-sitting?"

"Yeah, well, we all live together, my sis, the kid and me. I don't mind. It's family, the three of us, y'know?"

He held up two cigarettes. I took one and let him light it for me. Individual letters on his knuckles spelled out the word PATIENCE. "Thanks. Should you, you know, be smoking?"

He snapped his Zippo shut. "It's all good." He took a drag off his cigarette and smiled at me sidelong.

"Okay."

"Wanna see something?"

"Sure."

He leaned into me. "Check this out." He lit his lighter again and held it up to his wrist. On the inside of his forearm was the image of a winged baby.

"Is that your nephew?"

"Yeah, that's him. Cute, eh?"

"He is."

"Damn right he is." He put away the lighter. "He just turned two. He looks just like his mom."

"Where's his dad?"

Mohawk Guy made a face and shrugged. A helicopter passed overhead. The city gave off too much illumination to see actual satellites. As he gazed up at the night sky, I wanted to put my arm around his shoulder, but I didn't. "My nights off," he said, "I like sitting out here. It's quiet. Nobody can see you. It's like you're invisible, you know what I'm sayin'? You get to observe a lot of interesting things. Once I saw this drag queen pull down her panties and fuck this other guy right over there."

"No kidding."

"You coming from Fly?"

"Yeah."

"You don't seem like a Fly guy."

"I'm not."

He nodded. We both watched a cat cross the street. "The best thing about this neighbourhood is the raccoons. They remind me of home, y'know? There were these coons used to live in this big hollowed-out tree just behind our barn. Sis and me, we start feeding them. Hell, they'd come up and eat right next to our cats. They had these babies one year and trooped them right up to our back door. Then sis brought one inside the house. Big mistake."

"What happened?"

"Pop found out what was going on. He stayed up the next night and shot 'em. Then he torched that tree. We watched it go up in flames."

"That's fucked up."

"Yeah. Well, that man was a fucker. I don't blame our mom for leaving him."

Police sirens rose and fell faintly. "My parents," I said, "died in a car accident."

"Shit."

"One minute, they were there, telling us to go to bed on time and kissing us on the tops of our heads. And then they were gone. Just gone. Just like that. They were coming back from some party. I learned later their car rolled and caught fire. It made page two in the news. At the funeral, it was all closed caskets. We didn't understand at the time why it had to be that way."

"Shit."

"Our grandfather raised us after that."

"How'd that turn out?"

"It was okay. He's a good guy."

"Alright. Here's to good guys."

We knocked bottles. Mohawk Guy's hoodie was only partially zipped and I could see his bare chest underneath. I butted out my cigarette and dangled my beer between my knees. "So where's your girlfriend?"

He leaned back against the railing and tiredly stretched out his legs one by one. "In this city? Shit, I don't have a girlfriend. I work sixty hours a week. I don't got time for no girlfriend."

"You get all those hours at the bathhouse?"

"Naw. I bus tables at Black Eagle weeknights. They like me there."

"You sure you're straight?"

"Yeah, buddy. I am."

"That's too bad."

He glanced at me and smiled crookedly. "You think?" I noticed he was missing a tooth. He was good-looking in a rough trade kind of way. "I saw this guy get gay-bashed right over there," he said, pointing, "right outside Fly. There were three of them and they had him on the ground. It was bad."

"What'd you do?"

"I broke a bottle and went after them, and they took off. Someone else called 911."

"You just keep coming to the rescue."

"Yeah, well. That guy died."

"What?"

"The gay guy who got bashed, he died, like a year later. Overdosed on painkillers. I didn't get to him fast enough."

"I'm sorry to hear that."

"That didn't get into the news. You'd be surprised what shit doesn't get into the news."

"I guess so."

"Look, buddy, you can blow me if you want."

I picked at the label on my bottle. "I thought you said you were straight."

"I am."

"Oh."

"I just normally charge people."

"What kind of people?"

"People. People who'd pay to blow someone."

"Oh."

"There's no charge tonight."

"I dunno."

He shrugged. "I'm offering."

The label came free, mostly intact, and I folded it into a tiny square. "Sure. Inside?"

"No, like I said, my nephew's sleeping."

"Where then?"

"Right here."

"Right here? People can see."

"Did you see me?"

"No."

"Okay then."

"Alright."

Mohawk Guy unbuckled his belt and opened his pants. I set aside my beer and knelt on the bottom step. When he took it out, it was medium-sized, soft and uncut. I pulled back the foreskin and put it in my mouth. He tasted salty, musky. My arm rested on his thigh. It took a while before he started to get hard. By then, my other hand was in my own pants. In the end, I jerked both of us off, also using my mouth and my tongue. Mohawk Guy didn't say anything, but his breathing got harder through his nose. I could tell when he was getting close. Then I timed it so I came the same time he did. It trickled out of him in weak pulses. Afterwards, he pulled up his pants and buckled his belt.

"Thanks."

"You're welcome."

It'd been a long time since I'd come, and I'd dropped a huge load. I wiped myself using the bottom of my shirt and a crumpled napkin I found in my pocket. We finished our beers in silence. He offered me another cigarette, but I'd had enough. I wasn't a smoker. Across the street there was a movement in the shadows. As we watched, a huge raccoon crossed the front drive of an apartment building, followed by four baby raccoons. "Well I'll be damned," Mohawk Guy said. Down the block, someone stumbled out of Fly Nightclub and threw up. When I looked back, the raccoons were gone.

"Did you see that?"

"Yeah. They were cute little fuckers."

I sat up on the top step next to him. We sat like this for a while. I draped my arm over his shoulders. He didn't stop me or say anything. Eventually, he finished his cigarette and flicked the butt onto the front lawn. "Well," he said, "it was nice talking to you." He held out his fist and I pressed my knuckles against his.

I got up. "Good luck," I said. "You know, you still look good without your mohawk."

"Thanks. But I plan on growing it back."

"You do that." I started down the walkway. When I reached the sidewalk, I shouted back at him: "I'm counting on it." I could barely make him out. He was lying down on his back, one foot propped up over his knee. He'd pulled his hood up over his head and was smoking another cigarette. The ember glowed, a single point of light in the dark. I could still taste him in my mouth, his saltiness and his muskiness. I had an urge to go back and lie down next to him, to spoon him and wrap my arm around his chest and tell him everything was going to be okay. Invisibly, far above, satellites passed overhead. Instead, I turned and walked away.

⌒ The Free Times Café at College and Spadina was one of my favourite places. In the late afternoons, I'd pack my textbooks and laptop and go there to study. I'd order a pint and nurse it for hours. Sometimes I'd order food (their latkes were the best in the city). In the back Club Room the walls were covered with portraits of some of the more famous musicians who'd performed on their tiny stage over the years. Every night, seven days a week, they'd host live music, local and regional artists hawking their EPs or CDs out of a guitar or violin case. The venue didn't hold more than fifty people. It was intimate and dark, it was beautiful and perfect.

Last summer I'd introduced Pat to Free Times. He took it upon himself to get to know the owner Judy Perly who'd run the venue close to twenty-five years. She was short with big red hair, and could be spotted personally managing the space every night. This summer, Pat and Blonde Dawn planned their world premiere as a duo for the Monday Nite Open Stage. Back in our senior year, Pat's band Krypton had won second place in Sudbury's Teen Battle of the Bands. Once Krypton performed at the mayor's niece's house party with all five members wearing nothing but socks. (That show went on to become an urban legend.) Boys and girls fell in love with Patrick Garneau wherever he went. But when Pat told me his plans to perform at Toronto's Free Times, I was secretly worried how his talent might hold up in the big city.

The night he was to step up onto the Open Stage, I arrived early to make sure to get good seats. I'd brought Parker, Charles and Megan with me. Sign-up started at seven p.m., but by eight p.m., Pat was still nowhere to be seen. He wasn't answering my calls or my texts and the performers were about to begin. After three acts, I gave up on Pat, apologized to my friends, and resigned myself to enjoying the evening as best I could. There was still beer, great food and live entertainment. I figured Pat and I had simply gotten the date mixed up. When the final act came up, I had to do a double take. It was Pat and Blonde Dawn, each decked out in a black suit, sunglasses and a fedora. They'd been sitting in the back all along, and I hadn't recognized them in the crowd. Pat slung his old Martin over his shoulders, adjusted his harmonica on its neck rack, pointed me out in the front row and announced he wanted to dedicate their opening number to his brother Dan who'd broken up with his boyfriend back in February and hadn't yet gotten over it. Three more musicians, a bass, a trumpet and a saxophone, joined them on stage. "We do sincerely hope you'll all enjoy the show," Pat declared, "and please remember people, that no matter who you are and what you do to live, thrive and survive, there're still some things that make us all the same. You, me, them, everybody, everybody." After that, with Blonde Dawn on drums, Pat launched into a cover of "Everybody Needs Somebody to Love." By the third chorus, he had the entire Club Room on its feet, clapping, stamping, and chanting along. Then Pat attempted to haul me onto the stage. When I refused, Parker, Megan and Charles pushed me from behind. When I still refused, Judy Perly herself came out and escorted me up. *The Blues Brothers* had been one of Dad's favourites. Jake and Elwood Blues were among Pat's heroes. Even Liam could quote lines from that movie, and this song ranked up there as one of our all-time favourites.

Pat and I shared the mic, cheek-to-cheek, belting out the final refrain.

We brought the house down.

CHAPTER NINE

Wake Up to the Sun

On our twenty-first birthday, Pat convinced me to come out to a concert at the Kathedral on Queen West. The headliner was some band called Alexisonfire. The venue turned out to be a huge purple-painted cinderblock of a building with filthy, sticky floors. Pat bought me a Jägermeister and a beer and introduced me to a dozen of his friends. "The Kathedral," Pat explained enthusiastically, "it's like *Cheers* for punks." In the three years I'd lived in Toronto, I'd spent most of my time in campus pubs and cafés. I wasn't used to this bizarre display of tattoos and piercings. But Pat was Pat. He could be best friends with anyone in the world.

"So Pat tells me you're a doctor?" someone asked, a dark-haired guy in a Nickelback T-shirt.

"Um, no. That's a long ways off. I just want to be a doctor." The music was a swirling wash of electric guitars, the bass beat reverberating in my chest. Nickelback Guy was a little shorter than me, compact, with the clearest blue-gray eyes I'd ever seen. "What do you do?" I asked. He smiled and nodded. I drained my beer and shouted in his ear. "So what do you do?"

"I'm a bike mechanic," he said and kept talking for another minute, tapping me on the chest with the back of his hand for emphasis. His nails were painted black. I had no idea what he was saying. I just smiled and nodded. Pat and his other friends had disappeared. Nickelback Guy ducked away and left me standing alone. So much for my twenty-first birthday. Ten minutes later, just as I was thinking of leaving, he shouldered his way back through the crowd with another two Jägers and two beers. "Cheers." He grinned in a lopsided kind of way. "Happy birthday." I could lip-read that much. I noticed one of his front teeth was chipped. He ran the tip of his tongue across it. "Cycling accident."

I blushed, embarrassed he'd caught me staring. "Thanks," I said. We tossed back the shots and knocked bottles. He stood next to me as the opening act came on, the side of his arm pressed against mine. It was some local punk-house band called Kids on TV. Boys in wolf masks, underwear and knee pads pranced about on stage. Nickelback Guy leaned into me. "What do you think of these guys?"

"They're different."

"Well, I think that lead singer's fucking hot. Would you have sex with him?"

"Probably."

"Probably?"

Despite myself, I had to laugh. "Okay, he's hot."

"Definitely. It's David, by the way."

"What?"

"David Gallucci, that's my name. Just in case you've forgotten."

"Daniel Garneau." I shook his hand.

"I know who you are, mister." He looked me hard in the eye. His breath smelled like Jägermeister, cigarettes and cinnamon. I thought he was going to kiss me right then and there.

Pat draped his arms over both our shoulders. "How you boys doing?"

"Fine," we retorted in unison.

That night, David took me back to his loft and we were making out before the front door was closed, knocking over a framed poster of Che Guevara, scrabbling at our buckles and zippers, before moving to the mattress on the floor, trailing clothes behind us. I left before dawn while he still slept. It was good, really good, but I never expected to see him again. Yet a few days later he texted me, telling me he'd gotten my number from Pat, and asked if I wanted to go out on a date, a real date.

We met Saturday afternoon at the Art Gallery of Ontario. The last time I'd come to the AGO was when I'd brought Parker Kapoor, when Marcus Wittenbrink Jr. was still a distant mirage in my life. When I got off the streetcar, I spotted him across the intersection leaning against the giant bronze by Henry Moore. Today he was clean-shaven, wearing a pair of black jeans and a vintage blue dress shirt. For a moment, I didn't recognize him at all. I withdrew beneath the awning of the Village Idiot Pub and watched him as he checked his phone and lit a cigarette. One week ago, I'd had sex with this man. I recalled the nape of his neck, his pink nipples and taut chest, the inside of his thighs, pale and muscular, dusted in soft dark hair. I'd expected tattoos, but he didn't have any. His crotch had smelled musky and pleasantly sweet. When I'd drawn back from deep-throating him to catch my breath, we'd remained connected by a gleaming thread of precum. Pedestrians crowded the intersection separating us, a constellation of humanity. I imagined invisible lines of energy weaving between everyone: ex-lovers, work colleagues, distant cousins, hospital patients who'd shared the same recovery room, two people who'd exchanged glances once in an elevator years ago.

David spotted me and waved. Hello. Goodbye. It was all the same gesture. I waved back, drew a breath and crossed the street. It was just a couple hours at the art gallery, I reminded myself, nothing more. By way of greeting, I patted the side of his arm. It was David who drew us together and gave me a hug. That afternoon, he led me on a guided tour of the AGO. Apparently, he and his sister had come here for years. He showed me his favourite Renaissance pieces by Donatello, da Vinci, Raphael and Michelangelo. Logically, he concluded, the Teenage Mutant Ninja Turtles were also all gay. After we were done, we shared an espresso in the Parisian-styled café across the street. That evening, we walked into Chinatown where we had dinner at The Red Room, decorated with fairy lights, busts of buddhas and artwork by local Toronto artists. After two pitchers of Tsingtao, we ended up next door at the El Mocambo. It was a sold-out event, a Battle Royale of all-girl rock bands. But David knew the bouncer and got us both in.

Towards the end of that summer, David asked me to move in with him. But before I made any decision, he said he had a confession to make. He was perched on a stool on the gravel rooftop of his Kensington Market loft. The sun was hot and we passed a cigarette back and forth as I shaved his neck with a number two clipper. We ran power through an extension cord from inside the stairwell, the steel door propped open with a broken cinder block. Colourful graffiti decorated the concrete walls. "So what's this confession?" I asked after a minute.

David picked at the peeling decals on his stool. "So before we met, you know how I was friends with your brother Pat, right?"

"Right." I switched to a number one clipper and carefully began blending my way up.

"Well, did he ever tell you exactly how we met?"

"He told me you'd both crashed this frat party birthday bash where neither of you actually knew anyone, that you met in the kitchen and bullshitted each other all night before figuring out the truth. I've heard this before, David. Hold still."

"Okay." A seagull flew past carrying a bagel in its beak. "Okay, well, we both got pretty wasted that night."

"Alright."

"So, Pat and I, we just thought it was hilarious the two of us had met like that, you know?"

"Mm-hm."

"And you know your brother's pretty hot, right?"

Almost done. I took the scissors and carefully clipped a few stray hairs around his ears. "Yeah?"

"So I kinda messed around with him that night."

"Kinda messed around?"

"Well, I kissed him. Or he kissed me. We made out in the washroom, maybe for half-a-minute. I think someone might've slipped G into the keg. I need you to know this before you move in. He said he'd just broken up with his girlfriend, that he'd never kissed another guy before, and he wanted to see what it was like."

"That's not true."

"I know, he told me that later. He was just messing with me. He told me not to tell you, that you'd freak out. So does this, like, freak you out?"

I stood back. "Okay, all done." I unplugged the extension cord and began to roll it up. "David, look, Pat already told me all that before he introduced us."

"What?"

"Yeah, before that Alexisonfire concert. I know what happened."

"At the Kathedral? But you acted like you didn't know me."

"David, I didn't know you. Pat just said you were a really nice guy. What was I supposed to say? *Hey, you're the dude who made out with my brother?* He set us up. Pat can be an idiot sometimes, but he always has the best of intentions. I didn't want to go. I'm glad I did. Here." I passed him a mirror. "So, what do you think?"

"Holy crap, it's perfect. Where'd you learn how to cut hair like this?"

"From my grandpa. He cut all our hair."

"You're just a jack of all trades."

I whisked his shoulders with a tea towel. "I'm a man of many talents. That'll be five clams, kid."

David's eyes grew wide. "Gee, mister, I'm flat broke.

All tapped out." He pulled his undershirt on over his head. "I don't suppose you'll take an IOU?"

"Nope. Pay up, or my goons throw you off the rooftop." I put on my sunglasses, took one last drag off the cigarette and flicked it at David's chest.

"Ouch, harsh. Well, look, can I barter you for it?"

"I dunno, kid. You got anything I want?"

He squinted in the sunlight, hitching his thumbs into the top of his jeans. "I dunno. Maybe. What do you want?"

I studied the axe blade of his nose, the curve of his lips. I imagined him as a young Roman legionnaire, or an apprentice in da Vinci's studio, or a character in a Jean Genet play. "Everything."

"Everything?"

"You can pay in instalments."

"Instalments?"

I ran the tip of my scissors down the length of his arm. "We'll start with this." Taking my time, I pulled his undershirt out from his pants and began cutting my way up the front. His stomach muscles tensed. When I got to his throat, his Adam's apple rose and fell, but he didn't flinch. His cool, chrome-coloured eyes never left my face. When I was finally done, I set the scissors aside.

"Now I'd like a kiss."

"A kiss I can afford."

Our foreheads were touching, his hands on my hips. I traced my thumb across the stubble of his throat and pulled the remains of his shirt off his body. "But it better be good, or off the roof you go."

"Well, mister, I just better be a good kisser, then."

"I'll be the judge of that."

∼ Of course, I didn't move in with David. We'd only known each other three months. I'd also gotten to like my bachelor apartment. Some of the homeless people in the neighbourhood reminded me of Grandpa. One big guy who sold handmade jewellery reminded me of Liam. He said his name was Cree. When I asked him what that meant, he said that's what all the local Ojibwe called him, given how he was Cree and come up from the States. Then he whispered in my ear that his real name was Robert Burns, like the Scottish poet. I learned later he was on meds for schizophrenia. He'd carve little pendants, eagle feathers and wolf heads from scraps of wood. He wouldn't let me buy him a coffee, but he did let me buy one of his necklaces. Every time I saw him, I'd ask: "Hey Robert Burns, how's it going?" And he'd say: "Keeping it real, doc, keeping it real." Robert Burns would often hang out with his buddies in the nearby Allen Gardens, with its expansive lawn and century-old red oaks, sugar maples and beech trees. Seniors and dog owners also frequented the park. Sometimes I'd see groups of people practicing tai chi. In the evenings there'd be crack dealers and the occasional prostitute. The park offered something for everyone.

On a rainy afternoon in August, David and I met in the Allen Gardens Conservatory. We entered through the central Palm House with its banana trees, bamboo and gigantic cycads. We found a secluded bench in the back of the Tropical House, next to a small waterwheel and a pool inhabited by turtles and goldfish. "So I still don't understand why you won't move in," David said. "You need a place for September, I need a roommate. You're already staying over for like days at a time."

"Yeah, and then I go home. I like having my own space."

"Daniel, things are good between us. Aren't they?"

"They are. And I want it to stay that way. I don't want to rush this, okay?"

The air was moist and fragrant, the rainfall softly drumming on the glass roof. When David stroked my thigh, I pushed him away. "What's wrong?"

"Don't. Someone might see us."

"C'mon. There's no one here." Mischievously, he ran his hand up the inside of my shorts. "This is nice. You like this?" His fingers slipped beneath my underwear. "Well someone's happy." There were steel doors connecting all five greenhouses that made up the Conservatory. If someone came in, we'd hear them. I leaned back and swallowed. "I want you to move in," he insisted. "We'll just be two guys living together, like roommates."

"No, we won't be just two guys living together like roommates. We're lovers. We're boyfriends." I was distracted by what David's fingers were doing. "These things take time."

"I think about you every day."

"Me too," I said after a moment. It was the truth, but I'd been reluctant to admit it.

"I think about you when I jerk off. I have these fantasies. You want to know what my fantasies are?"

"Mm-hm."

"Ask me."

"What's one of your fantasies?"

"Well, I have a few. But sometimes I imagine you're a pirate captain, and you've captured me and I'm your prisoner. You need me to tell you where the treasure's buried."

"Where the treasure's buried?"

"Shut up and just listen. You need to know where the treasure's buried. You visit me down in the hold of your ship where your men have imprisoned me. I'm just this country boy who got pressed into the Royal Navy. I didn't sign up for this. My clothes are all torn and bloodied. You have your men strip me and wash me. Then they leave us alone. I'm naked on my hands and knees. My wrists are shackled and I'm chained to a post. But I'm loyal to the king, and won't give in to your demands. You kneel down behind me, spread my cheeks, spit on me and rub it in. No one's ever touched me this way before. I get excited, I can't help it. My hips arch. I'm so hard. I want to touch myself but I can't because of my chains. You grab my hair in your fist and pull my head back. At the same time, you push your thumb inside of me. You're pressing on me from the inside, massaging me. You know exactly where to touch me. It's a kind of torture and I'm moaning. I start to drip. I can't help it. The precum drips and runs down my shaft. But I still won't give in."

"Stop," I whispered. "Stop it, someone's coming."

David withdrew his hand, and we both simultaneously took out our phones. Two Filipino women pushing strollers manoeuvred down the narrow path, admiring the orchids and lush tropical plants.

"Do you know the artist Gauguin?" David asked.

"Who?"

"Paul Gauguin."

"No. Who's Paul Gauguin?" I watched the women out of the corner of my eye.

"Well, Gauguin, he was a French Post-Impressionist

who painted all these figures from the tropics. There's a painting by him called, *Where Do We Come From? What Are We? Where Are We Going?* It was his masterpiece. In the centre is this young guy, naked except for a loincloth, with his arms upraised reaching for an apple. His skin is golden, he's so beautiful."

"Was Gauguin gay?"

"Oh no, he had a wife and kids, and mistresses. After his marriage broke down, he started sleeping with the under-aged native girls who posed for him. The man was obsessed with sex and death."

"Death?"

David showed me an image of the painting on his phone. "Paul Gauguin, he tried to commit suicide, a few times. He hated the modern world. His whole life he struggled in search of something more simple, more meaningful. This golden man in the middle here, he symbolizes everything about being young and alive, searching for truth."

"Keeping it real."

"That's right, keeping it real."

The two women had paused close by, pointing out the fish in the pool to their toddlers. David leaned over and kissed me.

"I love you," he said.

"No, wait," I stuttered. David drew back. I cleared my throat. "I'm sorry."

"It's okay. You don't need to say anything."

One of the women approached us. She held out a camera and said: "Picture? Take picture?"

"Sure." I felt awful inside. I managed a smile and reached for the camera.

She stood back and gesticulated. "Closer, you sit closer." Dumbly, David and I posed as she took our picture. "My brother back home in Manila," she explained, "he is in love with boy. I hope they move to Canada. I send him picture."

Her companion asked a question in Tagalog, whereupon the two started up an animated debate. They were still arguing when they departed. Rounding the bend, they turned and waved back at us.

I listened to the rhythmic pulse of the waterwheel. I reached out and touched David's knee. I was afraid he might pull back, but he didn't. "Hey, I'm sorry." I felt pathetic. This time, without warning, he rose and straddled my leg, gripped my face and kissed me. I'd never been kissed this way before. I could hear the rushing of my own blood in my ears. When he finally let me go, his hands slid down to rest on my chest. I was sure he could feel my heart pounding beneath his palms. He bowed his head, breathing harshly through his nose. "I'm crazy about you, Daniel Garneau. You know that, don't you?"

I hadn't known that. I hadn't even thought that was a possibility until this moment. When he looked up, I saw my reflection in his eyes. "So, Daniel," he asked, "where are we going?"

"I don't know," I said. "I honestly don't know." If I could offer David nothing more than that, at least it was the truth.

◠ The deep buried truth was, as much as I hated to admit it, that I'd fallen hard for Marcus Wittenbrink Jr.

I didn't tell this to anyone. Not to Karen or Parker. Definitely not to David. Maybe if Derrick McNeil-Tsao was still in town, I would've said something to him, but M.T. had moved back to North Bay last spring. After my break-up with Marcus, I'd promised I would never let myself be hurt again. I kept the squash ball M.T. had given me mounted on a shot glass over my computer desk. I missed our Sunday afternoon games together, but kept going on my own. It was my form of meditation, smacking that little black ball around in that nine-by-six-metre white room.

One September afternoon, I was sitting alone in the sauna after an especially hard work-out when an older man with a moustache walked in. He might've been in his mid-forties, with abs like a washboard. I didn't recall seeing him around the gym. He adjusted his towel and sat across from me. "Hey," he said. "Hey," I replied and looked away. He was a handsome guy with big, chiselled features. I pictured him wearing a Stetson and lassoing cattle. I entertained an image of him riding me down, wrestling me to the ground and trussing me up like a young bull.

"You looking for a pardner?"

"What?"

"A squash partner," he said. "I've noticed you playing by yourself. You're pretty good."

"Thanks." I wondered how long he'd been watching me. Out of politeness, I asked: "Do you play?"

"Since college, on and off. It's been a few years."

"I just started two summers ago."

"I just moved to this gym, closer to work. I'm looking for a partner myself. We should go a few rounds."

Something in his tone and choice of words made me

meet his eye. He seemed friendly enough, sitting forward with his elbows on his knees. He had the broadest shoulders and the most perfectly defined arms. He was also pulling a Sharon Stone. I couldn't be sure if it was on purpose or not. What was sure was the fact that I was getting a hard-on, what with him sitting there like that on full display. I saw naked guys in the showers all the time. I wasn't even really attracted to this man, but it made no difference. Barnum and Bailey had pulled into town. I was mortified. I thought of icebergs and road-kill and Grandma in the nursing home. Nothing worked. I was trapped. There was no way I could stand up without it being obvious if it wasn't already obvious. If I was Harry Potter I supposed I could've simply disapparated. But I wasn't. I was Daniel Garneau, *muggle ordinaire*. I thought of Grandma naked in the nursing home. I thought of Grandma naked taking a dump on the can in the nursing home.

"You okay?" Moustache Man asked, looking concerned.

"Um," I stammered. "I'm fine."

"Maybe you should get a drink of water."

I wasn't about to miss my cue. "Yeah, I think you're right. Thanks. I'll do that." I got up and turned my back and shuffled sideways out of the sauna. By the time I got to my locker, I was in better shape. Normally, I would've taken another shower, but this time I towelled myself off and changed as quickly as I could. Just as I was leaving, I bumped into Moustache Man weighing himself. "Hey, how're you feeling?" he asked.

"Better. Yeah, thanks. It was, it just got a little hot in there."

"Obviously." Ninety-eight-point-five kilos of raw, seasoned steak. His steely eyes crinkled in a smile. "Let me know."

"Let you know?"

"Let me know if you want to go a few rounds." He stepped off the scales. "Squash?"

"Squash. Right."

"My name's Richard, by the way."

"Daniel."

"Nice to meet you, Daniel." When I shook his hand, his grip was like a bear-trap. "Cheers." He draped his towel over his shoulder. I couldn't help but stare at his enormous hairy bubble butt as he walked away.

Later, when I told Parker Kapoor what had happened, he made a face like he'd just sucked on a lemon, and nodded knowingly. "He definitely was having his way with you," he said. "These older muscle marys, they're dangerous. They're like large cats toying with their prey. You can't be too careful around them."

"Large cats?"

"Large predatory cats." Parker clawed the air and bared his teeth.

"C'mon, Parker, we don't even know if he was gay. He could've just been this friendly straight guy looking for someone to play squash with."

Parker leaned against a magazine rack, watching me play *Street Fighter II*. We'd come across the old game in a Mac's corner store, and I couldn't resist sticking in a quarter. Pat and I had put in hundreds of hours working up to fighting the Four Grand Masters.

"Was he hung?" asked Parker.

"Like a horse. His nuts were like these over-sized golf balls. I'm not kidding."

"That is impressive. I have to confess, Daniel, I didn't know you were a size queen."

"Parker, I am not a size queen! Look, I wasn't attracted to this guy. Just because I happened to get a hard-on doesn't mean I was attracted to this guy." I drop-kicked my opponent Blanka, winning two rounds easily, and moved on to the next challenge.

"Still, I'm impressed you got one in a sauna. That's not an easy achievement."

I threw up my hands. "Okay, maybe fine then, maybe I was turned on. But not for any obvious reason."

"Tell me more."

"I don't know. Maybe it was just the fact that we were two guys sitting in a sauna and his junk was all hanging out when, hello, it really wasn't supposed to? And see, if he was doing it on purpose, then that's hot, right? And if he wasn't doing it on purpose, well, then that's also hot, for totally different reasons."

"In other words it was kinky."

"Kinky?"

"Kinky. If Moustache Man was exposing himself on purpose, then he was being an exhibitionist. If he was exposing himself unintentionally, then you, my friend, were being a voyeur. Either way, it's kinky. It's all about sexual transgression. Of course, probably the most common kink is sex in a public place. It's exciting. We've all done it. Try to find a gay boy who hasn't. When was the last time you had sex in a public place?"

"That depends on what you count as sex."

"Cockandballs, Daniel. Anything involving cockand-balls."

"Cock and balls?"

"No. It's one word." Parker's mouth formed into a round O. He drew a breath and exhaled: "*Cockandballs.* That is the Zen pronunciation. *Cockandballs.* It is a state of oneness. Now you try it. Like this."

I formed my mouth into a round O. "*Cockandballs.*"

"Well done, Daniel. You're a natural. The Force of Faggotry runs deep in you."

"Parker."

"Just saying."

"Don't."

"Why are you smashing up that car?"

"It's the Bonus Stage."

"I'll be right back. You want anything?" I shook my head. "Creamsicle?"

"No thanks."

All four tires went flying. PERFECT. Eleven seconds to spare. *Yes.* I still had it.

Parker returned after a few minutes slurping on a super-sized slushie so ginormous he needed to hold it in both his hands. Now I was flying on to Japan to fight against Ryu. Pat always played Ryu. It was a rivalry that went back to when we were kids. "*Attack me if you dare,*" I muttered, "*I will crush you.*"

"I beg your pardon?" Parker said.

"Never mind."

"Public sex?"

"What? Oh, um, let me think. I suppose it was a month ago."

"And?" Parker worked his straw up and down like he was breaking up an ice jam.

"David gave me a hand job."

"And where was this?"

"In a greenhouse."

"A greenhouse?"

"Yeah, there were palm trees, fountains and everything."

"That sounds romantic."

"I suppose. Except I kept worrying someone was going to walk in on us. Some people did walk in on us. We never finished."

"And how was that?"

"It was okay. He was also talking dirty, kind of. We were pirates. Or I was supposed to be a pirate, and he was my prisoner."

"Kinky."

"No, Parker. No. It wasn't like that."

"Yo ho ho. Aaarr."

"No."

"Cockandballs! Three sheets to the wind!"

"Look, we weren't role-playing. It was more, like, he was telling me a fantasy of his. It was kinda hot."

Parker nodded. "Pirates rock. Did you know pirate society was democratic and egalitarian, inclusive of queers and women, and had health insurance?"

"No, I didn't know that."

"So, what's the best public sex you've ever had?"

"The best I've ever had?" I thought of my first Halloween in Toronto. I thought of the High Park hook-up-that-never-happened. I didn't count Marcus and Fang. I

thought of Mohawk Guy. But then I thought of something even better. "I did it in a Zamboni once?"

"You're not sure?"

"I did it in a Zamboni once."

"Daniel, are you making fun of me?"

"No, Parker, I'm not. I lost my virginity in a Zamboni."

"And how was that?"

"It was awesome."

"Enough said." Parker slurped from his slushie.

"Don't you want to know what happened?"

"No. Unless you want to tell me."

"It was my assistant hockey coach, Stephan Tondeur."

"You got fucked in a Zamboni by your assistant hockey coach?"

"No. I fucked him."

"I am impressed."

"Stephan was the first person I ever did it with. He
was my first, actually, for pretty much everything. He
was supposed to be grooming me for team captain. One
night, I said I wanted to take the Zamboni out for a spin.
I was joking, but he actually let me. He knew where they
kept the keys. He could've gotten fired just for that.
Then, while we were still driving around out on the ice,
he started to blow me. Then he took out some lube and
a condom, pulled down his pants, bent over the steering
wheel, and got me to fuck him."

"I need to take up hockey."

"Parker."

"This was grooming you for team captain?"

"I never got to make captain. The head coach kicked
me off the team."

"Because of what happened with the Zamboni?"

"No. No one ever found out anything about that."

"But it was because you were gay."

"Yes. Well, no, not directly. Because I got into a fight with three other teammates. Because I broke Gary Kadlubek's nose and knocked another player's tooth out. They were harassing me and saying I was gay. I'd had enough and just lost it. I'm not proud of what happened."

"Aaaaah!" Parker cried out.

"What?"

"Brain freeze." He clutched his head. "I've never thought of you as a violent person, Daniel."

"I'm not. But Sudbury's a rough town, and we went to school in a rough part of Sudbury. If anyone ever messed with us, me and my brothers, we'd kick the shit out of them."

Parker studied his high tops. "I don't approve of violence."

"Well, you wouldn't have made a very good pirate, then, would you?"

GAME OVER. M. Bison had demolished me with his Psycho Power. I'd gotten rusty. Good thing I wasn't playing against Pat. I straightened and turned to Parker. He stood looking downcast, wearing a T-shirt with a picture of Mahatma Gandhi decked out like a DJ in front of a console. "Parker. Listen to me. The truth is, I've only seriously gotten into three fights in my life. But I'd do it again if I had to. Grandpa taught us to stand up for what we believe in. My brother Liam, he got his black belt in kung fu by the time he was sixteen. We Garneau boys had a rep. We'd stand up to the bullies. Look, if someone ever messed with you, Parker, I'd kick the fucking shit out of them. You can count on it. Grandpa was a fighter, an amateur boxer in the merchant navy, back in the day. Are you okay? Hey, what is it?" Tears had welled up in Parker's eyes. He didn't wipe them away but let them roll glistening down his cheeks. "Parker, what is it?"

"No one," he said, "no one's ever said that to me before. Thank you. Thank you, Daniel." He flung his arms around me. I stood with my arms pinned to my side. Eventually, Parker disentangled himself. "I still don't approve of violence."

"Okay, Parker, I hear you. I hear you." In the end, we agreed to disagree on the matter. After that, the topic never came up again. But I wondered to myself if my life would've been different if I'd just known Parker Kapoor when I was still in high school. Maybe I wouldn't have gotten into that fight, then maybe I would've made team captain and ended up staying in Sudbury. Or maybe I wouldn't have thrown that big black dildo at Brett and we would've actually gone on to become real boyfriends, holding hands at Fan Expo dressed up as gay superheroes. But there was no point thinking about all the what-ifs. So what if Daniel Garneau had grown up during the golden age of piracy? Maybe then he would've made team captain. Maybe then he would've sailed the high seas, embarking on wind-swept adventures, swashbuckling and drinking and revelling with his comrades-in-arms. Yo ho ho. But that was a fantasy. The reality was here and now. I remembered Gauguin's man reaching for the apple. I reminded myself: *Just keep your eye on the ball.*

CHAPTER TEN

Your Ex-Lover is Dead

I met David's mother a week before Thanksgiving. She was an art critic for the *Globe & Mail*, and lived on her own in a elegant, Victorian semi-detached. I'd come over one Sunday morning to help clean out her rain gutters. Afterwards, she had us move the piano in the sitting room, and rearrange some furniture in the guestroom which had been David's old bedroom. She was a petite, severe-looking woman with impeccable make-up. Of course, I was obligated to stay for Sunday lunch. Three of her neighbours joined us, bringing over a plate of antipasto, fresh-baked focaccia and dessert. We ate with silverware off fine china, beneath a gold-framed portrait of Pope John Paul II. Mrs. Gallucci remarked how my parents must be proud I was applying to med school (I didn't mention this was my second go at it) and that I would make a good husband one day. Then someone asked me what I thought of Italian girls, and I replied I thought they were very beautiful and wonderful cooks. David had warned me not to mention his sister, so I didn't. I also remembered to twirl the spaghetti on my fork and not to put Parmesan on my fish, and to let the women clear my plates. We had a little wine and a lot of water. By the time we were finishing dessert and fruit and coffee, it was mid-afternoon and we managed to excuse ourselves with just a moderate amount of fuss, with some cannelloni and roasted lamb and tiramisu in separate sets of Tupperware.

"Ma thinks I'm a Don Giovanni," David said as we cycled south side by side down the tree-lined street, "which is why I don't have any steady girlfriend. She likes to tell me I'm just like my pa."

The sunlight flickered through the boughs. "How long were your mom and your dad married?"

"Two years. He was her third husband. My sister remembers him. I was still a baby when he died. We had a nanny who home-schooled us for a while. You know that framed print of Michelangelo's *David* in the front hallway? I used to imagine he was my pa. Then when I got older, I used to think of him as a big brother."

"That's nice."

"Yeah, well, after a couple more years, I'd think about that print whenever I whacked off."

"How old were you then?"

"Ten, eleven maybe. Sometimes I'd do it right at the dinner table, at least until my sister caught on. I'd get off on all those Greco-Roman and Renaissance male nudes: Ganymede, Antinous, Saint Sebastian, you name it. Ma kept art books and magazines right in the washroom. We went through a lot of toilet paper."

"Your mom mentioned a lot of the girls you dated. Did you actually date them?"

David laughed. "Of course, I did. I'd take them out dancing, buy them stuff. I even had sex with them. I was a horny little bastard. Didn't you?"

"No."

"So you've never slept with any girl before?"

"Um. No." I figured I'd tell David later about the Three Amigas. In that moment, I didn't think they counted.

"You've never even thought about it?"

"No, not really. Karen suggested it once, just to see what it'd be like. I'm glad we didn't."

"You sure she's not in love with you?"

"What?" I swerved to avoid a pothole. "What? Oh, god, no. What? No. I mean, no. Karen and my brother Liam have been together since high school. They've been on and off, but, Christ, David, why would you say something like that?"

"Just asking. Why on and off?"

"What?"

"You said Karen and your brother have been on and off."

"Liam's not the easiest person to get along with. He was on antidepressants a couple years. He was just a kid, but they were shelling out Prozac back then like there was no tomorrow. I think the forest saved him."

"The forest?"

"Being out in nature. Every springtime, Liam he'd be running around barefoot, and camping out back in our tree house. For a couple years he was obsessed with casting animal tracks, then he got into collecting skulls. Karen would hang out with us, we'd all go camping together. Grandpa would call us the Four Musketeers. But then

Pat started up his band, and I started playing more hock-ey. After that, it was just Karen and Liam. They'd go off camping weekends, in Killarney or up around the Good Medicine Cabin, just the two of them. Liam's hardcore. I think he'd live permanently out in the bush if he could. You know how some people cope with stress by hitting the gym or playing video games or partying? Well, Liam copes by being in nature."

"And what about you?"

"Me? Well. Like I said, it was hockey for a long time."

"And now?"

"I dunno. Sex works."

It was my attempt at a joke, but David regarded me thoughtfully. "You think so?"

"I like sex. I love sex. I mean, who doesn't? Sometimes it's not so great. But sometimes it's amazing."

"What's sex with me like?"

"Sex with you? Sex with you is amazing."

"You're not just saying that?"

"No, I'm not just saying that. You're amazing in bed. You're beautiful. You're one of the best lovers I've ever had."

"One of?"

"Aw, c'mon, David."

"I'm not jealous. I'm intrigued. What other amazing lovers have you had?"

I braked and pulled over to the side of the road. "Look, I really haven't had that many."

"Well, tell me about the ones you have had."

"You're serious?"

"Of course I'm serious."

"Tell me about yours."

"I asked you first."

"Okay. Alright." We got off our bikes and started walking east along College Street past Italian bakeries and cafés. "Okay." The sidewalk and patios were bustling this Sunday afternoon, and I spoke lowly, discreetly. "There was this one guy. We met at a bar. He was from out of town. He took me back to his room. He was an average-looking guy. He said his name was John, but he was really sweet and he had a great laugh. He took his time and really paid attention. It was like he was actually interested in me, and not just in getting off. It was different from any hook-up I'd ever had up until that point. It was, I dunno, erotic. I still get hard thinking about it."

"What did he do?"

I was embarrassed already, having shared what I had. "You want details?"

"Details would be nice. Ma always told us to get right up close to a painting and look at the individual brush strokes. Are you embarrassed?"

"No, I'm not embarrassed." We paused in front of a grocery store patio crowded with marigolds and giant sunflowers. "Okay. Well, he undressed me, slowly. He caressed every part of my body, with his lips and tongue. He was hard the whole time, but he didn't rush. I was ready to come before his mouth even touched my cock."

"And then?"

"We jerked each other off. After that, he had me lie down. He told me not to move and he gave me a massage, and eventually he got me off again. After I came that second time in his mouth, he didn't swallow but he held it all and we kissed. We kissed for a long time like that. I'll never forget that."

"Wow. So how long were you together?"

"How long? It was just one night."

"Just the one night?"

"One night. I never saw him again."

"I'm sorry to hear that."

"Really?"

"Sure. It sounds like you connected in a special way. It sounds like he was an awesome lover. It sounds like you learned a lot from him. I need to be with someone who's experienced, who knows what he likes."

"Okay."

"I need someone who can take charge."

"You like it when I take charge?"

"Yeah, I do. I like it when someone knows what they want and then makes it happen."

"What about you? What do you want?"

"I want to be your lover."

"You're already that."

"I want to fall asleep in your arms, and I want to wake up in the morning naked next to you."

"We already do that."

"I want us to last a lifetime. I want to know we're going to be together every single day until the day I die."

"David."

"What? You asked. You think I'm wanting too much? Or is it that that's not what you want?"

"David, don't."

"Don't what?"

"Isn't it enough to know that we're going to be there for each other when we wake up tomorrow?"

"It's enough, for now. But you asked me what I wanted. I told you the truth. Would you rather I didn't? Look, when we get home, I want you to fuck me. Can we do that?"

"Okay."

"And I want to be on my back, and I want us to kiss. I want to see your face while you're inside of me."

"Okay."

"And I want you to fuck me slowly and as deep as you can. I want you to make it last, for a long time. Do you think you can do that?"

"I'll try my best."

"You know, Daniel, you look like him."

"Who?"

"Michelangelo's *David*. Honestly, you do. I never realized it until now. You have his conviction."

"Conviction? Are you kidding me?"

"Sometimes you act like the little guy, like a boy, but you're not. You're a king waiting to happen. And deep down, some part of you knows it. But you're too humble to even think it, much less say it out loud. But you are just like him."

I didn't know what to say. I wanted to scoff at him, but David's sincerity stopped me. So I said nothing at all. When we got back to his loft, we took off our clothes and lay down in bed together, and after a while, I put on a condom and I did my best to make it last, just the way he asked, until it became awkward and almost painful for me. In the end, both his hands were grasping the back of my head, fingers knotted in my hair, when I felt his entire body tighten, jerk and spasm, and his orgasm spurting hotly against my chest, burning and shocking, while my tongue was in his mouth and while I was still moving inside of him, just the way he'd asked, and it was this final sensation between us that pushed me over the edge, past the point of no returning, and I was suddenly, involuntarily thrusting and thrusting as hard as I could, and I felt an indescribable release that broke me and seemed to go on forever in roiling, crashing waves, and I would've cried out except my mouth was locked to his, and we were together and we were lovers and we were one body, and it seemed to last a lifetime, just the way he'd asked.

⌒ When I went back to Sudbury for the holidays that December, I got the biggest surprise. Grandma was sitting in her easy chair in the living room, covered in a quilt. "Grandma," I blurted, "you're home!" Liam, who had picked me up at the bus terminal, walked in behind me. "Oh, I forgot to mention," he said, throwing his scarf over the coat rack, "Mémère's out of the nursing home, at least for the weekend. The washing machine's broken, and the upstairs toilet's clogged again. I've put three bottles of Drano in there already. Use the downstairs toilet." Grandpa poked his head out the kitchen, wearing an apron and reindeer antlers. The sleeves of his plaid shirt were rolled up and his big, callused hands were covered in flour. I could smell tourtières baking in the oven. "Salut, Daniel!" he beamed. He nodded towards the living room and winked. "Your mémère's home." He tossed me a beer bottle, which I caught one-handed, and disappeared back into the kitchen, humming to himself.

"What happened?" I asked.

Liam was peering out the front door, whistling for Jackson who had dashed off somewhere. "They changed her meds." He glanced over his shoulder. "Go say hi."

"Is she awake?"

"Of course, she's awake."

Someone had put on our old *Elvis Gratton* VHS. I was surprised the tape hadn't completely fallen apart by now. I set the beer aside, took off my snow boots and walked into the living room. I knelt in front of Grandma and waited for her to notice me. A plate of gingerbread cookies and a mug of tea had been set next to her. Both looked untouched. Eventually, her eyes flickered in my direction. "Hi, Grandma." I smiled broadly. "It's me, Daniel." I could tell she was trying to recall my face. "I'm Daniel, your grandson. It's good to see you." I rested one hand on her knee. She blinked a few times, then puckered her lips. I leaned forward so she could kiss me on the cheek. After that, she turned her attention back to the TV where Julien Poulin was struggling to extricate himself from a beach chair, his hairy fat bulging out of a skimpy bathing suit. Grandma craned her neck forward, squinting her eyes. I stood abruptly and backed away. "Liam, I don't think she should be watching *Elvis Gratton*."

"Why not?" said Liam said, brushing the snow off Jackson and extricating him from his winter doggie jacket.

"Well, look at her."

"What?"

"Liam," I exclaimed lowly, "look at her. I think she's, you know."

"What?"

"You know."

"What?"

"You know. Masturbating."

"What?"

"Look at her."

We both stared at Grandma sidelong. The section of quilt over her lap was moving up and down. She bit her lower lip and her eyes fluttered back in her head.

"Whoa," Liam said.

"No kidding."

"Look, we've been trying to get her settled all day. *Elvis Gratton*'s the only thing that's worked."

"Seriously. *Elvis Gratton?*"

"We brought her home yesterday and she was fine. But she woke up this morning and she was really disoriented. She was crying and shouting. *Elvis Gratton* calms her down. I've rewound that movie three times already."

"You're kidding."

"Mémère loves her *Elvis Gratton.*"

"Look, Liam, did you try *The Golden Girls?*"

"Do we have it here?"

"Shit." I'd taken our DVD box-set of *The Golden Girls* with me when I moved to Toronto. "Shit."

"Daniel, just let her be. I don't see what the big problem is."

"Liam, we can't let her keep doing that."

"Why not?"

"Why not? It's indecent."

"Well, Daniel, until you pointed it out, I had no idea. Listen, she'll stop on her own. She'll probably fall asleep in a few minutes."

I had a sudden image of Grandpa and Liam strolling about the house stark naked, and realized Liam and I did not exactly share the same notions of what amounted to common decency. "Fine." I raised and dropped my hands. "Fine." Grandma abruptly hiccoughed and burst out laughing. I noticed she wasn't wearing her dentures. In the kitchen, Grandpa was singing, "*O what fun it is to ride in a one-horse open sleigh, hey!*" Jackson ventured into the living room and sniffed at Grandma, his tail wagging. When she reached out from under her quilt and patted his head, he started licking her hand. "Merry Christmas, Daniel," Liam said. "It's good to have you back."

That Christmas Eve, after Grandpa and Grandma had retired for the night, Karen tramped across the street and joined us for our traditional drink. I hadn't seen her since I was up in Sudbury for Thanksgiving with the Miltons. Blonde Dawn had to work over the holidays and, despite my protests, Pat had made the decision to stay with her in Toronto. So it was just the three of us this year, lounging side-by-side on the living room couch, watching the blinking lights of the Christmas tree. Liam and Karen had smoked a joint earlier, and I'd polished off an entire bottle of Baileys on my own. Anne Murray was droning on, singing her seasonal favourites on the radio. No one bothered to get up to change the station. It actually wasn't all that unpleasant. Liam and I had cleaned and tidied the house (we found Grandma's dentures in the Christmas tree), split two cords of firewood, moved the broken washing machine out into the garage, and delivered a dozen of Grandpa's tourtières and sugar pies to the staff and residents of the nursing home. The fridge was stocked, the turkey was defrosting, and the drive was shovelled. Out the window, I watched a cab pull up in front of the house. "Well what do you know," Karen said. "If it isn't the prodigal son."

I opened the front door before Pat could ring the bell. He had his camping backpack slung over one shoulder and was grinning ear to ear. "Surprise!" he hollered. "Merry Christmas!"

All that Baileys had started to give me a headache. I said: "I thought you were spending Christmas in Toronto."

Pat dumped down his heavy pack. If he'd brought his dirty laundry home to wash, he was in for a disappointment. "It's good to see you too, Dan," he panted. When I said nothing, he shrugged. "Blonde Dawn convinced me to come home."

"Is that right?"

"She insisted."

"Pat, you made me bring all your presents up."

"Yeah, thanks for that. I really hope Grandpa likes his new bowling ball. You know, I had it custom-drilled, monogrammed and everything. I really didn't think I'd be seeing you guys."

"So what made you change your mind?"

"Like I said, Blonde Dawn. She and a bunch of her EMS coworkers are spending Christmas together. Technically, she doesn't actually even celebrate Christmas. You know her family's Jewish, right?"

"Yes, I did. Good for her."

"I also heard Grandma's home."

"Who told you that?"

"Karen did. She texted me this morning."

"She is."

"So how's she doing?"

"Fine."

"Grandpa must be thrilled."

"He is."

Pat glanced past my shoulder. "You going to let me in, Dan?"

"Pat, you should've come home."

"Dan, I am home." He pulled off his toque and scratched his head. "Look, I'm home. Okay?"

"It's important."

"Okay. I know that."

"Yeah, well. Maybe you need to hear it face to face."

"I hear you."

"Do you, really?"

"Dan, dude. It's Christmas. I'm home."

I'd wanted to spend the holidays with my boyfriend, but I'd left him to come back home. Still, I didn't have David's name tattooed over my heart. I'd never even said I loved him. Hell, I wasn't even ready to move in with him.

"Daniel." Liam and Karen were poised behind me. "You going to let Pat in or what?"

I opened the door wide and stood aside. Pat hauled his bag into the house and gave Jackson, who had bounded up, a smothering hug. He got up and wrapped his arms around Liam and Karen. "Merry Christmas! How's life on Manitoulin?"

"Rockin'," Karen said.

"How's your little sis?"

"Anne, she's fine. She just got her navel pierced."

"Sweet. Whoa, I see you guys got the tree up. Looking sugar crispy."

"Yup," Liam said.

"And Grandpa's been baking?"

"Yup."

"Smells great in here. Dan, it's good to see you." He opened his arms. "Merry Christmas?"

I wanted to give Pat a hug. Another part of me just wanted to smack him across the back of the head. After a few seconds, the former impulse won out. "Merry Christmas, Pat." Reluctantly, I took him in my arms and, to my own surprise, found myself squeezing him as hard as I could. For the first time in years, the family was back together again under one roof. "Welcome home."

On New Year's Eve, David and I stayed in, opened a bottle of Prosecco and cooked a meal together. David's loft was twice the size of my place with a far better view. More importantly, his entire building had central heating. The radiator in my hole of an apartment was touch and go at best. Close to midnight, we climbed the fire escape to David's rooftop, where we could see across Kensington Market and Chinatown all the way to the lake. The CN Tower and downtown skyscrapers were glinting, dark shadows, like giant angels haloed in stars, gathered and watching over us. The night was bitterly cold and we clung to each other, bundled up in our mittens and jackets. At the stroke of midnight, fireworks glittered over City Hall and seconds later we could hear their faint popping and crackling. Random voices shouted in the streets below. David and I kissed. "Happy New Year, mister," he said. "I love you."

Back inside, we gave each other our Christmas presents. I'd bought David a pair of ice skates; he'd gotten me a pair of Maple Leafs tickets. We both loved our gifts. While he opened a second bottle of Prosecco, David remarked: "By the way, I found this when I was over at your place." He held out a crumpled envelope.

I stared at it in my hands for a couple seconds before I recognized what it was. "David, what the hell?"

"I was just checking in on your apartment like you'd asked me to."

"Yeah, and you just happened to go through my garbage?"

"You always mix everything up, Daniel. I keep saying you should have an organics bin and a recycling bin. I was just separating your garbage."

"I didn't ask my boyfriend to separate my fucking garbage. I asked him to water my plants."

"Alright, Daniel. I apologize, okay? If that pisses you off, I really, sincerely apologize."

"Don't patronize me."

"Then don't treat me like I did something wrong. I wasn't snooping. You know I wasn't. It's just that. Well, that's him, isn't it?"

Reluctantly, I drew the card from its stained envelope. It was an invitation, cream-coloured and embossed in silver. I'd received it in the mail days before Christmas, just as I was leaving for Sudbury. I remembered shoving it back in its envelope and throwing it in the garbage. Maybe if I wasn't rushing out the door, I might've taken the time to reply. But I hadn't.

"Daniel, honestly, the only reason I looked twice at it is because my name's on it too."

It was true. The envelope was addressed to both Daniel Garneau and David Gallucci. I opened the card. It was an invitation to a New Year's Eve party from Marcus Wittenbrink Jr. I wondered how Marcus had found out my new address, and how he knew about David.

"You know we broke up on New Year's Eve."

David's eyebrows rose. "I thought you said you broke up on Valentine's Day."

"We did." I sighed. "But it all started on New Year's Eve." I'd never explained the details of our break-up, and David had never asked.

"Shit. Look, I didn't know that. I'm sorry. I get it."

"It's okay. It's not your fault."

"I've really fucked up tonight, haven't I?"

"No, no you haven't."

"Here, I'll take that." David took the card. "Let me get rid of it."

"Wait," I exclaimed. "Wait. David, what were you thinking? I mean, why'd you even bring that back here anyway?"

"Daniel, it's just that this Marcus guy, I dunno. It's obvious he still wants to be in your life. And sometimes, well sometimes, you talk like you still have feelings for him. And, I was just thinking. Maybe we should go to this party, you and me. Just to figure things out. Just so we can figure things out together. I'd like to meet him."

I was stunned. Any other person might've felt threatened by someone like Marcus. But David felt the opposite. I stood up. I didn't know what to say.

David rested his hands on my shoulders at arm's length. "You know I love you, right? You know that, don't you?" I nodded. "I'm in love with you, Daniel. I want us to work this through. We're just starting out. I don't want any ghosts."

"Ghosts?"

"My ma, sometimes she talks to my pa, and her other husbands. It's not cute. It's fucking weird. Sometimes, she argues with them, sometimes all three of them at once."

"For real?"

"She's been doing it for years, ever since my sister and I can remember. She thinks nobody knows. Sometimes, I swear, I'll be in the same room with her, and suddenly she's staring past my shoulder with this look on her face. I just don't want any ghosts, okay?"

"That's creepy."

"Damn right it is. Do you believe in ghosts?"

"Well," I said, "that depends on what you mean by a ghost."

"Something about a person in our past that haunts us. Something that won't go away by itself."

By that definition, my life was filled with ghosts. I retreated, gathering dishes into the sink. "Marcus and I were together five months," I finally said, running the hot water. "We broke up almost a year ago. It was an intense relationship. I don't think he's altogether mentally stable. Did I ever tell you about the first time I met him? He was covered in pig's blood and singing nursery rhymes. How fucked up is that?"

"Now that's creepy."

"Maybe your mom and Marcus should get together."

"Holy shit. You think?"

"He could cover himself in pasta sauce and recite catechisms for twenty-four hours non-stop. Ooh, now that would be sexy."

"Sexier than me?"

"I don't know. I've never had you covered in pasta sauce before."

David came up behind me, and circled my waist with his arms. "You've never tasted my meatballs either."

"Oh, I've tasted your meatballs."

"Bottle of Chianti, with a bit of bread and olive oil. I could fill a man up."

"I'm sure you could. Here." I handed him a dish towel. "Dry."

Carefully, David wiped down a carving knife and placed it in its rack. "So how about it?"

"How about what?"

"Going to this party?"

"You're serious."

David refilled our glasses. "Only if it's okay with you. It's a cold night. We could also just stay in, snuggle up, enjoy this bottle of bubbly, smoke a joint."

"I don't smoke pot, remember?"

"Okay. You have the bubbly, I'll have the joint. We can have fun with some pasta sauce."

"It'll be a bitch hailing a cab."

"We can call one. It'll be here in half an hour."

"I didn't RSVP."

"Do you think he'd turn us away?"

"Alright. Fine, then. Let's go. Call a cab."

"Really?"

I turned off the tap and dried my hands. I shrugged, trying not to sound too excited. "Sure."

"Okay." David tossed the dish towel onto the counter. "Okay, then. It's settled."

"Okay, then."

"Really?"

"Yeah," I exclaimed. "Really."

"So. What do you wear to these shindigs, anyway?"

"Marcus' parties? At this hour, David, I don't think it matters."

"What's that supposed to mean?"

"It means if Marcus' friend Marwa is catering, it's going to be, you know, a little bit crazy."

"I grew up Roman Catholic. I can handle crazy."

I paced the living room. "David, I'm serious. Maybe we should talk about this. If it's anything like last year, it really is going to be crazy."

"Okay."

"So what are the rules here?"

"Rules?"

"We're going as a couple, right?"

"Of course we are. What sort of a question is that?"

"What I'm asking is, what if some drunk boy, all coked up or high on E or whatever, starts flirting with you? What if he wants to get it on?"

"You mean like your brother Pat?"

"Something like that."

"Is that likely to happen?"

"It might."

"Well, you tell me. So, what if some boy wants to kiss me, or you for that matter?"

I hesitated, searching my feelings. I wanted to be honest with David. I wanted to be honest with myself. "Well, how would you feel if I said that would be okay, as long as you told me about it?"

"Just kissing?"

"Yeah, of course. I mean, nothing more than that."

"Well, if that were to happen, mister, I think you should be there to see it happen. I think you and I should stick together, no matter what happens."

"Okay."

"We walk in as a couple, we leave as a couple."

"Okay. That's the rule, then? We stick together."

"Daniel, you sure you're okay with this?"

"Yes. As long as you are."

"Look, we really don't have to go. Honestly, I'd be okay staying in."

"No, I want to go. Marcus' parties are famous. My friend Charles might even be there."

"We stick together."

"We stick together."

By the time the cab pulled up in front of Marcus' warehouse, it was close to two a.m. David had insisted on dressing us up. In the end, I let him put a little eyeliner on me and spike up my hair. I refused to let him paint my nails. I wore one of David's vests and a matching bow tie. He also had us go commando, just for the hell of it, which I'd never done before. I felt anxious, nervous and thrilled all at once. The fact that I was actually going to Marcus' party was weird enough. I wondered if he was

still with Fang. Charles must've given Marcus my new
address and told him about David. I started to text
Charles to see if he was there. As we rounded the corner
of Marcus' warehouse, I saw flashing lights and figured
the party was still in full swing. The inside of the cab was
all fogged up, and I wiped at the window with the palm
of my hand. A second later, I realized two police cruisers
and an ambulance were pulled up at the side entrance
parking lot. Yellow tape fluttered and people were gathered outside. I opened the car door and jumped out into
the icy snow before the cab had even come to a complete
halt. Frantically, I scanned the faces in the crowd. I spotted a short girl in fishnet stockings with wide, glazed
eyes, and hurried over to her. "Marwa! Marwa, what's
going on?"

It took a moment before she focused on my face.
"Daniel the Doorman," she said. Her eyes were all puffy
and her mascara had run down her cheeks.

"Marwa." I held her by the shoulders. "What the fuck
is going on?"

She turned and pointed. Through the crowd, I could
see paramedics placing a body onto a stretcher. I caught a
glimpse of a man's pale, naked limbs. "It was an accident,"
she said. "It was an accident."

"What was an accident? What happened?"

"Marcus," said Marwa, "he fell. It was an accident.
He was on the rooftop and he fell. Marcus is dead."

CHAPTER ELEVEN

Five Days in May

R umours of Marcus' death were greatly exaggerated. He'd fractured multiple bones and suffered a concussion, but was expected to make a full recovery by the spring. It was true, he could easily have died. He could've suffered a more serious head or spinal injury, but none of that happened. He'd fallen four stories into a snow bank piled up by the side of his building. Marcus Wittenbrink Jr. was the luckiest man alive. When I visited him in St. Michael's Hospital in early February, he was manoeuvring himself around in a wheelchair and asked if I would accompany him outside for a smoke. "Since when," I asked, "did you start smoking?"

"I was about to ask you the same thing," he replied, lighting my cigarette for me. We were bundled up just outside the Queen Street entrance, between the Eaton Centre and the Metropolitan United Church. We hunched next to a parked ambulance, shielding ourselves from the wind. Nearby, an elderly gentleman in bunny slippers, attached to an IV rack, puffed leisurely on a cigar. A few cyclists in ski masks braved the icy roads. A streetcar rumbled past, streaked with brown, salt-stained slush.

"My new boyfriend," I said, "he smokes."

"David Gallucci."

"That's right." I regarded Marcus sidelong. "You still with Fang?"

"I am, and another boy Joseph."

"Joseph?"

"The three of us, we're together."

"I see." So this Joseph was my replacement. "Well, I'm happy for you."

"Thank you. I've missed you, Daniel."

I nodded, tight-lipped. "And how are your parents?"

"Enjoying the seaside, I suppose."

"What do you mean?"

"They winter in Costa Rica." Marcus flicked ash from his sleeve. "New Year's in Santa Teresa is their tradition. They sent a money transfer, of course, to cover anything I needed."

I was dumbfounded. "They didn't come back?"

"Why?"

"Because they're your parents?"

Marcus said nothing. I should've been accustomed to his equanimity, but on this occasion, I wanted to shout at him, I wanted to shout on his behalf. But I swallowed it down, and all I said was: "I'm sorry."

"Trust me, Daniel, it is for the best."

"Is it?"

"It is, truly. I'm grateful for the space they afford me. Without them, I would not have a private room." He glanced up and winked.

"So, how's the food?"

"I've been ordering take-out."

"You can do that in a hospital?"

"You'd be surprised."

I wasn't, actually. Marcus Wittenbrink Jr. probably had the head nurse personally fetching his take-out for him.

"Daniel, thank you for visiting. I was starting to think you wouldn't come."

"Of course, I would come. Why wouldn't I come? I was just waiting for the right time. I figured the first month you'd have like a million visitors. I guess I just wanted you all to myself." I regretted that last remark the moment it was out of my mouth. I'd also wanted to say that I'd missed him too. Even in his injured state, Marcus was beautiful to me, like a bird with a broken wing. His nails weren't pared, and it seemed as if he hadn't shaved in a month. I did my best to change the topic, and lighten the tone. "That's an interesting look on you."

"What, this?" He stroked his thin beard and puffed delicately on his cigarette. "Surprisingly, people find it compelling. I think I might keep it after this is all over. What do you think?"

"I like it."

"The physiotherapists say I should be on my feet in a week, with the use of a cane."

"That's good news. Shall I get you a top hat?"

"I already own a top hat, and a frock coat."

"Why am I not surprised."

"Victorian garments would suit you, Daniel. You have a timeless quality about you."

"Timeless and simple," I said, "that's me."

"Yes, it is."

Back in his room, I helped Marcus out of his winter jacket and hung it up for him. He was only wearing his blue hospital gown underneath. He must've been chilled outside, but he hadn't complained. "Daniel, can you assist me, please?" He draped an arm over my shoulder and I supported him as he stood. In the end, I half-lifted Marcus back into his bed. His brow gleamed with perspiration. It took him a minute before he could catch his breath again. "Thank you."

"Are you okay?"

"I'll be fine."

I stood back awkwardly. I could tell he hadn't showered in some days, and he wasn't wearing deodorant. I wanted to bury my nose in his armpit, and lick the salt from his throat and neck.

He sipped from a glass of water on the side table. "There are metal pins in me now. See what they've done to me?" Gingerly, Marcus pulled up his gown.

"They've performed an arthroscopy," I observed. I also noticed he wasn't wearing any underwear.

"That's right." He traced his fingernails over his scars. "These aren't so bad, are they?"

I reached out and touched his scars, red and bruised-looking against his pale skin. "No," I lied, "you'd hardly notice them at all." Tentatively, without meaning to, I stroked and squeezed his thigh. His skin was warm, almost hot to the touch. The door behind me opened out into a bustling hallway. When I rested my palm against his hip, Marcus bunched his gown up in his fist and pulled it further aside. "See, Daniel, what you do to me?" When I didn't move, he took my hand and placed it over his exposed erection. The thick head of his penis was pierced at its base. Before meeting Marcus, I hadn't even heard of a Prince Albert, much less seen one up close.

I swallowed. My mouth was dry. "Marcus."

"I really have missed you, Daniel. You and David came to my party New Year's Eve. Why?"

"You invited us."

"You never RSVP'd."

"Sorry."

"Well, I'm glad you decided to come. I'm sorry about what happened. If I'd known you were coming, I would've waited for you. I'm sorry we missed each other. I truly am. I hope there is another chance the three of us might meet."

If I clambered onto the bed, I could straddle Marcus, spit in my palm, sit back on him and feel him push up inside of me. Instead, with an effort, I withdrew my hand. "Marcus. I need to ask you something. I don't want you to get offended. Okay?"

He gazed at me, unblinking.

"It was an accident, right? It was an accident, that night you fell."

Marcus covered himself with his gown, and turned towards the window. In that light, his brow and cheek seemed to be made of alabaster. After a while, he said: "Does it matter?"

"Of course, it does. Of course, it matters."

"Was it an accident," he said, "when Icarus fell?" Shyly, he searched my face.

I buried my hands in my pockets. "Marcus, I gotta tell ya, I have no fucking clue who Icarus is."

"He was a boy who grew up in a Labyrinth."

"He was like some Greek god or hero, right?"

"No," Marcus said. "No, he wasn't a god or a hero. He was just a boy."

"Okay."

"Yet," Marcus said, sighing, "Daniel Garneau, I am sure you could name every player on the Canadian Olympic hockey team, couldn't you?"

"Well that would depend."

"On what?"

"On which Olympics you're talking about."

"The last one."

I thought a moment, then named the head coach and the assistant coach and all twenty-three players on the last Canadian Winter Olympics hockey team. It wasn't hard. "What?" I shrugged. "Those guys are hot."

After that, we shared a laugh.

Before I left the hospital, Marcus made me promise I would introduce David to him sometime soon. When I gave him a parting hug, he squeezed my arm and pressed his lips against mine. It was a companionable gesture, like a kiss between friends. Nevertheless, it sent electrifying shock waves through me. I'd wanted to kiss him back, bite his lip, hold his tongue between my teeth. I'd not told the whole truth to David. In our five months together, Marcus Wittenbrink Jr. was, in fact, the most extraordinary lover I'd ever had. His Prince Albert was the least of the surprises I'd encountered along the way. If I knew what I wanted sexually, it was because Marcus had taught me to know. If I was able to take charge, it was only because Marcus had taught me how to take charge. I hadn't even begun to share with David the things I'd learned. If David only knew just how much I could take charge. But it was clear to me that David wasn't ready yet, and I wondered if he might ever be.

⌐ "I need your finger, Daniel."

I stuck out my finger and held down the gold ribbon that Parker was using to wrap his gift. The wrapping paper was satiny fuchsia, the box the size of a large toaster oven. Every year, for his own birthday, Parker would purchase a gift and wrap it the prior day. "That way," he explained, "in the morning, I wake up and voilà! There it is waiting for me. Then I make myself a mimosa (from a dealcoholized sparkling wine beverage, of course) and ring in the newest year of my life. This is a big year for me, Daniel. This spring, I'm one quarter century old."

"I take it that's not a toaster oven."

"Who can say? I'll find out tomorrow."

"But you bought it, Parker. You brought it home and you're wrapping it yourself."

Parker positioned the gift on the coffee table. "I have no idea," he murmured, carefully adjusting the gigantic bow, "what you're talking about."

"Didn't your family ever give you presents?"

"They would give me cheques which I was obligated to deposit in the bank. Birthday bank deposits are a tradition in the Kapoor family. You can read all about it in my memoirs."

"You still working on that?"

"Of course, I am. You're in it, you know. There, now doesn't that look just perfect? I love it already. Thank you for your help. I'm so excited. I love opening presents. We have time for a drink, don't we?"

I'd swung by Parker's condo to pick him up en route to a Saturday matinée. He lived on the fifteenth floor of a high-rise just north of City Hall. The place was tastefully decorated with vintage furniture and chrome fixtures. Black and white headshots of Hollywood stars from the 1950s and 60s adorned the wall. He had a turntable set up next to a mini bar, complete with a stainless steel martini set. "I like making virgin drinks for myself," Parker explained. "It's also for the guests." His face lit up. "Why don't I make us some cosmos?"

"Sure," I said, although I had no idea what a cosmo was. Two goldfish in a bowl occupied the centre of the dining room table, next to a towering vase of pink and yellow tulips. "Their names are Harold and Maude," Parker announced, scrubbing an orange in the sink. "They're in love. All my friends are in a pool to guess what month each of them will die."

"That's a little macabre."

"On the contrary, it helps me appreciate every day that they're alive. I've had them both exactly six years, since I moved out on my own. Did you know goldfish can live for decades, given the proper love and care? So, Daniel, what are your guesses?"

"What?"

"Who and when?"

"Oh, no."

"Just pick any two months."

"Can I abstain?"

"Daniel, please, humour me."

I rolled my eyes. "Harold in March, Maude in May."

"Thank you!" Parker made a precise note on a slip of paper on the refrigerator. After that, he busied himself assembling bottles and measuring out ingredients into two stainless steel shakers. "Tomorrow is the first of May. It's my favourite month, you know. Everything comes back to life in May and starts all over again. It's also my birthday month, of course. I was never allowed pets growing up. My parents thought keeping pets was cruel. Harold and Maude were my very first birthday gift to myself. I remember the day I brought them home, swimming round and round in that clear little plastic bag. They were utterly adorable. They still are. I used to hide them in the closet whenever relatives came to visit. But then one day Mother dropped in unannounced. She was in a tizzy and absolutely needed to consult with me on my eldest sister's wedding. (She's since consulted with me on all my sisters' weddings.) Well, she pretended not to notice them, right there literally under her nose, even when I served tea at the table. My hands were shaking, I was so upset. Finally, I couldn't stand it any longer. I stood up, threw down my napkin, and declared that yes, in fact, I was the proud owner of my very own goldfish, and that I would not be hiding my Harold and Maude from the family any longer. I was sure it hurt their feelings every time I put them in the closet. That day was momentous. It was a turning point for me."

"You are talking about goldfish?"

"I am."

"And what did your mother say?"

"Well, it was extraordinary. She stared at Harold and

Maude as if she were seeing them for the very first time. One thing let to another. In the end, pairs of goldfish formed the centrepiece for every table at my sister's wedding reception. The floral arrangements and saris were all selected to match them. Everyone thought it was delightful and magnificent. I'd never been more validated in my life. It was the most beautiful thing my parents had ever done for me."

"Wow."

"I know. Of course, when they finally go belly-up, I'll buy myself another pair. But those two are the first. I'm glad you've had a chance to meet them, Daniel. Kiss the bowl."

"What?"

"Like this. Kiss the bowl." Parker leaned over the table and kissed the fishbowl. He handed me a martini glass containing a pink liquid garnished with a delicate coil of orange rind. "It's such a fresh, bright and happy drink," he said, sighing, "don't you think?" I nodded appreciatively, leaned over and kissed the fishbowl. Harold and Maude bobbed up to stare at me. Parker held up his own drink. "To May."

"To May."

In the end, we never did go to our matinée. But Parker put on an LP of Paul Anka's greatest hits, and had us sit on his tiny, south-facing balcony overlooking Bay Street, drenched in sunlight. Eventually, he made me three more cosmos in a row. He didn't ask about Marcus or David, and to my own surprise, I felt no inclination to bring them up. But we wore our sunglasses and opened the collars of our shirts and took off our shoes and socks, and talked about our families, and our grandparents and their grandparents. And they weren't wrinkled and dusty dead people, but young and alive, dancing in the evenings under electric lights for the first time in history, and wearing the latest fashions in an era when men showing their nipples on the beach was indecent, and blacks in America were newly liberated, and the independence movement in India was gaining strength, and Freud was looking up ladies' skirts, and Manet was painting nudes, and the *Kama Sutra* had just been translated into English, and the Wright brothers were still just boys flying kites, and Rimbaud and Verlaine were tearing across Europe madly in love, and Oscar Wilde's trial was the scandal of the century.

After that, Parker invited me to stay for dinner but I told him I had to go home and study, which was true. But instead, I went downtown and bought a journal and the fanciest wrapping paper I could find. On the front of the journal was Henri Matisse's *The Goldfish* which the master had painted in 1912. I knew this because it said so on the inside back cover. On the inside front cover, I wrote, "Happy birthday Parker Kapoor, may your memoirs be full of poetry and light. Your friend, Daniel Garneau." Then I texted Parker and asked if I could meet him for coffee the next day and he said yes. After I wrapped his present, I went to bed and slept well and didn't dream at all. I woke up on the first morning of May, feeling remarkably refreshed and not hung-over at all.

⌒ By the end of May, I'd yet to introduce David to Marcus, as I'd promised. So it was an awkward moment when we bumped into Marcus, Fang and Joseph in a line-up at Toronto's Inside Out Film Festival. We had planned to see some generic, forgettable Hollywood blockbuster, but at the last minute opted for a Festival show, a screening of a compilation of short films. We figured they couldn't possibly all be bad or boring. I was surprised by the diversity of people in the crowd. David nudged me in the side. "Hey, isn't that your Marcus?" As discreetly as I could, I leaned over the red velvet rope and craned my neck. Marcus was turned away, speaking with another person I couldn't quite see. Too late, I noticed Fang had spotted me. He whispered something in Marcus' ear. Three faces turned in our direction. Then Marcus ducked under the rope and approached us. His hair had grown out and he sported a trim moustache and beard, perfectly matched by a silk shirt opened at the collar and pleated pants held up with suspenders. He walked slowly, with a limp, leaning heavily on a cane. "You must be David Gallucci," he said upon arrival. "I've heard so much about you." It was an outrageous statement, since it couldn't possibly be true, and I was immediately annoyed. David shook his outstretched hand and regarded me curiously.

"David," I said, waving, "meet Marcus Wittenbrink Jr."

David said: "I've heard a lot about you too."

"Have you, now?" Marcus said, smiling. "Nothing too scandalous, I hope."

"Not yet."

"If I didn't know better, I'd think your boyfriend here was trying to keep you all to himself."

I folded my arms. "I'm glad to see you're up and about, Marcus."

"You're looking well, Daniel. You seemed a little pale back in the winter. I enjoyed my cigarette with you."

"How's the leg doing?"

"Improving. How are you enjoying the Festival?"

"We've never been before." I made a point of holding David's hand. "We thought we'd check it out this year. See something different. And yourself?"

"Well. I've made this little film, an adaptation of the title poem from my book. It's a small project, nothing too ambitious. But it's kept me busy. You remember my book, Daniel, don't you?"

"*Tales From the Bottom of My Sole.*"

"That's right. You attended the launch at Hart House two years ago."

"That's an interesting title," David said.

Marcus leaned forward on his cane. "It's about love, in dark places."

"Dark places?"

"Darkrooms, to be precise."

"It's about photographers?"

"No," I said. "He means darkrooms in bathhouses."

"Most of my male friends are in this film," Marcus said pleasantly, "or at least their feet are. You know, of course, how in a darkroom you sometimes step barefoot into ejaculate on the floor? Sometimes it's fresh and still warm. More often it's cold. The experience may fill us with horror and disgust, or perhaps something else: desire, connection, intimacy, lust. There's always a story, one that happens here." He touched his breast. "I like to imagine that in the end, all these stories are about our relationships with love."

"Oh," David said. "*Sole.* Not *soul.*"

"That's right. I hope you enjoy it."

"Enjoy it?"

"My film. It's on the Mixed Shorts bill you're seeing today."

David turned to me. "Did you know that?"

"No," I said truthfully, "I didn't know that."

"Really?" Marcus raised an eyebrow.

"Really?" David said.

"Really. I had no idea." I sounded more defensive than I'd intended to. "Marcus, congratulations. I didn't know you'd been working on a film."

A balding gentleman in a lavender scarf turned around. "I'm, I'm so sorry, but I couldn't help but overhear your conversation," he said. "That's why we're here, actually, you see, to see your work." He clutched his partner's shoulder, a short Middle-Eastern fellow with startlingly white teeth. "My husband and I met in a bathhouse. Your book, it's meant a lot to us." He fumbled in his side-bag and withdrew a slim volume. "I don't suppose you might consider ..."

"Of course." Marcus produced a gleaming fountain pen. (It was like a magic trick.) "It would be my pleasure." He opened the front cover. "Daniel, would you mind?" He handed me his cane, turned me around and bent me over, and autographed the book against my back.

"We really, really are quite the fans of yours," Scarf Guy effused. "Thank you, thank you so very much. Actually, would you, I mean, do you mind if?" He thrust his phone at me, and drew Marcus in between him and his husband. I handed Marcus' cane to David, ducked under the rope, stood back and took their picture.

"Thank you so much. We really appreciate it."

"You're more than welcome," Marcus said. "Now, let me tell you something that's not in the credits." He drew near conspiratorially. "All the ejaculate you see in the film, it's authentic." He winked. "I should get going, my lovers are waiting for me. Thank you for coming." He touched David's elbow. "David, it was a pleasure meeting you. Daniel." He retrieved his cane and limped back to the front of the line.

"You two are friends of his?" Scarf Guy asked.

"Yes," said David said.

"No," I said.

"He is," David said, pointing at me.

Scarf Guy regarded me expectantly. "So, are your feet in the film?"

"What? No. No, my feet are not in the film."

"Oh." Scarf Guy's face went blank. "Well, then." He turned his back. The line was starting to move. I had a vision of body checking Scarf Guy into the sideboards as hard as I could. The truth was, my feet could've been in the film. They should've been in the film. Marcus had asked all his male friends to be in his stupid film, but he hadn't asked me. Even worse than feeling excluded and shamed, I felt envious. It was juvenile and pathetic, but I couldn't help it. Why hadn't I been given the opportunity to walk over Marcus' cold and slimy jizz in front of the camera? After everything I'd done and been through, I'd at least deserved that opportunity.

"He seems like a nice guy," David said, perusing the program. "Oh look, here he is: '*Tales from the Bottom of My Sole*. English language. Canada. Runtime 19 minutes.

Directed by Marcus Wittenbrink Jr. No animals were harmed during the making of this film. Nor does this film contain any footage of Daniel Garneau's feet.'"

Then I felt like body checking David. But I didn't. Instead, I bit the bullet, accompanied David into the theatre, and watched eight short films back to back. The shorts were from all over the world, ranging from two to twenty minutes. Marcus' piece was the only Canadian entry in the lot. In the end, when the houselights finally came back on and as the audience applauded, I sat mutely in my chair. Although I hated to admit it, Marcus' *Tales* had been by far the strongest, most honest, creative and moving piece on the bill. And it was clear to me that the jizz on the bottom of Marcus' feet was the story of my life.

⌒ That summer, I decided I would move in with David in the fall. I'd lost count of the times I'd been woken up in the middle of the night by shouting or screaming in the alleyway outside my bedroom window, or the sound of bottles smashing. Going to school and working part-time at the group home was hard enough without having to lose sleep like this. The turning point came when I arrived home one evening to find a large man in a hoodie slumped over against my front door. For a few seconds, I thought he might be dead. The entrance to my basement apartment was at the bottom of a narrow concrete stairwell, and any casual passer-by might not notice a body in that alcove. Immediately, I set my bike aside, and took out my phone to call 911. Then the man raised his arm. "Hey doc, how's it going?" I recognized that voice. It was Robert Burns.

"Robert Burns, Jesus Christ."

"It's just Robert Burns, doc."

I descended the stairwell. "Are you okay?"

It was a stupid question. He was not okay. It was obvious he'd been beaten up badly. Blood gleamed in his hair and one eye was swollen completely shut. When I fumbled with my phone, he gripped my ankle. "No. Don't."

"I'm calling an ambulance."

"No, don't. No ambulance."

"We need to get you to a hospital."

"No ambulance. No hospitals."

"Okay, look, Robert Burns, the Sherbourne Health Centre is just around the corner."

"I'm just banged up. I'm okay. I'm okay." He gripped the door handle and pulled himself to his feet. He would've fallen if I hadn't caught him in both my arms. "I just need a place to lie down, catch my breath."

"Robert Burns, seriously, we need to get you to a hospital."

"No!" he screamed, his voice breaking. "No!" He flailed and shoved me aside. "No fucking hospital!"

"Okay." I stood my ground, and wiped the spittle from my face. "Okay, no hospital. Look. Hey." I put away my phone. "No hospital."

"You're a doc, doc. Can't you just. Can't you just fix me up? I just need a place to wash up. Maybe get a few stiches. Fuck." He had slumped down again against my front door. Now there was blood on the handle.

"You know I'm not a doc, right? I just got into med school. I haven't even started yet."

He looked me in the eye. "Please. I'm asking."

Then I realized something I'd never realized before in all my encounters with Robert Burns since last summer. Maybe it was because I'd held him in my arms. Or maybe it was because of the way he'd screamed at me. Or maybe it was simply the naked look in his eye in that moment. I was shocked and shaken I hadn't realized it before now. I keyed open the door and helped him inside. Most of the blood had come from a cut on his head. He smelled like he'd pissed himself. I gave him a T-shirt, a sweatshirt, sweatpants, socks and a pair of my underwear, and told him to take a shower which he did. I also gave him a plastic bag to put his dirty clothes in. He was in the washroom an hour before he finally came out. During that time, I wiped down the chair he'd sat in, as well as the front door. Then I went to get my bike which I remembered I'd left on the sidewalk. But it was gone. Jesus fucking Christ. I went back inside. I called Blonde Dawn, but there was no reply. When Robert Burns finally came out of the washroom, I took out my first aid kit and cleaned and bandaged his injuries as best as I could. He had a few serious contusions. I thought he might have a broken rib from the way he was breathing and holding himself but I didn't ask to examine him more closely. Instead, I rummaged out some leftover mac and cheese and microwaved it in a bowl. I set this on the kitchen table along with a beer. He ate slowly, in silence, as I watched.

After a while, I said: "Robert Burns, what happened?" But he didn't reply. I knew better than to ask if he wanted to call the police. After he finished his beer, I gave him a glass of milk. "Look," I said, "hospitals can be shitty places." He chewed methodically. "Some doctors can be assholes." He glanced up at me and down again. "I promise you, I promise you, if you go to the Sherbourne Health Centre you'll be treated okay."

He didn't say anything but finished his mac and cheese. He pushed his empty bowl and glass away. "I'll take it under advisement, doc." Then, without another word, he got up, pulled on his shoes, picked up his garbage bag of dirty clothes, and left. The front door clicked shut behind him. I sat for a moment, drumming my fingers on the table. "You're welcome," I said.

Two weeks later, my bike showed up on my front walk, chained to an iron fence and secured with an industrial padlock. It'd been cleaned and tuned up. One of the loose brake cables had been replaced. I had to check twice, but there was no mistaking the fact that this was my bike. An envelope had been slipped through the mail slot on my front door containing a small key. I unlocked my bike and brought it back inside.

I didn't see Robert Burns for the rest of that summer and figured he must have moved on, maybe gone back to the States. He'd said he was from Montana. But then one morning late in August, while passing through Allen Gardens, I spotted him across the street coming out of the Sherbourne Health Centre. I cycled around and caught up to him at the intersection. "Hey Robert Burns, how's it going?"

"Keeping it real, doc, keeping it real."

"Haven't seen you in a while."

"Been around."

"You like my new bike?"

"It's not new."

"Well, you're right about that. This was the first bike I got when I moved to Toronto. Bought it off Kijiji. It has a lot of sentimental value." I nodded towards the Sherbourne Health Centre. "They treating you okay?"

Robert Burns turned and observed the building behind him. He squinted at me in the sunshine. "Got four stiches in my head." He parted his hair to show me.

"Looks all healed up."

"That's a Medicine Wheel."

"What?"

He pointed at the ring on my finger. "That's a Medicine Wheel."

"Yeah, it is."

"Your girlfriend give you that?"

"No. A friend did."

"Your boyfriend?"

I watched the black squirrels in the park scrambling after each other. "No," I said. "Just a friend."

"The Medicine Wheel, you know what it means?"

"I have an idea."

"You still got the feather?"

I pulled out the little wooden eagle feather which I'd bought off Robert Burns over a year ago.

"You got any Indian in you?"

"My grandmother's Métis."

"That means you got one-sixteenth Indian blood in you."

"I suppose it does. She was a school teacher. She

taught English. She pretty much passed as white her whole life."

"Good for her. You do what ya gotta do to survive."

"She's got dementia now. I don't think she remembers much of who she was anymore."

"That ain't so bad."

"Maybe for some people." I tucked the eagle feather back under my T-shirt. "You're a good man, Robert Burns. I want you to know that."

He studied his shoes. "You know I'm not, doc." When I didn't say anything, he grinned and shook his head. "Doc, I know you know. I saw it in your face, that day you took me in." I still didn't say anything. Robert Burns pointed behind him. "I just got a needle in my butt. Hurt like hell. You know what for?" I shook my head. "It was my T-injection. You know what that is?"

"Testosterone."

"Naw, man, T's for Thunderbird. I just got my Thunderbird-injection. If things go right, they're gonna help me get my top-surgery come spring. You know what that is?"

"A mastectomy."

"Naw, man, c'mon. That means top-of-the-world, top-o'-the-mornin'-to-ya, top gun, top notch, top dog. That's right. So fuck these bindings. I am so sick of them. I am so fucking sick and tired of it all. Sometimes, you get so sick, eh, you get tired of walking Mother Earth. Ever get that sick, doc?"

"Can't say that I have."

"Don't. It sucks. You know why I carve my feathers and wolf-heads?" I shook my head. "So I don't carve myself. Check it out." He rolled up one sleeve of his flannel shirt. Dozens of white scars covered the inside of his forearm. "I hear voices they tell me to carve myself, eh. But I carve my feathers and wolf-heads. There's a lot of medicine in that."

"I think you're onto something there." He rolled his sleeve back down. "Here," I said. I took off my ring and handed it to him. "You take this."

"I can't take that."

"Sure you can. I'm giving it to you."

"Fuck that. Your friend gave that to you."

"Yeah, and now I'm giving it to you. Look, I'm moving at the end of the summer."

His broad brow furrowed. "You leaving town?"

"I'm moving across town."

Robert Burns blinked and ran his hand over his face. He reached out and took the ring. He examined it in his big stubby fingers. After a while, he said: "You need anything."

"Okay," I said. "I'm going to go now."

"Alright, doc. Don't be a stranger."

"Keep it real."

"I always do."

I rode away. I needed to start packing. I never was one to leave things to the last minute. Rounding the corner, I glanced over my shoulder and waved. Robert Burns, who was still standing where I'd left him, raised his fist. The truth was, I was going to miss this neighbourhood. I was going to miss the Conservatory in Allen Gardens, St. Lawrence Market just a few blocks south, and the Gay Village on Church Street just a few blocks north. But most of all, I was going to miss its colourful characters, and people like Robert Burns. I knew his was one of just countless stories out there. But like Karen had said, I'd still barely scratched the surface of everything this city had to offer. And it was time to move on.

CHAPTER TWELVE

This Could Be Anywhere in the World

David's loft was just around the corner from where he worked at Bikes on Wheels on Augusta Avenue. I'd been spending so much time at his place over the last year, moving in didn't seem like such a big change. There was a lot more sunlight for all my plants. Also, living in Kensington Market, I was closer to Pat and Blonde Dawn, and a lot closer to school. (After four years of undergrad, starting med school didn't even seem like that big a change, just more classroom lectures and more studying.) I'd missed the neighbourhood Karen and I had staked out as our own. Sneaky Dee's and Free Times were both just blocks away. In the end, David was right. It really was like we were just two regular guys sharing rent. The only difference was we also shared a bed.

Towards the end of October, Pat organized a dim sum outing in Chinatown. David and I rolled out of bed one Sunday morning, strolled ten minutes over to Spadina Avenue and hiked up a circular stairway to the second floor. The restaurant turned out to be a cavernous hall decorated with red lanterns, with a raised stage at the far end adorned with a golden dragon and phoenix. There must've been over three hundred people, young and old, Chinese and non-Chinese, packed into the space. It was buzzing and chaotic, elegant, tacky and totally fabulous. I'd never been to dim sum before, and David told me I was in for a treat. We'd invited Parker, and Megan and Charles. Pat and Blonde Dawn had also brought along a few of their friends. We were the perfect party for a table for ten.

I recognized one of Pat's friends as the saxophone player from the Free Times Café, who reintroduced himself as Bobby Lam. As the only Chinese person at our table, he was our default go-to guy when it came to identifying the contents of the bamboo steamer baskets and stainless-steel platters being pushed around on carts by ladies calling out, "*Har gow!*" and "*Shumai!*" Pat was more than eager to try everything, and he'd gesticulate and order two of every dish that passed by without even waiting to see what was inside. We had shrimp dumplings and sweet-and-sour pork, crispy fried squid, and sticky rice wrapped in lotus leaves. My favourite was the steamed BBQ pork buns.

More than once, Pat exclaimed with his mouth full: "I have no idea what the fuck I'm eating but this shit is delicious!" Then Bobby would lean over, examine his plate and illuminate him. Megan passed on the pig's blood and half a dozen other items, but the rest of us followed Pat's lead and tried at least a bit of everything. (Parker's favourite was the chicken feet.) There was tea and more tea to wash everything down.

In the end, we stayed for hours, catching up and chatting and debating the merits of chopsticks versus forks, paperbacks versus e-readers, and The Beatles versus The Stones. Everyone agreed that Toronto offered some of the best selections in ethnic foods in the world, and conceded that lightsabers were in fact the ideal weapon of choice when battling zombies. At this point, Bobby mentioned how many of the locals believed the building was haunted, given that it was once an old Chinese morgue and funeral home. Megan shrank back, wide-eyed, in her seat. Then David remarked how his Roman Catholic mother talked regularly to her dead husbands, which prompted Charles to offer-up a mini-lecture on séances and ectoplasm. At this point, Megan uttered a mouse-like squeak and excused herself from the table. No one seemed to notice, including Charles who continued on enthusiastically about Toronto's Haunted Walk and real-life modern-day ghostbusters.

I excused myself from the table, and found Megan outside pacing the street corner, puffing on a cigarette. Today she was wearing a black turtleneck and a red beret with matching mittens on a string that dangled from her wrists, flopping about whenever she'd gesticulate. "You okay, there, Megan?"

"No, I'm not okay. I'm not," she said. "I don't know why Charles has to go on and on about ghosts when he knows it creeps me out. And those chicken feet are absolutely disgusting! I don't know how people can eat those things. I know it's so not PC for me to say that, but I really don't give a flying monkey's ass. You think they have monkey's ass on the menu? I wouldn't be surprised if they did. Sweet and sour monkey's ass, sticky rice monkey's ass in lotus leaves, crispy barbecued flying monkey's ass-on-a-fucking-stick. Honestly! I tried ordering a plain garden salad (with no tomatoes since you know, Daniel, I can't stand the texture of raw tomatoes), but did you know those cart ladies don't even speak a word of English? I'm also PMSing right now. So that just explains everything, doesn't it? At least that's what Charles would say. 'Megan, sweetie, you're PMSing. This will pass.' I hate it when he says that."

"You two fighting?"

"What? No, Daniel. That's the problem. We never fight. My ex-boyfriend Chris and I, we used to fight all the time."

"And that's a good thing?"

Megan sneezed. "Well, no. It was awful." She searched her pockets and pulled out a crumpled tissue. "But we'd have make-up sex afterwards. Make-up sex is the best. It's just the best. But Charles, he just, like, he goes along with everything." She dabbed at her eyes and blew her nose. "If I complain about something, he'll listen and understand and apologize if he needs to, and he'll be so calm and nice about it. Sometimes it drives me crazy. I want my knock-down fights. I want my make-up sex."

"Okay," I said.

"Look at me. I don't even smoke! I just bummed this off an old Chinese guy with one tooth right now. Here, take this away from me, please."

She handed me her cigarette, smeared with lipstick. "Charles," I said, "is a really nice guy."

"I used to want nice. I remember that. I remember when that was all I wanted."

"You two have been together, what, two-and-a-half years?"

"Well, since that dinner party of yours. I suppose it's been that long. Has it been that long? How are your friends from upstairs, the ones who were pregnant? What were their names?"

"Mike and Melissa."

"That's right."

"They had their baby, little Benjamin. They moved into a condo up in North York. I don't really see them anymore." I butted out the cigarette.

Megan sniffed. "I miss Karen. She was my best friend. Well, she still is. But you know how it is."

"Yeah. Well, she's my best friend too. I miss her too."

"Charles is going to be a professor one day. Professor Ondaatje. Doesn't that sound nice? I think about having his children. Seriously, I do. I could be Mrs. Ondaatje, couldn't I? He says he's a devout atheist. Can you be an atheist and still believe in ghosts? I could be an atheist. I have an open mind, right? But Daniel, I just don't know what I want these days. Maybe I'm just being too nitpicky. Do you think I'm being too nitpicky?"

"I wouldn't know."

"Karen said you and I can both be a bit uptight sometimes."

"She said that?"

"Of course, there is one thing about Charles I can't complain about."

"What's that?"

"He's huge. But I guess you would know that. Honestly, compared to Charles, Chris was a cocktail sausage."

Megan whispered: "Did I ever tell you Chris always had to use a cock ring?"

"Yes, you have."

"Well, Chris always had to use a cock ring, just to keep it hard. I think he had something wrong with him down there."

"He tried to kiss me once."

"What? Who?"

"Chris."

"My Chris?"

"Your Chris. A few summers back, during Pride. He tried to kiss me. He was drunk."

"Oh my god, do you think Chris is gay?"

"Well, I don't know. Pat's convinced no one's completely straight. I figure most guys are mostly straight. I think Chris might fall into that category."

"What was it like, Daniel, when you and Charles were together?"

"Charles and me?"

"Megan nodded.

"Um." I scratched my head. "It was … nice?"

"When you two kissed, would he do that thing with the tongue?"

"What thing?"

"You know, that thing."

"Oh, that thing. Um, yeah, he would."

"Did you like it?"

"I didn't mind."

"Would he, like, go down there, on you, with you?"

"Um, sure. Why? You?"

"No. Well, sometimes. Not as often as I'd like. Except

then he'd do that same icky thing with the tongue." Megan rolled her eyes.

"Well, why don't you tell him you don't like it? He can't read your mind, Megan. Tell him what you would like. Tell him what to do."

"Oh, I couldn't do that!"

"You're a teacher, Megan. Just think of him as one of your students."

"I teach pre-K to grade three, Daniel."

"Exactly."

"You know, Karen and I kissed once?"

"Oh?" I was genuinely taken aback.

"It was awkward. I mean, I thought it'd be, you know, like all that." Megan screwed up her face and shook her head. "We were able to laugh about it afterwards. She made me promise not to tell you. Honestly, I don't think I could ever do it with a girl. Ew!"

"Yeah." I nodded. "Ew."

"Daniel, what was it like with Marcus and Fang?"

"What do you mean?"

"Well, you know. When the three of you were together. What was sex like?"

"Who says Marcus, Fang and I were together?"

"Daniel, are you kidding me? Everyone knew the three of you were together. There's nothing wrong with that! Really, I'm not judging you at all. It's the opposite, in fact. I mean, first of all, I think guy-on-guy sex is so hot. Sometimes I'd get Charles to watch gay porn with me. I used to think about the three of you doing it all the time. And Marcus, he's so attractive. Not that you're not attractive, I mean, you are. But Marcus, he's like this angel, he's like this Greek god. In fact, I was thinking, well. Do you think Charles would ever be into a threesome, like, with another boy?"

"You should ask Charles."

"Would you sleep with us?"

"What? What? Megan, hold on. Look, I'm with David."

"Well, do you think you and David might sleep with us? I just need, I think, I mean. I mean we're friends right, all of us? But you gay guys sleep with your friends all the time, don't you? And I was just thinking, Charles and me, we're kind of in a slump right now. And he's not into open relationships, and I'm not either. But I thought maybe like just this once. And I trust you. And David seems really nice. And there's no harm in asking, right?"

"Megan. No. No, I don't think that would be a very good idea."

"Okay."

"Look. Megan. Have you tried a strap-on?"

"What?"

"A strap-on. I think Charles might enjoy that."

"Why would he enjoy that?"

"What do you mean, 'Why would he enjoy that?' Charles, he would enjoy that. He likes it."

"Likes it?" Megan blinked and raised one hand. "Oh no. No, he told me that he's, you know. Oh no. He told me that when he was with other men, it was exclusively, you know."

"What?" Now I was more than taken aback. "Charles never topped me. He was always the bottom. I never bottomed for him, not once, not even close. Not that there's anything wrong with being the bottom. But that never happened between us. Did he tell you he was the top in our relationship?"

Megan nodded.

"Okay. Well." I folded and unfolded my arms. "Well, that. That's a lie. And I'm disappointed. I'm really disappointed. And, Megan, you should get a strap-on. In fact, don't tell him. Just get it. And I think you should surprise him with it when he's least expecting it. Trust me, he'll love it. In fact, I'll help you pick one out."

"Oh, Daniel, would you?"

I rested one hand on her shoulder. I could've said a lot of things to her in that moment. I could've told Megan that Charles had all the sex appeal of IKEA furniture, and that when it actually came to performance in bed, despite his vast and esoteric intellect, what Charles needed most was someone to take him by the hand and lead him like he was in pre-K. But instead, I simply smiled and said: "Hey, what are friends for?"

⌢ Grandma was sick. It'd happened suddenly and without warning. She'd been able to leave the nursing home without any fuss and come home for Thanksgiving. But by November, she had moved into hospice care, and was sleeping almost all the time. A week before Christmas, the chaplain was called in. In the early morning of Christmas Eve, Grandma passed away. Grandpa was at her side, holding her hand when it happened. Liam, Pat and I were crashed out on a couch the head nurse had let us drag into Grandma's room. I woke up first, blinking blearily. Pat was snoring, drooling on my shoulder. The flowers crowding the windowsill shone, luminous. For a few seconds, I didn't know where I was. The sunlight was blinding on the white sheets. I squinted and rubbed my eyes. Gradually everything came into focus. I got up and went over to Grandpa, knelt and held his shoulders. After a minute, Liam and Pat did the same. Grandma was ninety-one years old.

I texted Karen who arrived forty minutes later along with the Miltons. To my surprise, Karen's little sister Anne also showed up. As usual, she was dressed all in black, but on this occasion it seemed appropriate. I remember the red exit signs, the sound of the nurses' heels on the linoleum floor, the oil in Grandpa's unwashed, thinning hair. The staff knew exactly what to do, what we needed, and how it was to be done. In the end, I was the one who spoke with the doctors and the funeral director. Mr. Milton was helpful, as was Karen who had managed arrangements for her father's burial two years ago. The Miltons stayed with Grandpa that afternoon and all evening.

Late that night, when everyone had gone home and Grandpa had gone to bed, Karen knocked on the front door and I let her in. The four of us sat silently in the kitchen. In the last few days, I'd cleaned the house from top to bottom. Liam had jerry-rigged the downstairs toilet with a coat hanger so it was working fairly reliably. The furnace, however, was acting up again. At Grandpa's insistence, the three of us had taken his pick-up and gotten ourselves a Christmas tree. It just didn't seem right not to have one. It was smaller than usual this year, and we'd taken our time decorating it. Tonight, Liam made a big pot of Labrador tea. A plate of store-bought shortbread cookies sat untouched next to it. After a while, Pat emptied his cup and set it upside-down on the table. "Well, that hit the spot."

"Yep."

"Yes sir."

"Yesiree."

The window over the sink rattled. A draft was moving through the house again. Jackson padded into the kitchen and looked from one of us to the other. He whined and rested his chin in Liam's lap.

"Look, guys," Pat said. "Anyone want a drink?"

"Definitely," we said in unison, "for sure." Chairs scraped, tea cups were cleared, a bottle of Canadian Club was cracked open and four glasses appeared.

"Hey guys," Karen said, checking her phone while I poured. "It's Anne. She wants to know if she can join us."

We stared at each other. When we were little, the five of us used to always hang out. I remembered rescuing Anne's stuffed giraffe after Gary Kadlubek threw it onto the train tracks. But by the time we got into high school, she was doing her own thing. "Yeah," we said. "Sure." I tucked my shirt into my pants. "Of course."

When Anne arrived, she was wearing an Avril Lavigne T-shirt and cargos. Her hair was dyed blue and one side was shaved. She kicked off her combat boots, strolled through the living room and peered out the back door before settling in the kitchen. "Nice tree," she said. She handed me a Tupperware of shortbread tied with a ribbon. "Here. My mom baked these for you guys."

"Thanks," I said. "You want a drink?"

"Sure. What do you have?"

"Well, we're having whiskey. Here." I handed her a glass with a shot in it.

"What? No milk and cookies?"

"Not tonight."

"Some party. Cheers." She threw back her shot before I could ask if she wanted any Diet Coke or ginger ale to go with it. She handed back the glass and wiped her mouth on the edge of her wrist.

"Hey, look, Annie," Pat said. "Thanks for coming out this morning. It meant a lot to us."

"Really?"

"Really."

"Well, thanks for having me over."

Pat poured everyone another round. "Remember when the five of us used to play hide-and-seek?"

"Yeah." Anne smiled shyly. "That closet in your bedroom had that squeaky floorboard. It was always a dead giveaway."

"Shit. I remember that."

"I remember," Anne said, "your grandpa used to clean and sharpen his lawnmower blades right at this table. The first time I saw that, it scared the hell out of me."

"No kidding," Pat said laughing, "that's right. You started bawling your eyes out."

"How's he doing?"

"Grandpa? He's doing okay."

"He's a survivor," Liam said.

Anne poked at the fridge magnets. "So when's the funeral?"

"In two days."

"You're going to the funeral?" Karen said.

"Of course, I'm going to the funeral."

Karen nodded, her lips compressed into a thin line. I looked back and forth between the two. "What's up?"

"Oh," Karen said, shrugging. "It's just that she wouldn't go to her own father's funeral. That's all."

"Would you rather I didn't go?" Anne said.

"That's not the point, is it?"

The room had gotten colder. I wondered if the furnace was acting up again, but I didn't think so.

Liam drew himself to his feet. He looked haggard and his eyes were bloodshot. His beard needed trimming. I had a vision of him hauling traps and trudging across the wilderness through a blizzard in furs and snow shoes. "Guys, I'm pretty tired. I think I'm going to hit the sack. Karen, if you want to stay up, go ahead."

"Whoa whoa whoa!" Pat said. "Hold on, it's not even midnight yet. We all gotta stay up until midnight."

"Who said that?"

"We always stay up until midnight. It's our tradition. C'mon, guys, it's Christmas Eve. It's our tradition."

"Except last year," I said. "Pat, you weren't even planning to come home for Christmas."

"But I did come home," Pat said. "I came home, asshole. I came the fucking home! Look, I haven't missed a single Christmas in this house in my entire life, so fuck off! You're always on my fucking back." Tears were running down his face. "I'm here, aren't I? We're all here."

We were all taken aback.

"Liam," Karen said.

"Hey, look," Liam said, "I'll stay up. It's no big deal." He reached across the table, collected all our glasses, lined them up and started refilling them. Except he wasn't being careful and was spilling all over the table. Karen had to kick me twice in the leg to get my attention.

"What?"

She gestured with her eyebrows. "Pat." I drew a breath. "Pat, I'm sorry." But Pat only knuckled away his tears and wouldn't look me in the eye.

Liam hesitated over Anne's glass. "How old are you anyway?"

"I'm fucking nineteen," Anne said. "I've been drinking since I was twelve."

"Oh." He poured her a double-shot. He set the half-empty bottle down and raised his glass. We all picked up our glasses. "Here's to Grandma."

"To Grandma."

"To family," I said. I put my arm around Pat's shoulder.

"To family."

"To us," Karen said.

"To us."

"Hey, it's midnight. It's Christmas. Merry Christmas everybody."

"Merry Christmas."

⌒ Three days after the funeral, as I was loading up the car for the drive back to Toronto, Grandpa brought a cardboard box from the house.

"Here, Daniel, I've been buying these in bulk for your mémère. It'd be a waste to throw them out."

He set the box down in the trunk, patted my shoulder, and walked away through the lightly falling snow.

Puzzled, I opened the box which was neatly packed with slim white cartons. I pulled one out. They were fresh scent, vaginal cleansing douche kits. Pat and Liam emerged from the garage hauling our old dresser. I closed the box, threw my jacket over top of it and pushed it to the back of the trunk. I was still blushing as we wrapped the dresser in an old camping tarp and strapped it up on the roof of the car. That piece of furniture was older than we were, covered in faded hockey stickers and decals which we'd collected for years. Grandpa had insisted David and I could use it in our loft.

"Just strip it down," he said. "Give it a stain and it'll be good as new." But there was no way in hell I was going to strip it down. I was planning to keep the dresser exactly the way it was.

When I got back to Toronto, I dropped Pat off at the Ferry Docks. Blonde Dawn was in Florida with her family, and Pat was spending New Year's Eve again with his friends on the Island. When I thanked him for the loan of his car, he reminded me it was actually Blonde Dawn's car, and to return it by the weekend.

"Pat," I said, leaning over the passenger's seat. "Thanks. Happy New Year."

"Happy New Year," he said, and closed the door.

Back home, I keyed into the loft as quietly as I could. A huge pot of chili was simmering on the stove. I could smell it from down the hallway. The table was set with folded sheets of paper towel, a basket of focaccia and a bottle of red. Broken Social Scene was playing on the stereo. I could hear the shower running in the bathroom. I pulled off my snow boots, hung up my jacket, stripped naked and knocked on the door. David peered out from behind the curtain, soap suds in his hair and eyes.

"I was wondering when you'd be home." He squinted. "How was the funeral?"

"It was good," I said. "I missed you."

He glanced down at me. "Looks like it."

"Merry Christmas."

"Merry Christmas."

I kissed him, gently at first, and then more passionately. I'd been gone almost two weeks. "You'd better not be jacking off in there."

"Hey, we both promised not to."

David drew back the curtain. I observed the water streaming down his torso, hips and thighs. I'd kept my promise, and it looked like he had too. I reached out and cupped him in my palm, swollen and heavy.

"See?" He smiled, biting his lower lip. "I am a man of my word. They're about as blue as they get." We both noticed the drop of pre-cum oozing from the tip of my own erection. He touched it appraisingly and licked his fingertip. "So, mister, are you coming in or what?"

I stepped into the stall and closed the curtain. He wrapped his arms around my waist and swung me under the showerhead. The water was scalding hot. I almost came just from that embrace. I'd missed him so much. A few minutes later, when he had me in his mouth, I did come. Then I drew him to his feet and we kissed bruisingly as I took him in my fist, tasting my own sticky saltiness, until he shuddered and gasped out loud, almost grunting, again and again. Afterwards, he lay limply in my arms, but by then I was hard again. I turned David around, took up some soap and began to wash him. I groped for a condom in the medicine cabinet, tore it open and put it on. At that moment, the hot water gave out and the shower turned icy cold. As fast as we could, we clambered out, swearing and laughing at the top of our lungs.

Later, over dinner, I told David about Grandpa. "Liam's going to stay with him, at least for a few weeks."

"Those two really get along, don't they?"

"They're two of a kind, alright." I grated a block of hard Romano over both our bowls.

"How's your grandpa doing, anyway?"

"He's doing okay, as well as can be expected. You know, they were married fifty-nine years."

"No shit. That's incredible. What was she like?"

"Grandma? I just remember she was a lot of fun. She loved to laugh. I mean, we were still kids when she started getting the dementia, right? So it's hard to say what she was really like. But in all the pictures of her when she was younger, she looked like a Hollywood starlet. Everyone says Dad got his good looks from Grandma. She was a glamorous gal. One thing's for sure: she loved to be in nature, and she loved to go for walks. It got to be a problem. Grandpa and my parents would put up childproof locks and signs, but nothing worked. Once she disappeared for almost thirty-six hours. The police found her wandering along the highway, halfway to North Bay. Somebody must've given her a lift. She was really dehydrated, scraped up, and had no idea where she was."

"Whoa. That must've been scary."

"It was. Then after Mom and Dad died, it was just impossible to keep her safe. Three boys were a handful enough. She'd forget to turn off the gas stove. She'd wander off in the middle of the night. The whole neighbourhood and the police got to know her. She started getting erratic. Sometimes she'd get confused and ask where Mom and Dad were. Around that time, Liam started cutting himself, and Pat got caught lighting fires in the dumpsters behind the school. Then child welfare threatened to take us away. That was when Grandpa finally made the decision to put her in the nursing home."

"That must've been hard."

"Well, the home was only thirty minutes away, and we'd visit all the time. They loved her in the home. She'd read poetry to all the other residents. Grandpa likes to tell people they were high school sweethearts. Technically it's true. They met when he was fifteen. What most people don't know is she was actually his high school English teacher. He wasn't the best student so she'd keep him after school to tutor him. Well, one thing led to another. When word got out, it was a small town and you can imagine what it was like back then. She got fired of course, and eventually had to move. She ended up in Toronto, cutting up rubber in a tire factory. But Grandpa, he followed her. After he graduated high school, he followed her and moved in with her. He was nineteen and she was thirty-two when they got married. Then when our dad was still just a baby, Grandpa got conscripted into the merchant navy. They didn't see each other for two years."

"Wow. That's awful."

"Well, everyone was part of the War effort back then. Everyone made sacrifices. Grandpa wrote her every day, usually from the East Coast, but sometimes from as far away as ports in Russia. She kept all his letters. When the dementia started getting really bad, he'd read them to her at the nursing home, and then she'd remember who he was. What? What is it?"

"You know, you and I will be old one day."

"One day."

"We should write to each other."

"What do you mean?"

"We should write letters to each other, love letters, like your grandparents did."

"Wouldn't it be easier if I just texted you?"

"Daniel, I've never gotten a real letter before. I want to open the mailbox and find a letter with a stamp on it from my lover. I want to smell your cologne on the paper, and see your hand-writing. I want to get letters the way your grandma got letters. From Russia with love."

"Oh, James," I said, laughing.

"Promise we'll send each other love letters."

"You're serious?"

"Of course, I'm serious. Why are you always asking if I'm serious?"

"I guess because I'm so used to Pat messing with me. He used to yank my chain all the time."

"Oh, I'll yank your chain alright." David's stretched out his bare foot and pressed it up against my crotch. "But I'm serious about the letters. Look, I'll write the first one."

"Alright." I took his foot in my lap and began to massage his toes.

"You know," David said, "you never finished what

you started." He nodded towards the bathroom. "Maybe I should write a letter of complaint, for sexual non-harassment."

"How about a letter to the building manager about that hot water tank?"

"I love you."

I pressed my thumb deeper into his arch. I listened to faraway sirens and the faint, clattering rumble of a passing streetcar. Fifty-nine years was incomprehensible to me. It was more than twice as long as David or I had even been alive. If David moved to another city, would I follow him? Grandpa was only eighteen when he left everything he knew and followed after the woman he loved. Then when he was my age, he was already risking his life, fighting in a war across the ocean against the Nazis. What was I risking and what was I fighting for?

David searched my face. "You okay?"

I nodded. "I love you too."

David sipped from his wine glass.

"What?" I asked.

"You know what, mister. Hey, you ready for dessert?"

"You made dessert?"

"No, but my ma did. It's her cannoli."

"That reminds me. Grandpa had me bring back a couple of his sugar pies. He remembered you liked the last one I brought back from Thanksgiving."

"Pie and cannoli, then." David got up and rummaged in the freezer. "There's Rocky Road too. You ready for a sugar blast extravaganza?"

"Alright," I said. "But after." I got up, closed the freezer door and took David by the hand.

"Where are we going?"

I led him to the bedroom where I pushed him down onto the mattress, and started unbuckling his belt. "Let's just say," I said, smiling, "I don't want to get any letter of complaint."

Later that night, long after David had fallen asleep, I got up out of bed carefully so as not to awaken him. I put on my coat, climbed the stairwell to the rooftop and had a cigarette. The snow had stopped and the city for once seemed at peace. Christmas lights still twinkled here and there, in people's windows and balconies. Tomorrow, I'd get David to help me bring the dresser up. I was just starting to build my life with him. For Christmas, Grandpa had given me a slim book of poetry entitled, *Leaves of Grass*.

"It belonged to your mémère," he said. "I want you to have it."

I was sure Grandpa already knew I was gay. It didn't matter whether he'd figured it out on his own, or if Pat had told him. I wondered if it hurt Grandpa that I hadn't come out to him yet. I promised myself I would the next time I saw him. That sudden decision thrilled me in the most unexpected way. I was almost tempted to wake David up and let him know. Instead, I went back downstairs and had a drink of water. When I took off my clothes and crawled back into bed, David shivered and complained sleepily: "Oh Christ your hands are cold. Where'd you go?" I spooned him from behind and held him close. "No where," I whispered in his ear. "Go back to sleep. I'm here."

CHAPTER THIRTEEN

Sudbury Saturday Night

I n January, I was in the U of T Bookstore, picking up textbooks for the new semester. From the outside entrance, overblown with snowdrifts, the building was austere and unremarkable except for its size. But inside, marble staircases led up into a Great Hall awash in warm sunlight, with an ochre and gold ceiling flanked by decorated stone arches. It was a room that recalled a Venetian palazzo or the innermost chambers of Hogwarts. This particular bookstore always seemed a little bit magical to me, and over the years, I'd never gotten tired of its monumental architecture and endless flow of students and academic types. I was standing among the medical textbooks, admiring the ceiling when someone behind me said: "It used to be the old Reference Library."

I turned. "Excuse me?"

It was a girl on one knee, rearranging the shelf display, wearing a slim blue dress and horn-rimmed glasses. Her hair was stylishly coiffed and she had a beauty mark on one cheek.

"This building," she said, hefting a particularly thick

textbook, "the Koffler Student Centre, it used to be the old Toronto Reference Library. It was built in 1909 in the Beaux Arts neoclassical style. The university acquired it in 1977."

"The ceiling," I said, "it's like cake frosting."

"Cake frosting?"

"Oh, that's an architectural term."

"Really?"

"It is. It means: in-the-manner-of the-icing-of-a-cake, particularly in the Duncan-Hines style of the late twentieth century."

The girl took off her glasses, and pursed her lips. "Okay. I suppose I deserved that."

"Are you an architecture student?"

"No. I just work here." She stood and languidly smoothed out the wrinkles in her dress. "Are you?"

"No. I just like cake."

"I see."

"Yep."

"It's just that every time you come in here, it seems you're admiring the ceiling." She glanced at the textbooks in my arms. "How are you finding med school?"

"Expensive."

She extended her hand. "I'm Nadia, by the way."

"Daniel."

She tilted her head to one side. "You really don't remember me at all, do you?"

"I beg your pardon?"

"We've met before, two summers ago, at Sneaky Dee's. I was with my girlfriend Sam. We played a game of pool?

Your brother bought us drinks. We all took a cab together to that gay bar."

"Fly."

"That's right. You left without saying good-bye."

"Shit. I remember. Nadia, of course. Nadia. I am so sorry. That was rude of me. I was really drunk. That was not a good time for me."

"I know. You'd just broken up with your boyfriend."

"Who told you that?"

"Your brother."

"Well, it'd been a few months."

"Bad break-up?"

"Yes. No. I mean, just weird. The thing is, my best friend had also just moved away, and I was living on my own in this really sketchy neighbourhood, and, well, you know how it is."

Nadia raised her eyebrows. "You tell me."

"Well, it was a very distracted time of my life."

"Distracted?"

"Yes."

"Okay." Nadia nodded.

I cleared my throat. I was not enjoying this conversation. "So do you work here?"

"Mm-hm." She put her glasses back on and started shelving books again.

"You've seen me before?"

"Well, I'm usually working the register up front. I see a lot of people come and go. I've noticed you come in a few times."

"But you are a student."

"English major."

"My grandma was a high school English teacher."

"That's nice."

"She passed away a couple weeks ago."

"Oh, I'm sorry to hear that."

"On Christmas Eve."

Nadia put down her books. "Oh."

I shrugged. "She was pretty old."

"What was her name?"

"Her name?"

"She had a name."

"Well, we just called her Grandma or Mémère. But her name was Josette."

"And is your grandfather alive?"

"Yeah. His name's Tom. Thomas Garneau."

"Thomas and Josette. That sounds really nice. Were they a nice couple?"

"More than nice. They were amazing. They were extraordinary. They were so in love. They were married fifty-nine years."

"That is amazing. Please pass my condolences on to your grandfather."

"Thank you." I drew a breath. "She was cremated." I had no idea why I was still talking. It was like I was inside my body watching myself talking.

"Okay."

"He plans to scatter her ashes up by the family cottage. We used to go there a lot, the whole family, when we were kids. It's pretty run down now. We don't use it too often anymore."

"A lot of good memories there."

"Yeah. A lot. The truth is, I haven't been up there since I was a kid. Liam, that's our other brother, he keeps talking about how he's going to fix it up one day and maybe move up there permanently to live. He calls it the Good Medicine Cabin."

Nadia rested one hand on a shelf. "'I went to the woods because I wished to live deliberately, to front only the essential facts of life, and see if I could not learn what it had to teach, and not, when I came to die, discover that I had not lived.'"

"That's beautiful," I said after a moment. "What is that?"

"It's a famous quote by Thoreau, from *Walden*. Henry David Thoreau was someone in search of a state of grace."

"A state of grace?"

"That's right. You might say it's what we're all looking for."

"Living deliberately."

"Mm-hm."

"The title of that book, can you write it down for me? Maybe I'll get it for my brother."

"Here, I'll show you." Nadia walked past me and I followed. She led me to the literary nonfiction section where it took her less than a minute to pull out a slim, green volume. "Here you go. For the price of a coffee and a slice of cake."

"I'm shocked."

"You can also buy it used if you like. Save yourself a dollar or two."

"No. I can afford this. *Walden; Or Life in the Woods*. Thanks, I'll take it."

"So, can I buy you a slice of cake?"

"Excuse me?"

"I'm on my lunch break in ten minutes." She studied me calmly, resting one hand on her hip.

I wanted to let her know I was gay, but I realized she knew that already. In fact, the more I thought about it, the more I realized this girl knew more about me than most people did. She was beautiful, confident and smart. "Um, sure. Okay," I said. "Sure."

Later that evening, over dinner at home, David asked me what was on my mind. "Why do you think anything's on my mind?" I replied.

"Well, for starters, I just told you I'd jacked off in the cacciatore, and you thought that was nice."

I stared at him with my mouth full of bread. "I did." I chewed and swallowed. "Sorry. This really is delicious, by the way. Sorry."

"That's okay." David reached over and wiped some sauce from my chin with his thumb. "So what is on your mind?"

"I met this girl."

"Alright."

"I mean, we'd met before. But today we went out for coffee. She bought me cake."

"You love cake."

"I know."

"Okay."

"Well, we had an good time."

"Okay."

"I felt like I was cheating on Karen."

"Interesting."

"Do you think I was cheating on Karen?"

"What sort of dumbass question is that?" David laughed. "Dude! C'mon. What do you think?"

"Well, it felt like I was."

"Take it up with Karen. But no, for the record, you weren't cheating on Karen. Did this girl give you a ring?"

"No."

"Well, there you go."

I stared at my plate. "I don't have it anymore."

"What?"

"Karen's ring."

"You lost it?"

"No."

"I remember you used to wear it all the time."

"I did."

"So where is it?"

I poked at my cacciatore. "I gave it away?"

"You what?"

"I gave it to this guy."

"A guy?"

"It's not what it sounds like. It was this homeless person. He was this native guy, Cree. He really liked my ring."

"The ring Karen gave you as a graduation present? The one she got custom-made for you?"

"Yeah."

"Well. You must have had a good reason."

"I did."

"Alright. Did you tell Karen?"

"No. Not yet. I don't think she's noticed yet."

"But she will."

"Probably."

"You better tell her before she notices."

"I guess so."

David got up and brought back two fresh beers from the fridge. "So you had a good time with this girl."

"Her name's Nadia. She invited me out on her lunch break. She's slept with Pat."

"What?"

"She's had sex with Pat. It was just a thing."

"Small world."

"Well, I was with Pat the first time we all met. I think Nadia might've slept with him more than once. She didn't go into details. But she did tell me she and her best friend got into a really bad fight over it. It almost ruined their friendship. Apparently Pat was sleeping with both of them at the same time."

"Did he know they were best friends?"

"Yeah."

David drank from his bottle. "Hmm."

"Well, they made up, Nadia and her best friend. Now they both think Pat's an asshole. Nadia says it's people like Pat who give guys a bad name."

"Okay. Can't blame them."

"It was an asshole thing to do."

"Not cool."

"She didn't hold it over me though."

"Glad to hear that."

"I mean, he's my brother, right? But Pat, he's like, he's got this image of himself. He's always been this golden boy. He always thinks he's right. But sometimes I don't think he realizes how he makes other people feel. I want to think that, because the alternative is, he does know how he makes people feel and he actually doesn't care. And then that really makes him an asshole."

"You're brother's a good guy. He's just, well. He's like a straight version of me."

"Did you sleep around a lot?"

"I did." David sat back. "I did. Until I met this one guy. A friend set us up. We met at a concert downtown. It was his birthday. He'd just turned twenty-one. He was tall, dark and handsome. He had this amazing smile. He had great teeth. He flosses every day, you know. He was sexy as hell. It was love at first sight, for me anyway. He's going to be a doctor. I let him practice on me all the time. I'm going to marry him one day. He's going to wear my ring. One day. Definitely. I'm going to make it happen."

"David, you're twenty-three years old. And you want to get married?"

"Not tomorrow. But one day."

"How can you be so sure?"

He grabbed his crotch. "Because I can feel it here." He rested a hand on his stomach, and on his chest. "And here, and here." He touched his brow. "Then you can't help but start thinking it here. You know what I mean? I also want us to be dads."

"You and me, you know we're just, we're just kids playing at being adults, don't you?"

After a moment, David put down his fork. "Is that how you feel abut this?"

"What?"

"This, Daniel." He opened his arms. "Us."

"I don't know what to feel."

"Why the fuck is it so hard for you to feel?"

"Because," I exclaimed. "Because my life is fucked up."

"Well I'm sorry to be the one to tell you this, but everyone's life is fucked up. Everyone's. You're not that special. You don't have some monopoly on fucked-upness. We're all fucked up and we're all doing the best we can. Your grandparents did it, Nadia and her friend are doing it, and you and I are doing it."

"They were drinking, you know."

"What?"

"My parents. My mom and dad, they'd been drinking. It was Saturday night, and they were coming back from a party. They rolled their car because they were drunk and they were driving. Then their car caught on fire. Thank god they didn't hurt anyone."

"How do you know that?"

"Grandma told me. I was twelve years old. I was just a kid. Why would she say that to me unless it was true? She told me and then she forgot she even told me. I think Grandpa must've told her. That's how they died. And that's the reason why Grandpa had to put Grandma in the nursing home. He couldn't take care of her and us at the same time, not by himself. So he had to make a choice. So he put her in a fucking nursing home."

"Do your brothers know?"

"No! I've never told them that. I'm never going to tell them that. You're the only person I've told in my entire life. I haven't even told Karen that. You can't tell anyone, David. I am so, so angry at my parents, David, you have no idea."

"Okay. Okay. Come here." When I stood, he walked around the table and held me. He stroked my head, and he pressed his nose against my ear. "It's okay," he said. "It's okay." I was shaking and I was crying and I was so ashamed, but he kept saying it was okay, over and over again. After a while, I started to actually believe him. And the moment I did, I stopped crying, not all at once, but gradually. He kissed my neck, and my jaw, and the tears streaming down my cheeks. Then he stood back and held me by the shoulders. His eyes were locked to mine, but I didn't want to look at him because I knew I was all red-faced and puffy. "It's okay," he whispered.

"Oh, shit," I said breathlessly. I blew my nose in a napkin.

"You wanna sit down?"

I sat down on the couch. David sat next to me, one hand on my knee. I put my hand on top of his. I felt empty and hollow. I couldn't remember the last time I felt this way. Eventually, I drew a big breath and straightened. "Well, that was weird."

"Don't," David said.

"What?"

"It's okay."

Then when he said that, I started crying again, the way rain might start again, after a thunderstorm lets up briefly. I cried this way for a while, curled up on the couch next to him. Then, feeling exhausted and completely spent, I lay down in his lap and fell asleep.

⌒ In March, I met Charles at Mick E. Fynn's, a sports bar just outside the Village, across from Maple Leaf Gardens. It was one of our old haunts and we sat at our

favourite table close to the big screen TV. Sporting paraphernalia and neon beer signs decorated the walls. Charles
had been something of a recluse lately, having started his
dissertation. We hadn't seen each other since dim sum
back in October, and I was surprised at how fit he looked.
Charles explained to me how, since the New Year, he and
Megan had both been on a strict diet and exercise regimen.
"You two seem to be getting pretty serious," I said.

"Why do you say that?"

"Well, for one thing, you've been together how long?"

"Three years this month."

"That's a long time."

Charles blinked owlishly. "Can I confide in you,
Daniel?"

"Sure. Of course you can."

"It hasn't always been easy."

"It never is."

"For a period of time, I was starting to question whether or not Megan and I were even sexually compatible."

"Oh?"

"She's very fastidious."

"Okay."

"And controlling."

"I'm sorry to hear that."

"Oh, no, don't be. We've worked it out. Things are
better than ever. We've both been opening up, getting in
touch with our needs."

"Your needs?"

"Back in November, Daniel, we got ourselves a strap-
on. After that, for Christmas, we went out shopping
together for all sorts of toys."

"Sounds like fun."

"We've also been taking a tantric yoga class for lovers."

"Seriously?"

"It has been quite the adventure, if I do say so myself. I'm wearing a butt plug right now."

"What?"

"I'm wearing—"

"No, I heard you the first time." I sat back. "Charles." The waitress brought us another round and cleared our glasses. "Like, right now?"

Charles sipped from his Guinness and nodded, knuckling the foam from his lip.

"How does it feel?"

"Stimulating."

"Like, how stimulating?"

Charles folded his large hands on the table. "Well, there is a pleasurable sensation of fullness. I can also place additional pressure on my prostate at any time, just by doing so." Surreptitiously, he picked up the drinks menu, and shifted in his chair.

"Wow."

Charles shifted again, setting down the menu, and regarded me expectantly.

"Wow. I mean, you'd never know."

"That is the idea. Megan also likes the idea of me going about my whole day plugged."

"When do you take it out?"

"When she tells me to take it out. I've grown accustomed to it now. Over time, it starts to become part of your lifestyle, something you just do, like putting shoes on before leaving the house."

"Really?"

"It's more discreet than, say, a collar, and more intimate. Sometimes she also has me wear her underwear."

"Sometimes?"

Charles nodded.

"Right now?"

"I am. Megan's a petite woman and I'm a large man, so it is somewhat uncomfortable. But between the plug and the woman's lingerie, I'm aroused almost all the time. These last five months have been transformative for us."

"Gee, Charles. I don't know what to say. I'm happy for you guys. This sounds great."

"It is great, Daniel. I've proposed to her."

"What?"

"I asked Megan yesterday to marry me."

Pool players in plaid shirts and torn jeans slapped each other on the back, and raised a toast. The Major League season was about to start, and the networks were showcasing home-run highlights from past games. "Charles," I said, "holy shit, that's fantastic. Congratulations."

"She didn't say yes."

"What?"

Charles drew a shaky breath. "She didn't say no, either. She said she needed time to think about it."

"Okay. Okay, that happens. It's a big decision. People need time to think about these kinds of things."

"I was so sure she was going to say yes. She was giving every indication we were compatible partners." Charles broad brow glistened. "Do you think I was premature in asking her?"

"Well, it has been three years."

"I used to think," Charles said, "the basis of sexual and romantic attraction could be adequately explained by evolutionary psychology and cognitive neuroscience." He got up and started pacing. "What are human emotions but the measurable operations of brain chemicals: dopamine, oxytocin, adrenaline, vasopressin? Except now, I'm not so sure." He made a pained expression and shook his head. "I can't put my finger on it, but I'm starting to think there is something more."

I pinched the bridge of my nose. "Um, I should hope so. Charles, sit down."

"Even talking about it," Charles observed, "raises my heart rate." He sat down, pulled out a pad of paper and started scribbling notes.

"Charles, what are you doing?"

"Systematic self-observation. This in invaluable data. I need to document this."

"Charles, put that away. Stop. Charles." Other patrons glanced in our direction. When he didn't stop, I clamped my hand over his. "Charles, just put that down, okay? Stop being an academic, just for a second."

Charles stared at me. "This is what they mean by 'lovesick,' isn't it?"

"Is that how you feel? Then I suppose so."

"I can recall every detail," he said, "of the very first time I laid eyes on her: her red mittens, the snow on the collar of her jacket, her clumpy, poorly applied mascara. I can even remember the perfume she was wearing. It was a quantum moment."

"You're in love with Megan. You've fallen in love with her."

"I have. We both deduced that after the first night we spent together."

"And is she in love with you?"

"She told me she was. She told me she loved me."

"Then that's wonderful."

"Then why didn't she say yes?"

"Well. These things take time."

Charles sat back in his chair. "The subtleties of human courtship," he said, "can be so confusing." He rummaged out a ring box from his jacket pocket and opened it. "I wondered if it was too small or too big. It was an impulse purchase." He mopped his brow with a trembling hand. "Do you think it's big enough?"

Before I could answer, Charles fumbled and dropped the box. He knelt, picked it up off the floor and held it out. The diamond was enormous. I stared at it in shock.

"Yes. Yes, definitely."

"Are you sure?"

"Yes."

Passing our table, our waitress stopped in her tracks, open-mouthed. The pool players also stared in our direction. All around us, conversation had ground to a halt. "Oh my god," the waitress said, clutching her tray. "Oh. My. God."

"Wait," I began.

One pool player raised his pint. "Awesome."

The rest of the bar patrons around us followed suit. On the big screen TV, and on all the monitors over the bar, fans in their stands rose cheering to their feet. The bartender just shook his head and continued stacking glasses. Strangers came up to congratulate us. Drinks were on the house the rest of the night.

⌒ In April, Pat and Blonde Dawn invited David and me to the Lunacy Cabaret, a monthly fundraiser thrown by Zero Gravity Circus out in the downtown east-end close to Little India. Bobby Lam played in the house band and was able to get us free tickets. The event was vulgar, bawdy, and brilliant. There was clowning and sketch comedy, juggling, song-and-dance routines, and a belly-dance-hula-hoop-spinning act that was nothing short of astonishing. A tiny, muscular Asian guy performed aerial silks right over our heads. Even the obviously under-rehearsed numbers were entertaining. Many of the drunken audience members were dressed up in costumes themselves. Drink tickets were cheap and the raucous house was packed.

After the show, the audience cleared the metal folding chairs, and a dance party ensued. The cabaret took place in the main training space, with mirrors and circus paraphernalia adorning the walls. David and Pat vanished backstage with Bobby, leaving me on the crowded dance floor with Blonde Dawn. Soon we were both pogoing exuberantly hand-in-hand. I asked her about her tattoos and she explained them to me. Each one had its own story. She pulled off her blouse (she was wearing a black sports bra underneath) to show me the ones on her torso. Then Pat shouted across the room and tossed her a top hat (I had no idea where he got it), which she caught and put on at a jaunty angle without missing a beat.

A crash resounded across the room. Some unshaven guy in a tutu had stumbled into one of the heavy wall mirrors. There was broken glass everywhere and blood streaming down his forearm. Blonde Dawn and I pushed through the crowd, helped him up and sat him in a chair. A drag queen in a flamenco dress called 911. One of the bartenders found a towel and we elevated his arm and put pressure on the wound. Tutu Guy kept declaring his love for Blonde Dawn, eliciting laughter from his friends. To her credit, she remained professional, efficient and calm. Someone found a first aid kit, and she dressed his wound. When the paramedics finally arrived and escorted Tutu Guy away, he blew her kisses and people cheered.

Long after midnight, the four of us strolled down the block arm in arm, and stopped for a slice at Pizza Pizza. A skinny teenager with bad acne served us, and we settled ourselves into a booth just inside the entrance. "Hey, Dan," Blonde Dawn said, "you were good tonight."

"You were great. I was just your sous-chef."

"You both were amazing," Pat effused. "And you were the bomb."

"You two were like superheroes," David said. "You saved that guy's life."

"I wouldn't go that far."

"It was a little risky," Blonde Dawn said. "We'd been drinking, there was a lot of blood, and we went in without gloves."

"What are you guys saying? You did the right thing!"

Blonde Dawn studied me soberly. "Would you do it again, Dan?"

"Yeah," I said, "of course, I would."

Pat crammed the last of his pizza into his mouth. "Well, shit, man, there you go. You both deserve medals."

"We did make a good team, didn't we?"

"You betcha."

Blonde Dawn and I high-fived each other. Someone rapped on the front window. It was Marcus Wittenbrink Jr. surrounded by an entourage of revellers. He waved and touched the brim of his top hat. When Pat waved back, Marcus conferred briefly with his companions and entered the restaurant. Tonight, he was wearing a burgundy velvet frock coat and sporting a silver-headed cane. He'd waxed his moustache into Salvador Dali-inspired points that would've looked ridiculous on anyone else. On Marcus, they just looked incredibly sexy. He doffed his hat and bowed with a flourish. "Madam, I believe I have something that belongs to you." Dramatically, he produced a single glinting, golden hair. "This," he declared, holding it up, "is yours, is it not?"

Blonde Dawn wiped her mouth on a napkin. "That was your hat I was wearing."

"Guys, this is Marcus the Marvellous," Pat announced. "Marcus the Marvellous, this is Blonde Dawn and my brother Dan. You've met David."

"You," I asked, "were at the Cabaret tonight?"

"I was. How did you enjoy the show?"

"It was good. Here, I'll take that." I leaned across the table and snatched back the hair.

Pat glanced back and forth between us. "You two know each other?"

Marcus struck a tragic pose. "Once, Daniel and I, we were lovers."

"No shit." Pat's jaw dropped. "Shut the front door! You and my brother?"

"Alas, he broke up with me on Valentine's Day."

"Seriously." Pat regarded me accusingly. "Dude."

I cleared my throat. "How's Fang and that other boyfriend of yours?"

"Fang, Joseph and I are no longer together," Marcus replied. "I am a free agent, as they say. David here tells me you two are living together now?"

"That's right."

He squeezed David's shoulder and whispered in his ear: "Is he treating you well?"

"No complaints here," David said.

"Well, congratulations then." Marcus straightened and adjusted his cravat. "And congratulations on saving a man's life tonight. Blonde Dawn, your actions were extraordinary."

Blonde Dawn bowed her head. "Why, thank you, sir."

Pat beamed. "She's a paramedic."

Marcus' face lit up. "Then that is serendipity. You were heroic, madam, both you and our Daniel. This world of ours needs more heroes. I'm glad you enjoyed the show. David, if you and your friends change your mind, you know where to find us. Goodnight, gentlemen." He put his hat back on and left.

"Marcus the Marvellous?" David said.

"He's in character tonight," Pat said.

"He's a character alright," I muttered.

"Is that guy for real?"

"Dan, you broke up with him on Valentine's Day?"

I sighed. "Pat, fuck off. Blonde Dawn, yes, he's for real. Here." I handed her the strand of hair.

Blonde Dawn made a face. "What am I supposed to do with this?"

"It's yours."

"It's a hair."

"Well it's your hair. I didn't want him to have it."

"Just in case," Pat said, wiggling his fingers. He flared his eyes and twirled an imaginary moustache.

"Pat, like I said, fuck off."

"Captain Heartbreaker, sir." Pat saluted. "Fucking off, sir!"

"Pat, what part of 'fuck off' don't you understand?"

"Boys," Blonde Dawn said, "stand down. Or I'll have to put you down, both of you."

Pat barked like a dog and licked her cheek. When she turned around and smacked him, he grabbed her face and kissed her. David and I watched them making out for half a minute before we got up and went outside to share a smoke. By then, their hands were up beneath each other's shirts. Behind the counter, the pizza guy held out his phone and took their picture.

"That was hot," David said.

"That's my brother."

"I know. I've kissed your brother. He's a good kisser." He lit a cigarette.

"Don't get weird on me please. There's already been enough weirdness tonight."

"So, Marcus is single again."

I crushed a pop can under my heel, and kicked it across

the street. "David, you even just saying that is weird. And why didn't you tell me Marcus was there tonight?"

"I just bumped into him backstage. Pat actually was the one who introduced me."

"How the fuck does he know Pat?"

"I dunno. I think they might've just met? It happens. Look, Marcus and I talked for maybe two minutes. Then you got busy doing your good Samaritan thing. I was going to mention it."

"Well, why didn't he come up and say hi to me?"

"Daniel, I think you've been pretty clear with him about wanting some space."

"Then why do I sometimes think the guy's stalking me?"

"Fuck, whoa, Daniel, that is so paranoid. The guy's friends with half the circus crowd. He lives just a few blocks from here. We're the ones on his turf. And for the record, he did just come up and say hi. I thought he was pretty decent about it. I'm not sure what more you want from him."

"I suppose you're right."

David leaned against a lamppost. "I am right."

"Okay."

"I love you."

"I love you too."

"You want to fuck him, don't you?"

"What?" I exclaimed. "Who? Marcus?"

"Yeah, Marcus."

"I never said that."

"You don't have to."

"David, don't even go there." I paced up and down the sidewalk.

"Okay. I'm just saying."

"Saying what?"

"That you want to fuck him."

"What the hell are you talking about?"

"It's pretty obvious."

"What?"

"You're not denying it, are you?"

"David, he's my ex. It's over."

"Yeah, it's over. But it's pretty obvious you're like still carrying a torch for this guy. Look, don't worry. I'm not jealous. Would you rather I was jealous? If you feel threatened by him because you think I feel threatened by him, then don't. But I will tell you something."

"What?"

"Earlier tonight, he invited all of us back to his place. He told me to tell you Marwa would be there. Who's Marwa?"

"Some girl. What'd you say?"

"I said we had plans, but we'd take a rain check."

"Why'd you say that?"

"I said that, Daniel, because we haven't hung out with Pat and Blonde Dawn in like months. I want to spend some quality time together, just the four of us. Because family comes first. Is that okay?"

I nodded.

"Are you okay?"

"Sure."

David took one last drag and flicked the butt out into the street. "Are we okay?"

"Yeah."

Blonde Dawn and Pat came out of the restaurant. Pat

lit a cigarette, and draped himself over our shoulders. "Ready to rock 'n' roll, boyzengurls?"

"That pizza guy in there took your picture," I said.

"No he didn't."

"Yeah, he did."

"No he didn't."

"Yeah," I insisted. "He did."

"No, Dan. See, here's where you're wrong. Pizza Guy was video-recording us."

"Oh." I blinked. "Oh. Then, hey, that's okay then. You really don't mind having your make-out session plastered all over YouTube tomorrow morning?"

Pat looked at Blonde Dawn. "Is that okay?"

Blonde Dawn plucked the cigarette dangling from his lips. "Let the little cheese-faced fucker jack off all he wants to us." Her hair was all messed up, and she adjusted one bra strap. "I really don't mind."

"Alrighty then." Pat kissed David and me both on the cheeks. "We've got a bottle of mezcal at home with our names on it. You gentlemen get the cab, we've got the rest covered."

David hailed a cab and we all went back to Pat and Blonde Dawn's place where we stayed up half the night. The three of them smoked up, and we danced for a bit. Then we arm-wrestled and I beat everyone (although Liam could always beat me). Then Pat pulled out his karaoke machine and we all sang The Barenaked Ladies' greatest hits at the top of our lungs (except for *The Old Apartment*, which I insisted on singing solo). After that, David and I crashed in their guest room (which was really my old bedroom). I woke up the next morning to the smell of coffee and bacon, and David passed out on the floor next to me. When I shuffled out of the bedroom, Pat was in his underwear, wearing a pink, fur-trimmed bathrobe, draining grease into a mason jar. Blonde Dawn was in the washroom blow-drying her hair. There was buttered toast, Danishes, scrambled eggs and orange juice on the table. I had a killer hangover. But in the end, it had all been worth it. After all, like David said, family comes first.

CHAPTER FOURTEEN

We're Here for a Good Time

Late in April, Karen came down from Manitoulin to visit for the weekend. We met Saturday afternoon at the Moonbeam Coffee Company in Kensington Market. Our plan was to pick David up after he was done work, meet with Pat and Blonde Dawn, and step out for dinner. A recent rain shower had left the air smelling like fresh laundry. After the long winter, the sunshine on my face felt amazing. Down the street, Hasidic Jews dressed all in black and old Chinese ladies picked through the fruit and vegetable stalls. Students on bicycles rattled past. I hadn't seen Karen since Grandma's funeral. She looked good. Her hair was cut short in a fresh, stylish bob. She wore a T-shirt emblazoned with the yin-yang symbol stitched in red and gold, faded jeans and old hiking boots. She tossed her sunglasses and keys onto the patio table. "Wow, a whole box of your grandma's douche kits," she said, tearing open a packet of sugar. "I suppose that is a little weird. Still, it sounds like something your grandpa would do. They're pretty much the same as enema kits, right?"

"More or less." I glanced around, but none of the other patrons seemed to be paying any attention to our conversation.

"Did you know douching puts women at risk for cervical cancer?"

"Daniel, a lot of things put people at risk for a lot of things. You're a med student now. I don't know why you of all people are being so squeamish about this."

"I'm not being squeamish." A flock of pigeons rose storming from the rooftops, scattering the sunlight. I twisted at the fabric of my hoodie and lowered my voice. "Look, it's just that it's really personal, you know? I mean, what's going through Grandpa's head when he decides I can use Grandma's douche kits? He's thinking about me getting fucked up the ass, for chrissake. That's what he's thinking."

"Or fucking somebody else up the ass."

"Whatever. It's like, whoa, Grandpa, don't go there. Please. It's worse than imagining your own parents having sex."

I regretted my words the instant they were out of my mouth. To Karen's credit, she simply made a face and sipped from her coffee. "Okay, I get what you mean. Look, your grandpa's a practical man. He loves you. He accepts you for who you are. You're lucky to have someone like him. Most people don't."

"You're right." I drummed my fingers on the table. "You're right. I should just focus on that."

"So between you and David, who is fucking who?"

"Karen, c'mon."

"Just asking." Karen raised her eyebrows. "What? Daniel, hello, this is me you're talking to."

"We're, you know, versatile, sometimes."

"Versatile sometimes?"

"Well, most of the time I'm on top."

Karen's eyes crinkled into a smile. "And sometimes you're not."

"And sometimes I'm not."

"So, do you have any naked pictures?"

"What?"

"On your phone. Do you have any pictures of you and your hot Italian Catholic boyfriend?"

"I don't have any naked pictures."

"I don't believe you."

"Karen, I'm not going to show you our naked pictures."

"Oh, so you do have naked pictures."

"I never said that."

"But you do." Karen folded her arms and leaned forward. "Now you have to show me. Look, it doesn't have to be anything crazy or kinky."

"Oh really?"

"Just sexy."

"Sexy?"

"I want to see something sexy. You and David are good-looking guys. We shouldn't be ashamed of our bodies. We should celebrate them. Daniel, come on."

"Karen."

"Yo, just chill uptight boy."

"'Yo, just chill?'"

Karen leaned back, cradling her coffee. "I work with a lot of youth on the rez."

"Don't call me uptight. I hate it when you call me that. You told Megan you thought we were both uptight."

"I told her, Daniel, that I thought both of you could learn to relax more."

"Okay, fine." I took out my phone and flipped through my albums. "Hold on, let me see. Oh, here, okay. I'll show you this one." Discreetly, I held it out. It was a selfie I'd taken of David and me on our backs on our bed, grinning from ear to ear.

"Oh my god. Are you two covered in shit?"

"What? No! Karen, Jesus Christ. That's sugar pie. We were eating Grandpa's sugar pie off each other."

"What are those chunks?"

"That's cannoli, and Rocky Road ice cream."

"Oh, okay. For a minute there. Whoa. I'm all for kinky shit, but hey."

"It's not shit."

"Alright, okay. Well this is romantic then. You two boys look happy together. You really do. David's also a lot less hairy than I thought he'd be." Karen tilted my phone sideway. "Now that is one sexy treasure trail. Does he trim his chest?"

"No, he doesn't trim."

"What about down there?"

"Down there, maybe just a little bit."

"I thought so. All you gay boys trim."

"Karen, that's so not true. And straight guys trim too, you know. I don't want to talk about this anymore."

"Daniel, I tell you everything Liam and I get into. I trim, and I shave my pits. I really shouldn't. It's all this internalized white oppression. Liam never trims. He's a shag rug down there. And have you seen his ass lately? It definitely was not that hairy five years ago."

"Karen, I don't want to hear about my brother's ass. Anyway, I thought you two broke up again."

"We did break up." Karen handed me back my phone. "We're broken up."

After a moment I asked, "Is he okay?"

"Liam? He's fine. He's doing his thing. He spends his time between your family cottage and my aunt's farm. My aunt's practically adopted him. Oh, and I'm fine too, by the way. Thank you for asking."

"Are you okay?"

"When am I not? Look, Liam and I, we're still friends. This winter we went through a rough patch. He's back on his meds. He's doing fine now. I'm there if he needs me, and he has other people in his life too."

"Liam's back on his meds? What kind of meds?"

"Zoloft."

"Fuck."

"It's an antidepressant."

"I know what Zoloft is." I massaged my temples. I'd sensed something wasn't quite right with Liam back during Christmas. But with all the drama around Grandma and the funeral, I hadn't bothered to check in with him. Liam always played his cards close. "He doesn't talk to me about these things."

"He doesn't talk to anyone about these things."

"I've tried in the past, you know."

"I know."

"How bad was it?"

"Bad enough that he agreed to go back on meds."

"Does Grandpa know?"

"No."

"And he's better now?"

"He's better now, Daniel."

You were the one who convinced him?"

"And my aunt."

"Really?"

"She's been a big influence in Liam's life."

"I'd like to meet her."

"She's an amazing woman. She's the one who taught me how to drive a tractor. She competed in the 1972 Olympics in women's cross-country skiing. She's also the only Elder on the Band Council with a university degree."

"She sounds amazing."

"I'll introduce you one day. You should come up and visit this summer."

"How is life on Manitoulin?"

"It's a whole different world. I get a lot of respect. There aren't that many young people who stay on the Island anymore. But just between you and me, the truth is, the main reason I moved out there is to be closer to Liam. How ironic is that?"

"Karen, maybe you should start dating other guys."

"Who says I'm not? Who says I don't have some perfectly nice Manitoulin boy on the go, who opens doors for me, speaks fluent Ojibwe, tags me on Facebook, and actually answers my phone calls?"

"If you did, Karen, you'd tell me."

"I would?"

"Yeah. You're my best friend."

Down the lane, a dreadlocked busker started belting out an old Ronnie Hawkins tune. "I am your best friend, Daniel Garneau." Karen put on her sunglasses again. The clouds in the sky floated past like giant cotton balls. "I've missed you."

"I've missed you too."

She raised her face to the sun. "I do declare, I am looking forward to meeting your shuga-pah boy."

"Karen, you cannot tell David I showed you that picture."

"But, darling," she drawled, peering over her sunglasses. "It's sweet."

"Karen."

"No pun intended, honey."

"Don't. I'm serious. Promise."

"Okay."

"I mean it."

"Alright. Chill. I promise."

⌒ That evening, after three rounds of boilermakers, David remembered the sugar pie pic and insisted I show it to Karen, Pat and Blonde Dawn. The five of us huddled in a booth at Sneaky Dee's, sharing photos on all our phones. Karen had pictures of her and Liam smoking salmon they'd caught out on Providence Bay. Pat and Blonde Dawn scrolled through pics of the two of them hefting steak stroganoff poutine at a Rush concert at the Air Canada Centre. The waitress arrived with our fajita orders: sizzling cast-iron skillets loaded with thick slices of chicken, red and green peppers and caramelized onions, with sides of refried beans and rice, warm tortillas, guacamole, sour cream, salsa, mole and fresh-chopped tomatoes with cilantro and onion. After that, the topic of conversation turned to food and one thing led to another. Karen stayed the night at Pat and Blonde Dawn's, since they had the extra guest room. The next morning, the five of us met again on the patio of Aunties and Uncles with its quaint décor and white picket fence, which I must've walked past a hundred times. According to *NOW Magazine*, the tiny restaurant served up one of the best brunches in the city, and we weren't disappointed (they even made their own ketchup in-house). After five years in Toronto, I was still making amazing discoveries within blocks of where I lived. After that, Karen hugged us all goodbye, and hit the road for the long drive back home to Manitoulin.

"She's great," David said, keying back into our loft.

"You think so?"

"Of course she is." He flopped down on the couch and opened a copy of *Pedal Magazine*. "She can drink, she plays a mean game of pool, and she laughs at all my jokes."

"I'm glad you two hit it off. Karen's like family, her and her little sister."

"Who's her sister again?"

"Anne. Anne Fobister. If she gets into OCAD, she'll be moving to Toronto this fall."

"You know Karen's in love with your brother Liam."

"Why do you say that?"

"Isn't it obvious?"

"Is it?"

"It's just the way she talks about him."

"Well, they're not together anymore."

"That's beside the point. A lot of people who love each other don't stay together. And a lot of people who don't love each other, well, they end up staying together their whole lives. It's fucked up, but that's the way it is."

"That's sad."

"It's pathetic, that's what it is. Now Pat and Blonde Dawn, they make a great couple. Those two were meant for each other."

"Even though they're having sex with other people?"

"Pat's told you that?"

"Yeah, he's told me."

"Well, maybe it's because of that."

"What do you mean?"

David sat up. "Just because two people are in love doesn't mean they're not going to be attracted to other people. It's human nature. Those kind of feelings don't just suddenly stop. We're told that if we're truly in love with someone, we're not going to want to be with other people. But that's bullshit. That's a myth. It's a myth that's ruined a lot of good relationships."

"So what are you saying?"

"What I'm saying is that monogamy is way overrated."

"We're monogamous."

"We've acted monogamous, Daniel. But we've talked about opening up. Negotiating an open relationship takes a strong bond and a lot of trust. I'm in love with you. I'm crazy about you. Just thinking about having sex with you makes me hard. You're the person I want to spend the rest of my life with. At the same time, face it, you and I both also think about screwing other people. Why? Because we're healthy, normal young guys, that's why."

"But do you want to have sex with other guys?"

"Of course I do, and so do you. But we don't because

we're afraid of what it might mean to our partners. But the truth is, a lot of couples you think are monogamous are negotiating non-monogamy all the time. They just don't talk about it."

"We've talked about it."

"Yes we have. We just haven't done anything about it. Don't get me wrong, Daniel. I'm happy with you, more than happy. I'd also be happy eating Italian food the rest of my life. I love my Italian. You know what I mean?"

"Except you're not going to be eating just Italian the rest of your life."

"Exactly, given the option. Opening up should never be black-and-white, but it's all about negotiating options. For instance, Pat and Blonde Dawn have a don't-ask-don't-tell policy. That wouldn't work with me. I'd want to know. Hell, I'd want to be there. This morning, at Aunties and Uncles, Karen asked if we always eat off each other's plates. Have you noticed we do that? It's true."

"I suppose we do." It was true. David and I shared a lot of things. Some things we'd negotiated (like where I'd shelve my textbooks and ginormous DVD collection), and other things we hadn't (like wearing each other's socks and underwear). It just worked out that way. "So, is there someone else," I asked tentatively, "you want to have sex with?"

"You mean specifically someone I've been thinking about? Apart from you, Dean Winchester, and Tyler Durden," David said, laughing, "no. No there's not."

"Who are they?"

"Daniel. Let's just say, out of those three people you're the only one who's actually real, okay?"

I sat on the armrest of the couch. "But you think I want to have sex with Marcus."

David put down his magazine. "Don't you? C'mon, seriously. Don't you ever fantasize about him?"

"What makes you think that?"

"Because you say his name in your sleep."

"Fuck off. No I don't."

"Yeah, you do."

"The hell I do."

"You want me to record you the next time it happens?"

"The next time? Really?"

"Daniel, it's okay. It doesn't bother me. I've told you a hundred times, I'm not the jealous type."

"But what if I am?"

"I didn't say you were."

"No you didn't. I did."

"Are you?"

Three heartbeats passed. "I don't want to be."

"Then that just takes practice. C'mere." David pulled me down next to him and wrapped his arms around me. "I love you so much, Daniel Garneau. I love the sound of your voice. I love how you smell. I love the way you bite your lip when you cut my hair. I love sticking my tongue in your belly-button. I love downing tequila shots with your brother Pat and his girlfriend Blonde Dawn and your best friend Karen. I love the look on your face when you're inside of me. I love the way you eat your Cream-sicles, and I love the way you snore."

"I snore?"

"No one's ever told you that before?"

"What do I say?"

"What?"

"When I say Marcus' name."

"Nothing. You just mumble his name sometimes. He's important to you. He's on your mind."

"I'm sorry."

"Don't be. I trust us."

"He's like a ghost."

"Your relationship with him is a ghost. The guy is real."

"He's complicated."

"Aren't we all?"

"I'm not sure," I said sighing, "I want Marcus Wittenbrink Jr. in our lives, David."

"Okay. I'll leave this up to you. You know how I feel." His ran his fingers through my hair, and kissed the side of my head. "We have a whole Sunday afternoon to ourselves, mister. What do you want to do?"

"Why don't I take you to my gym and I'll teach you how to play squash?"

"Can I blow you in the sauna afterwards?"

"It's not that kind of gym."

"Can we shower with other naked men?"

"Probably."

"Alrighty then. I'm in. Let's do it."

And so we did.

⌒ At some point during the winter, Pat and Blonde Dawn had formed a band called Three Dog Run. Bobby Lam on saxophone (and half a dozen other instruments) and a bass player named Rod Rodriguez filled out the roster. They practised out of Rod's garage up in the Annex.

Rod was a short, balding thirty-something who sported an enormous, ZZ Top beard. The four made an odd-looking ensemble, but they sounded terrific. On more than one occasion, they'd used the Free Times' Monday Nite Open Stage to fine-tune their act. By May, David was designing a press kit and creating a Facebook page to promote the band.

"So what are you, like their publicist?" I asked.

"No," David said, bent over his laptop, "not even. I'm just helping out." He printed out an image and thrust it at me. "Here." It was a black and white, stylized silhouette of three puppies inside a spiral circle. "What do you think?"

I sat up on the couch, and sipped my Sunday morning coffee. "I like it." I examined it at arm's length. "I really like it. You designed this?"

"Of course, I designed it. I'm more than a pretty face, mister."

"I'm impressed."

David leaned over my shoulder. "It's playful. It's cute but not too cute. I just added the studded collars to give it an edgier look." He jumped the couch, pushed aside my textbooks and sat down next to me. "See here, the swirl, it kinda hints at a Seventies groove. Their band, it's all about fun and feeling good, right?"

"Pat's going to love this."

"It's going to have to go through Blonde Dawn first."

"Really? I didn't know that."

"I'd originally designed this three-headed dog logo, but Marcus said it looked too much like Cerberus, this monster that guards the Greek underworld. Way too heavy metal. Blonde Dawn agreed."

"Marcus?"

"He's been helping get the demo tape out. He knows people. Pat needs all the help he can get."

"Since when has Marcus been involved in this?"

"Daniel, you've been really busy with school. Look, it's not a big deal. We met at Lunacy Cabaret, remember? We're all friends on Facebook."

"Fuck this Facebook crap!" I stood up. "Why didn't you tell me Marcus was friends with Pat? Pat's my brother. Marcus knows that, he knew that from the start. I swear, I bet he lent Pat that hat on purpose."

"What the hell are you talking about?"

"I told you I thought Marcus was stalking me, and you told me he wasn't."

"He's not, Daniel. Get a fucking grip."

"So like have you been hanging out with him, and Pat and everyone?"

"Daniel, the last time I saw him was the last time we both saw him."

"And what about Pat?"

"What about Pat? Pat can be friends with whoever he wants."

"Obviously."

"What's that supposed to mean?"

"Nothing. Is there anything else I should know?"

"Well, since you asked: Three Dog Run cut its demo tape at Marcus' loft a few weeks back."

"What?"

"They needed a space to record."

"Holy shit."

"It's not a big deal."

"When was anyone going to tell me this?"

"Daniel, relax."

"You know, when you tell me to relax, it doesn't help. It actually has the opposite effect. That's just an FYI. I don't need another person in my life telling me to relax."

"If you have that many people telling you, maybe you should start listening."

"Fuck you."

"Fuck yourself."

I threw the print-out back at David and retreated to the bedroom where I flung open the closet. David followed me. "What are you doing?"

"What does it look like I'm doing? I'm changing. I'm going out to study. Some people are in school." I pulled off my sweatpants and threw them in the hamper. "Some people need to study."

"Stop," David said. "Stop."

I sat down on the bed, breathing hard, my T-shirt still wrapped around my arms. My bangs were in my face. I could feel the heat in my cheeks.

David stood uncertainly in the doorway. "What," he finally said, "just happened there?" I tossed my shirt on the floor. After a moment, David knelt on the bed behind me and wrapped his arms around my chest. "Daniel, what just happened there?"

I shook my head.

"I think I know what happened." He pressed his mouth against the back of my neck. "I think," he said, "my Daniel got jealous."

I didn't say anything.

"It's okay. You've been busy. You're in med school for chrissake. It doesn't get more busy than that."

"Jealous?"

"Mm-hm." He squeezed me and massaged my shoulders. "But it's all good. Cause there's absolutely nothing to be jealous about, okay?"

"This is just the beginning, you know."

"What's that?"

"Marcus. You don't know him. He has to be the centre of attention. The guy's got the hugest ego."

"Dude, so does your brother. Look, Marcus is just helping out. Blonde Dawn will keep them both in place. She doesn't put up with any bullshit."

"No, she doesn't."

"You have a hard time trusting people, don't you?"

"I'm working on it."

"Can I tell you a secret?"

"What's that?"

"I'm in love." David straddled me from behind. "And Blonde Dawn's in love. And Karen's in love. We're all in love. We're all head over heels in love with the Garneau boys. And you three boys love each other."

I tried to get up, but he wouldn't let me go. I rolled my eyes. "This," I muttered, "is such a chick-flick moment."

"Fuck that."

"I'm fucking right."

David pushed me over and yanked down my underwear. "How about I fuck this?"

"Fuck off!" I laughed, despite myself.

"Oh I'll fuck, alright." David was suddenly wrestling me on the bed. "Anytime, mister, anywhere. Bring it!"

"Is that a dare?"

"That's a double-dog-do-it-up-the-derriere-dare!"

"Anytime, anywhere?" I eventually let him pin me on my back. "The rooftop!" I gasped.

"What?"

"Let's do it on the rooftop."

"Right now? In broad daylight?"

"Right now."

"Who's fucking who?"

"We'll flip a coin, on the rooftop."

That morning, when we flipped the coin, the golden loonie caught the sunlight and fell glittering over the edge, like pirate treasure lost to the endless, swelling sea. After that, we had no choice but to take turns fucking each other on the rooftop while the pigeons watched. We wore sunglasses and baseball caps pulled down low over our faces. We used half a dozen condoms, and half a bottle of lube. Afterwards, we shared a cigarette and a bottle of soda, and strolled around in the buff in our sneakers admiring the view. We waved at people in the streets below, and they waved back at us. I thought of Grandpa and Liam hanging out naked in Sudbury together. For the first time, it didn't seem like such a perverse thing to do. It was kind of liberating in fact. A passenger jet passed overhead, and we waved at it. The next time I saw Liam, I figured I owed him an apology. This summer, I'd convince him to come down to Toronto. He needed a change of scenery. Spring was in the air, the cherry

trees in High Park were in full blossom, kids were riding
their bikes, the dog parks were crowded, and I was having
some of the best sex I'd ever had in my life. I felt like I was
in love. It wasn't easy, not by a long shot. But it was
beautiful. For the first time in the longest time, I felt like
I had the golden apple in my grasp.

⌒ For Pride Weekend that June, David and I threw a
rooftop party. When Karen and I had lived in Little Italy,
our apartment was too small for parties, but our loft in
Kensington was the perfect size. Technically, we weren't
even allowed on the rooftop, but Rick our building manager was a metalhead who also managed Graffiti's Bar &
Grill down on Baldwin Street, and as long as we kept the
noise to a decent level, no one complained. Rick had a
permanently dishevelled and pissed-off look about him
(like he'd just spat out a swig of bad milk), but David
assured me he was a decent guy.

We had about thirty people over, including a few of
our neighbours, and I got to meet a number of David's
work friends from his bike shop. Rod lent us a neon pink
inflatable kiddies' swimming pool which we set up on
two-by-fours. We brought up my giant palm, and blew up
two dozen beach balls which we'd bought in a dollar-
store in Chinatown. It was a hot and muggy day, and guests
spent the afternoon dipping in and out of the pool and
lounging in lawn chairs. We'd asked people to bring their
favourite classic cassette tapes which we played on an
old boombox. Eventually, Pat and Blonde Dawn arrived
and set up a keg in our kitchen. We spent half an hour

trying to figure out how to tap the thing before David called in Rick who showed us how to do it in less than a minute. After that, we all shared a cheer. When we invited him to join us, he informed us in a monotone that his new Japanese love doll had arrived in the mail and he was taking it for a test run, but that he might drop by that evening. I spotted Rick later fixing a broken fence in the back laneway and came to the conclusion he'd been joking.

By sundown, only about a dozen people were left and we'd moved the party indoors. Everyone pooled their loose change, and someone ran down the block and brought back Indian take-out. Samosas, Tandoori chicken and naan for everyone. Rick dropped by and had a drink and shared a joint. He and Pat got to talking, and Rick said he'd look into Three Dog Run playing at Graffiti's. When I asked Rick about the hot water tank, he regarded me sourly and said he'd also look into it. After that, he left for work, and by midnight everyone was gone. "It's Pride Weekend," David said, emptying ashtrays and picking up plastic cups and greasy napkins. "People have other parties to go to." It was also sweltering in the loft, even with all the windows opened and three fans going. Pat and Blonde Dawn had returned the keg. Half the food was uneaten and we piled the leftovers in the fridge. One of Pat's friends had puked all over our bed, and no matter how much I Febrezed it, the smell of vomit, beer and curry wouldn't come out. I hauled two garbage bags to the dumpster out back; rats scurried away from me in the dark. When I returned, I found David hunched over his laptop with a weird look on his face. "What is it?" I asked.

"Oh boy."

"What?" I wiped the sweat from my brow with the bottom of my tank top.

He lowered his screen. "Ok. I need to show you something. But Daniel."

"What?"

"Just stay calm."

"What is it?"

"You have to promise not to freak out."

"That doesn't help."

"Just promise. Look, it's all good. It's really not a big deal. It's actually kinda funny."

"David."

"Promise."

"Okay. Fine. I promise." I folded my arms and breathed through my nose the way Liam had taught me once. I was a yogi master, a prince of Shambhala, an enlightened sadhu above the petty concerns of humankind.

David didn't look convinced, but he knew he wasn't going to get any further with me. "So, earlier tonight," he said, "Rick takes me aside and tells me about this home-made video. He said his bartender had shown it to him. It'd been going around on the Internet."

"Okay."

"Well, he thought we ought to know about it."

"Okay."

"Check it out." David opened his laptop, pressed a few keys and turned it towards me. "The guy had recognized Rick's building."

For the longest time, I simply stared at the screen. Eventually, I said: "Are we in trouble?"

"Well, he told us not to do it again."

It was footage of David and me, grainy and shot from another rooftop. Every few minutes, the handheld camera would pull out and pan across the cityscape before coming back to us. Someone had scored the video with a Michael Bublé cover. The morning sun in the sky cast lens flares over our heads. I'd never seen myself from this angle before, and realized I didn't actually look half so bad. The camera tracked us as we strolled around in the sunshine waving to people in the streets below, at birds flying high, and the CN Tower beyond. Towards the end, the camera zoomed in slowly on the two of us kissing. I remembered that kiss. It had been a great kiss. The video had more than a few hits. It had gone viral.

"You can't make out our faces at all," David said.

"I can see that."

"Look, anybody can climb up the fire escape and get to that roof."

I simply sighed.

"You okay?"

"Do I have a choice?"

"It's actually kinda hot, don't you think?"

The truth was, it was more than hot. Now I understood why some people recorded themselves. I could tell David was trying his best not to laugh. I didn't know what to say. All I could think was that, with this one single video, I'd attracted a larger audience than Marcus Wittenbrink Jr. ever had in his entire career.

And the feeling was triumphant.

CHAPTER FIFTEEN

Rockin' in the Free World

That July, Three Dog Run threw a fundraiser to finance their first EP. They performed on a makeshift stage outside the Ward's Island Association Club House by the Island Café where the staff served up ginger mojitos, microbrews and home-cooked meals. Local, long-haired children played soccer nearby beneath the trees. David and I spent that afternoon serving up hotdogs for a toonie. A roster of artists had come together for the day-long event. Toronto was in the middle of a heat wave, and it had been a stifling, overcast day. But as twilight settled, patio lights were lit and the crowd grew more festive. Ward's Island was a ten minute ferry ride from the city's harbourfront, and both David and I had put out an open call on Facebook, inviting everyone we knew. Across Lake Ontario, the CN Tower and Toronto skyscrapers glittered, reflected in the dark waters. Karen and Liam were due to arrive on the next boat and I waited for them at the ferry dock, within sight of the Island Café.

My old neighbours Mike and Melissa had driven down from North York and spent the day on the Islands.

Mike looked a little bit sunburnt and windblown, but otherwise great. Fatherhood seemed to suit him. He walked apart from the crowds with Benjamin in his arms, rubbing his back. "Benny's got a tummy ache," Melissa explained, sporting a sunhat the size of a small umbrella. "Too much ice cream. He'll be less fussy once we get him to bed." She leaned on my shoulder and pulled off her flats. "Oh my god, my feet are killing me. I should've worn my cross trainers, what was I thinking?" She rummaged in a side-pouch of Benjamin's stroller and pulled out a Band-Aid. "Michael," she shouted, "how's he doing?" Mike, who was pointing out ducks at the water's edge, raised his arm and gave a thumbs-up signal. "We've got Benny in daycare for now," Melissa said, bandaging one toe, "but it's costing a fortune. Michael's going to quit his job and stay home full-time. He knows his way around the kitchen and laundry room better than I ever did. Me, I've got a dozen restaurants and drycleaners on speed dial in my phone. I'm pregnant again, did I mention that? God, I miss my wine spritzers. But I love being pregnant, you have no idea. Just look what it does to my boobs. I've got more college boys checking me out now than when I was in college. Oh, and the girls, they just adore Michael when he's out with Benny. What a DILF. Honestly, nothing is sexier than a man with a baby. You know, when we first got pregnant, he was such a mess. But it was his idea to plan for this second. I always knew he had it in him. Daniel, you'd make a great dad. Would you and David ever want kids?"

"Kids?" The question took me completely off guard. "No," I stammered, "no, I'm still in school. To be honest, it's not something we've ever discussed. I didn't know the two of you were expecting again. Congratulations." The ferry pulled up to the dock and the passengers disembarked. I spotted Karen and Liam and hurried forward to greet them. While Mike and Melissa introduced Benjamin to Karen, I gave Liam a high five and a hug. "Hey, look at you. Welcome back to Toronto. When did you two get into town?"

"A few hours ago," Liam said, scanning the grounds. He wore a plain white T-shirt and baggy, cut-off jeans. He'd also gotten a haircut, trimmed his beard and cleaned beneath his nails. He actually looked like someone who might've grown up in civilization.

Jackson leaned against his leg and whined. I knelt and rubbed him behind the ears. "Hey there, big guy." He licked my face. "Is he going to be okay," I asked, "with all this noise and people around?"

"He'll be fine," Karen said. "And Jackson will be too." She winked at Liam who managed a smile.

Melissa folded and hefted Benny's stroller. "Suburbia calls. We're off. Say bye-bye, Benny." Benjamin stared at us with his big blue eyes. Mike waved his chubby hand. "Bye-bye." Mike lifted him onto his shoulders as they boarded the ferry. When I called out, "It was great seeing you guys," it was Benjamin who gave a thumbs-up sign.

After that, I walked Karen and Liam up the path to the Island Café. Liam kept Jackson on a short leash in the crowd. Other dogs roamed freely underfoot. They'd both brought small packs and sleeping rolls. "Pat and Blonde Dawn offered their place," Karen explained, "but we're going to camp out on the beach. It's going to be a full Buck Moon tonight."

"Here, on the Islands? Is that legal?"

"No. But people do it all the time." Karen poked me in the butt. "I've got a few spots in mind. Don't worry about us."

On the outdoor stage, beneath the strings of patio lights, a five-piece jug band was playing enthusiastically, banging away on a banjo, a washtub bass and other home-made instruments. "So where's Pat?" Liam asked.

"He's around, somewhere. Three Dog Run opened this afternoon. They'll be the closing act tonight. Can I get you a drink? Lemonade, cider?"

"How about a beer?"

I glanced at Karen. "You sure about that?"

"I can have a drink, Daniel," Liam said.

"Okay. Okay, no problem. You two go find Pat. I'll get us three beers."

Stars began to appear from behind the pink-purple clouds. Someone lit tiki torches at the crossroads to the paved pathways. At the bar, I bumped into Parker wearing a Hawaiian shirt and his Ray-Bans. "Parker," I said, "isn't it a little dark for sunglasses?"

"I'm trying," Parker whispered, "to look casual." He leaned stiffly against the white railing, sipping on a Shirley Temple. "Do I look casual?"

"No, Parker, you look ridiculous." I took off his sunglasses and tucked them into his shirt pocket. "What are you doing?"

Parker's eyes swivelled in his head. "Behind me, five o'clock, is he still there?"

"Is who still there?"

"C.B. in a Tilley hat."

C.B. was our code for "Cute Boy." I glanced past Parker and spotted a strawberry-blonde boy with a freckle-faced girl in a denim dress. "I see him. He's looking our way." I waved and smiled.

"Daniel Garneau," Parker exclaimed without moving his lips, "what are you doing?"

"I'm being friendly. So should you. Oh, here comes his friend." The girl stepped up to the bar between us and retrieved a napkin. She spat out her gum and tucked it into a pocket of her skirt. "Hi," she said shyly to Parker.

"Hello."

"My cousin Kyle and I were just noticing your shirt. We think it's really nice."

"Thank you."

I leaned in. "My friend Parker here thinks your cousin is really nice too. Parker, why don't you go say hi to cousin Kyle." I gathered up my three beers. "Cheers." I walked away without looking back.

I found Karen, Liam, David and Blonde Dawn by a picnic table close to the stage. Pat, who was jamming with the jug band, on a kazoo, waved at us, stomping his feet. Some children and adults were dancing together, while most people were sitting in disorderly rows of plastic lawn chairs. "Hey, David," I said, "this is my brother Liam."

"We've met. Cheers, everyone."

Pat leapt off the stage, dodged through the audience and gave Liam a crushing bear hug, lifting him off the ground. "Hey little brother, welcome to the Islands! Glad you could make it." He grabbed the cup from my hand and drank thirstily. "Thanks for coming out. Wow!" he gasped. "This is amazing. You guys are the best."

"Here's to your EP."

"Here's to the Garneau boys," Karen said. "Hold on, let me get a shot of the three of you."

"Hey yo, Saxophone Man," Pat shouted, "get a picture of the six of us!" Bobby Lam, who happened to be passing by, juggled the handful of phones thrust at him, and the next minute was spent posing for photos and trying our best to keep Jackson in the frame. After that, Pat jumped back onto the stage with my beer. "Here." David handed me his cup. "I'll get us another."

"Thanks."

Charles texted saying he and Megan were about to board the next ferry. When I met them at the dock, Megan showed off the engagement ring on her hand. "He proposed again," she exclaimed breathlessly. "Like, I mean just now on the ferry, Daniel, and I don't know, I don't know what came over me, but this time I just said yes. I said it. I said yes."

I grinned at Charles. "Dude."

Charles stared back at me, his big eyes watering. He raised his hands and let them fall again. "She said yes."

"Wow." I opened my arms and hugged them both. "Guys, congratulations."

"Where's Karen?" Megan said. "Is she here yet? I have to tell her."

A familiar voice spoke behind me. "Hey there, Daniel the Doorman."

I turned to find myself face to face with Marwa. "Guys, look," I said, "Karen's here. She's up by the stage. She'll be thrilled to see you both. I'll catch up with you." Charles and Megan set off towards the Island Café. This evening, Marwa's gleaming curls were the colour of cherry cola, and she wore a strapless, white sundress that showed off her cleavage and perfect tan. "Well," I said, "if it isn't the Meatball Queen."

Marwa twirled and smiled coyly. "The one and only."

"Marwa, what are you doing here?"

"I came to see you."

"Were you on that last ferry? I didn't see you."

"No. We walked in from Centre Island. I came with Marcus. He's getting drinks."

"I see."

"How have you been?"

"Alright."

"So, Daniel, do I get a hug or what?"

"Marwa, of course." When I squeezed her, she felt fuzzy and warm like a peach. I was surprised how much I'd actually missed her. The last time I saw Marwa, Marcus was being carted away in an ambulance, over a year-and-a-half ago. "Wow, you smell amazing."

"Thank you. So do you."

"I smell like B.O., charcoal and wieners."

"Classic yet contemporary."

"I am the Hotdog King, I'll have you know."

"You've been helping your brother out with this fund-raiser?"

"Here and there."

"You're a good man, Daniel Garneau."

"I've been told that before."

Marwa looked past me, and we both watched as Marcus walked slowly but steadily down the path from the Island Café. He wore a sleeveless shirt with a colourful

Yakuza print, and a pale leather satchel at his hip. He was clean-shaven and had cropped his hair military-style.

"Hello, Marcus."

"Daniel." He handed Marwa a drink. "It's good to see you."

"No more cane?"

"No more cane. It has been a long convalescence."

"I'm happy for you."

"Thank you for the invitation."

"Hey, thanks for coming. That's a new look."

Marcus ran a hand over his shaved head. "Yes, I suppose it is. Do you think it is too austere?"

"Austere? No, not with that shirt. You look good."

"Do I?"

"You look great."

"Thank you. As do you."

Impulsively, awkwardly, I stepped in and gave Marcus a hug. "My brother's in from Sudbury."

"This is your second brother, Liam?"

"Liam. That's right."

"The 'wildman-of-the-woods.'"

"Did I call him that?"

"No, but Patrick has. Liam Garneau," Marcus said to Marwa, "is Daniel's brother who lives off the grid."

"He would if he could." I smiled. "I think he tries his best."

"There you are," David called out, approaching. "Hey, Marcus, how's it going?"

"I am well. It's good to see you again, David." He stroked Marwa's cheek. "David, this is my very old and dear friend, Marwa." He adjusted a bang that had fallen over her brow. "Marwa sometimes is my muse." He raised a toast. "Here's to the artistic process. I've brought a gift for the band. Are they about?"

"Somewhere," David said, draping his arm over my shoulder. "They're scheduled to go back up in an hour."

"What's this gift?" I asked.

Marcus raised a finger to his lips. "It is a surprise. But let me show you."

He handed Marwa his drink, opened his satchel and withdrew a black T-shirt. Ceremoniously, he unfolded it and held it up, displaying the three-puppies logo David had designed.

"Holy shit, dude!" David exclaimed. "That looks awesome!" He grabbed the shirt from Marcus' hands. "When did you do this?"

"I had thirty made up this morning. I've brought four for the band. And one for yourself."

"Thirty? Whoa. We have a budget for this?"

"Like I said, these are a gift. When Three Dog Run wins their first Juno, I except a VIP pass to all their concerts."

"Fuckin A!" David laughed. He pulled his own T-shirt off over his head, and put the new one on. "What do you think?"

"Here." Marcus tucked in the tag sticking out of David's collar, and rearranged the shirt on his shoulders. He patted his chest, and stood back appraisingly. "Beautiful."

"Very nice," Marwa said.

David glanced at me. I folded my arms and shrugged. "Looks great."

"Come on, let's go find the band! They can wear these on stage tonight."

Marwa and I watched Marcus and David disappear into the crowd. "Your boyfriend," she said, "he's cute."

"Thanks. So are you."

"That's sweet, Daniel." She looked up at me sidelong, biting her lower lip. "You okay?"

"Of course I am." I drained my cup and tossed it into a nearby garbage can. "Why shouldn't I be?"

"Just asking."

"So how is Marcus?"

"He's working on a new project. He won a big Ontario Arts Council grant for it. It's major. But he won't tell me what it is."

"Oh?"

"Ever since the accident, he's been different. More secretive. He keeps to himself a lot these days."

I wanted to ask if he was seeing anyone, but all I said was: "He seems well."

"He isn't seeing anyone, in case that's what you're wondering."

I caught myself reflected in Marwa's enormous eyes. "Is he happy?" I asked.

"Daniel. Marcus is never happy."

The ferry horn sounded last call before pulling out. "And how are you doing?"

"I," Marwa said, "have been baking cupcakes."

"Cupcakes?"

"Mm-hm. Lots of them." Marwa handed me her card. "I've even hired an assistant."

"Well." The card was hot pink with delicate, swirling script. "*Cherry Bomb Bakery*. Impressive."

"Thank you." Marwa performed a curtsey. "Everyone loves to eat, right? Who doesn't love cupcakes?"

"Who doesn't love cupcakes."

Marwa looked in the direction Marcus had gone. "When he was in the hospital, I'd have him test my samples. Raspberry chocolate truffle was his favourite. I'd also bring him home-cooked meals, and take-out: Swiss Chalet, dark meat with extra dipping sauce."

"I know."

"He likes to tell people he's vegan."

I sighed. "I know."

"His leg was hurting him by the time we got here. I told him he should've brought his cane, but he insisted he didn't need it. I gave him something to help with the pain. Don't tell him I told you."

"You still catering Marcus' parties?"

"I cater a lot of people's parties. Is there anything I can get you?"

"Out here?"

"Try me."

"What are you, like a walking pharmacy?"

"Does your boyfriend like to party?"

"David? I think so."

"Look. Marcus is having a few people over tonight. Why don't you and David join us? It'll be fun."

My heart began to thud in my chest. I tried to sound casual. "I dunno."

"Why not? I'll take care of you both. I promise."

"I know you will. That's what I'm afraid of."

"Daniel."

"Marwa, I like you. You've been really nice to me. It's just that I don't entirely trust myself. When I've been on favours, I've done things I've regretted."

"So we won't get you high. Just come on over and have a few drinks with us. Are we that scary?" She bared her teeth and clawed at my chest.

"No," I said, laughing, "you're not that scary."

"That's too bad. I've always wanted to be scary. I always kind of thought of myself as a Wild Thing."

"Wild Thing?"

"You know, from that children's book."

"I can picture that. You, Marcus, Fang. Wild Things, definitely."

"Oh, Marcus, he's not a Wild Thing, despite what people think. The truth is," she whispered, "he's just a boy."

"From Burlington."

"That's right."

"I see."

"He really misses you, you know."

"Does he?"

"Daniel, I've known Marcus his whole life. You had a big influence on him."

"I know. I'm the first person who's ever asked him out. Woohoo. I suppose I'm also the only one who's ever broken up with him too. Is that right?"

"That's right."

"Bummer. Welcome to the real world."

"Daniel, why did you ask him out?"

"My best friend, she put me up to it."

"Your best friend?"

"Karen. She's here tonight. I'll introduce you."

Marwa hooked her arm through mine, and we strolled along the waterfront. "Should I be jealous?"

"Karen and I grew up across the street from each other. We've known each other since we were kids."

"I'm jealous."

"You and Marcus grew up together."

"That's true. I remember Marcus, he was this skinny, nervous, excitable boy. He was sick all the time. He'd get these nose bleeds that would land him in the hospital for days. It was awful. He used to get teased and beat up a lot."

"I didn't know that."

"I was his only friend. He used to stage private performances just for me. I've lost track of the number of Marcus Wittenbrink Jr. world premieres I've attended."

"Sounds like fun."

"It was. For the both of us. His parents didn't approve of me. They were these big shot lawyers, see. Back then, I was this sketchy goth chick. They took one look at me and figured I was bad news."

"And were you?"

Marwa giggled. "Of course I was."

"I've met his parents."

"Oh, I'm sorry. Look, Marcus hates talking about his past. Don't tell him I told you all this."

"He's lucky to have you."

"Well, we're a lot of things to each other." Marwa picked up a piece of driftwood and, with surprising force, hurled it overhand across the lake. "Except, I wouldn't call him my best friend."

"No?"

"No." Her eyes sparkled. "I wouldn't."

"What would you call him then?"

"Oh, that's easy." Marwa smiled up at me wistfully. "Marcus, he's leader of the wild rumpus. He's Max, King of All Wild Things."

∿ Just before Three Dog Run was to take the stage, I found myself waiting outside the single-occupancy washroom at the back of the WIA Club House. When the door finally opened, to my surprise I encountered Parker emerging hand in hand with Kyle. "Oh," Parker blurted, "Daniel." I could've sworn I saw him blush. "Daniel, this is Kyle. Kyle, this is my friend Daniel."

"Hey Kyle, nice hat."

Kyle, who looked like a shaggy Christopher Robin with facial hair, smiled shyly. "Thanks."

"Parker," I said, "what's a DILF?"

"A DILF? That's a Dad I'd Like to Fuck. Why do you ask?"

"Oh, okay, thanks. That makes sense." I clapped them both on the shoulders. "You guys having a good time?" Both nodded. "Parker," I said, pointing, "you're flying low. Excuse me." I squeezed past them and closed the door behind me. I stood over the toilet pissing for what seemed like a whole minute. After that, I soaked a handful of paper towels in cold water and wiped down my neck and armpits. I wished I'd brought my deodorant. When I finally stepped out, Marcus was waiting. "Oh, hey."

"Care for a bump?"

"What?"

He held up a tiny Ziploc bag of white powder. Fang had always been the cokehead when the three of us were together. I glanced around nervously. Marcus squeezed past me. His hand rested on the doorknob. "You coming?"

I followed Marcus back in and he bolted the door. The washroom was cramped enough for one. I did my best not to press myself up against him. Marcus spent some time crushing the contents of the bag with his lighter against the edge of the sink. "I don't mean to sound un-grateful," I finally said, "but can we hurry this up?"

Marcus regarded me mildly. "Now that just sounds ungrateful."

"Marcus."

"David did a good job with the logo."

I nodded. "You pay for those shirts yourself?"

"I did."

"Why?"

"Because I used to be like them. Because I've been fortunate to have had people believe in me and support me along the way. Now that I've achieved some modicum of success, it's good to be able to give something back. Here." He'd dipped the end of a key into the bag and held it out for me.

I opened and closed my mouth. Finally, I leaned over and snorted the bump. After that, Marcus helped himself. "Is that the only reason?" I asked.

"What do you mean?"

"Why Pat and his band? Why them? Thirty T-shirts? C'mon. You barely even know them."

"What do you want me to say, Daniel? Because Patrick reminds me of you?"

"Pat's not like me at all."

"That's right. Patrick's his own person, as are Dawn and Rodrigo and Robert." Marcus helped himself to a second bump, sniffed, and held out the key.

"No," I said. "No thanks."

"If it bothers you that much, give the word and I'll walk away. I'll take back the T-shirts. I won't talk to them again. Ever. Will that make you happy? Is that what you want? Because I'll do it."

"What? No."

"Then what is it, Daniel? Tell me, what is it?"

"I'm with David now."

"I know that."

"Are you sure you know that?"

"Daniel, don't be arrogant. It's not becoming."

"Do you really, honestly think I'm being arrogant right now?"

"No, I suppose not," Marcus said, his gaze downcast. "My apologies."

"But you think I'm being an asshole."

"I didn't say that."

"But you're thinking it."

"You can choose to believe that if you wish."

I reached for the door. "We're done here."

"Did you ever care for me?"

"What?"

"Did you ever," Marcus said, "care for me at all?"

"What the hell sort of question is that?"

"It's just that you seemed to be able to walk away from us so easily."

"You and Fang seemed to be getting along just fine."

"I didn't mean Fang and me. I meant you and me, the

two of us. When those elevator doors closed, you just seemed so cold and far away. You just didn't seem to care at all."

"What? What? Are you kidding? Are you, are you like kidding me?" I backed up, banging my head painfully against the towel dispenser. "Marcus, you were the one who kept pushing and pushing. You knew I wasn't into the three-some thing, but you kept pushing."

"Fang is a good person."

"This isn't about Fang!" I shouted. "This is about you and me, and what we meant to each other. We were sup-posed to be partners, we were supposed to be boyfriends. What happened on New Year's Eve was a mistake, a stu-pid mistake. But that's all it was. I didn't plan for it to happen. You were the one who took it and ran with it! I know you think I'm this, I'm this imbecile living in the Stone Age, but I happen to like the idea of being boy-friends. I am so sorry I'm not as enlightened as you are, but some people just aren't cut out for your New Age bullshit excuse for fucking around with whoever you hap-pen to get a hard-on for. That's what I walked away from. For the record, I loved us. I loved us, Marcus. But the two of us just wasn't good enough for you, or maybe it was too scary for you. Real relationships, the real ones that mean something, they're scary, they're fucking scary as hell. You were the one who shut down. You were the one who walked away from us." I scrabbled at the bolt. When the door swung open, I half fell out of the wash-room. On the far side of the Club House, Three Dog Run launched into their opening number, an energetic cover of a Sam Roberts tune.

I strode away without looking back, trying not to break into a run. Then I did break into a run. Rounding the building, I searched the crowd for David. Eventually, I spotted Karen towards the back, sitting comfortably up in the nook of a tree. "Where's David?" I asked.

"I thought he was with you. You okay?"

"Yeah. I just need to find David. Where's Liam?"

"He went for a walk. Jackson was getting a little spooked. Daniel, what's wrong?"

"Nothing's wrong." I clutched my head. "I'll tell you later."

"Daniel, you're crying." She jumped down from the tree. "What's wrong?"

I started to back away. "I gotta go."

"Go where?"

"I'm going to find David, alright?"

"Oh my god, you're bleeding."

There was blood on my hand. I touched the back of my head and my fingers came away wet. "Shit." On stage, Pat flailed at his guitar, craning his neck over the mic. The audience was on its feet. Karen took me by the hand and led me away to the nearby soccer field. I kept insisting, "Karen, it's nothing. It's just a scratch. I'm fine. Seriously."

She sat me down in the middle of the field, soaked a napkin with a water bottle and dabbed at my scalp. "What happened?"

"I got into a fight with Marcus."

"You didn't hurt him, did you?"

"What? No! Not, like, no we weren't fighting. We were just arguing and I must've hit my head. Look, I didn't even notice until you pointed it out." I pulled out my phone, called David, got his voice mail and hung up. Then I tried again and left a message: "David, it's me. Call me back."

"Well," Karen said, "it doesn't look too bad. What were you fighting about?"

"Us. Why we broke up."

"Daniel, you and Marcus broke up over two years ago."

"I know."

"For real?"

"I know. It's fucked up. You'd think we'd be over each other by now. And the craziest thing is that David seems to like the guy. I mean, what's not to like, right?"

"Marcus can be charismatic. Here, hold this." Karen had me press a fresh napkin against the back of my head. "Would you ever talk to David about this?"

"Oh, David talks about Marcus all the time."

Karen frowned. "Really?"

"I know. I mean, what kind of boyfriend keeps talking about your ex-boyfriend? Like, I mean, who does that, for chrissake? Sometimes, I think David wants to sleep with the guy."

"Does he?"

"I don't know. He's convinced I do."

"Is David the jealous type?"

"No. In fact, he's the opposite. That's what makes everything so weird."

"So do you?"

"Do I what?"

"Do you still want to sleep with Marcus?"

I stared at Karen. Now my head was starting to ring. Blinking jets passed high overhead, and farther beyond, satellites spun around the planet Earth. Hello. Goodbye. "Of course I do," I exclaimed. "If I didn't, there'd be no problem. That's the problem." The stars spiralled, dizzying. I inhaled into my lungs the moist fragrance of summer grasses, wildflowers and blooming trees. The sensations of the world filled me up to bursting. I wasn't sure if I wanted to laugh or cry.

My phone rang. "David, where are you?"

I could barely make him out over the music in the background. "The sound engineer, he's sick," he said. "He's hurling down by the dock. I'm on the mixer."

"What, right now?"

"Yeah, I'm mixing for Three Dog Run right now. I've never mixed before in my life. Where are you?"

"I'm over in the soccer field."

"What are you doing over there?"

"I'm talking with Karen."

"The band's on stage. They're playing already."

"Yeah, I know. I can hear them."

"How's my mixing?"

"It's fine."

"Daniel, is everything okay?"

"Yeah, everything's fine. I love you."

"I love you too. Hey, you sure everything's okay?"

"Yeah. I'm sure. I'll meet you after this song, alright? You're doing great."

"Alright. Hurry up."

I hung up. "He's on the mixer."

Karen took both my hands in hers. "Look, I should go find Liam. He wasn't looking so good earlier. Are you going to be okay?"

"Yeah. I should go too. I think David needs me."

"Daniel, I'm sorry."

"For what?"

"For getting you involved with Marcus. If I hadn't pushed you to ask him out ..."

"Oh, Karen, no. No, that was, that was cool. You were great. If it weren't for you, I would never have asked him. But, I mean, I want to thank you for that. Thank you. You're good for me. You're my best friend. Don't be sorry. I regret a lot of things in my life. But I don't regret asking Marcus out."

"You sure about that?"

I nodded. "I love you, Karen Fobister."

"I love you too." She stood up and helped me to my feet. "How's your head?"

"It's okay." I checked the napkin, but I'd stopped bleeding. "I'm okay."

"You sure?"

"Yeah. Really, I am. Thank you."

"Alright." Karen backed away. "Okay. Catch you on the flip side."

I waved and watched as Karen headed off. "Catch you on the flip side."

⌒ Close to midnight, David and I caught the last ferry back to the city. The fundraiser had been a success, and there was a lot to celebrate. Charles and Megan had taken the earlier boat. Pat, Blonde Dawn and the rest of the band were staying overnight with friends on the Island. Apparently, so was Parker. Good for him. Karen texted to let me know she'd found Liam and Jackson, and that all was well. David and I sat side by side on the main deck, sunburnt and exhausted, our hands buried in our pockets, our tired feet stretched out. David wore his big headphones, the hood of his sweatshirt pulled down low over his face. Two people strolled up. It was Marwa and Marcus.

"Mind if we join you?" Marwa asked.

"Hey," David murmured, lifting one earpiece. "We were wondering if you guys were on this boat."

They settled on the opposite bench facing us. A wind had sprung up, and the ferry rocked as it ploughed steadily across the channel to the mainland. Marwa slipped off her jewelled sandals. Clutching them to her breast, she lay down with a contented sigh, resting her head in Marcus' lap. Absently, he stroked her hair, gazing out the window. David put his headphones back on.

Eventually, Marcus and I regarded each other. His hazel eyes were flecked with gold. I knew I'd been angry with him earlier that evening, but that feeling was vague now and far away. He and David looked nothing alike, yet I saw something strangely similar in the way they held themselves, and in the way they'd both gaze upon me. Marcus' shaved head accentuated the precise proportions of his skull and jaw, the curve of his neck. He had one bare arm flung out over the back of the bench. I remembered more than once, long ago, resting in Marcus' lap just as Marwa did now. I noticed his knuckles were freshly bruised and crusted with blood, but I didn't think to ask what had happened. Calmly, we observed each other, breathing in unison, until the ferry arrived at the Harbourfront dock and both Marwa and David roused themselves and we all stood and gathered our belongings and waited for the corrugated metal gangplank to lower, before stepping off the boat back onto solid land, poised at the concrete edge of the luminous city at night. Then when the four of us hugged goodnight, I made a point of kissing Marcus on the lips. And this time, it wasn't a kiss between friends or ex-lovers. After that, I took my David's hand in my own and walked away.

CHAPTER SIXTEEN

We're All In This Together

That August, we planned a Garneau family road trip up to the Good Medicine Cabin to scatter Grandma's ashes. Over a hundred people had come out to her funeral: staff and residents of the nursing home, neighbours, and friends. Even some of Grandma's former students turned up, a few with grandchildren of their own. Grandma hadn't taught high school in over fifty years. One of them was Grandpa's classmate who introduced himself as Frank. He sported a diamond-studded tie pin, and a carnation in his lapel. During the reception at the nursing home, Frank caught up to me by the potato salad table (I counted six different selections). He produced a whiskey flask and poured a generous portion into his coffee. "Care for something stronger?" he asked. Taking my blank stare for an affirmation, he topped off my own cup. "This," he said winking, "was a gift from your grandpa. See here." I peered more closely at an inscription on the flask: TO F. MY BEST MAN, T. "That's right. I told my folks I was going camping, and drove myself all the way down to Toronto just to see them hitched."

"Wow." I sipped from my coffee. I had to admit, the addition was an improvement. "You two were close?"

Frank chuckled. "Oh, your grandpa Tom and me, we were a tight pair. He was a bull back in the day, star kicker in our senior year. I was quarterback. And your grandma Josie, well, I gotta tell ya, she had this classy chassis that would put Liz Taylor to shame. No disrespect, mind you. Every straight-shootin' boy in school had his eye on her. But Tom, he was on the hook." Frank tapped the side of his head. "It's craziness, you gotta understand, a kind of insanity. Being in love."

"Especially with your English teacher."

"Oh." Frank blinked in surprise. "He told you that, then, did he? Not everyone knows that, not anymore these days." He lowered his voice and elbowed me in the side. "Well, you have it right. Long and short of it, your grandpa was real gone. He didn't care what anybody said. After graduating, he took off after her. I'm proud to say, I was the one who lent him the money to buy his bus ticket. Counting the justice of the peace, it was just the four of us at their wedding. That night, I slept on the couch. I'll tell ya, the walls were paper thin in her apartment, I could hear everything. They apologized for it the next morning." Frank laughed. "I whipped up breakfast and served them in bed. Oh, we had a blast. Yes we did. Tom and Josie and me, we were odd balls, I'm not ashamed to say that."

"Odd balls?"

"Well," Frank said, leaning in, "let's just say, the three of us, we didn't care much what the world had to think." He plucked a devilled egg from a silver tray and popped it into his mouth. "I helped your grandma Josie raise your

father while Tom was off fighting the Nazis. Then after
the War, I helped build them that cottage of theirs up
north. It took us two years, but we got it done. Back then
you built things to last. Oh, the summers we'd spend up
there. Your grandma, she christened it the Good Medicine Cabin. You could drink the lake water then, sweet
as rain. There was fishing, partridge, jackrabbits. Now,
Josie, she could shoot a gun better than any man I knew.
I remember plugging your father's ears with cotton whenever we took him out hunting with us."

"He's never talked about this."

"Oh, he would've just been an ankle-biter, not more
than three or four. I'd doubt he'd remember much. I
moved away after that, to New York City."

"No, I meant Grandpa."

Frank squinted across the dining hall at Grandpa who
was chatting with a small group of women, most of them
in wheelchairs: Grandma's poetry club at the nursing
home. The late-afternoon sun slanting in through the
floor-length windows edged them in a brittle, pale light.
"No," he reflected. "No, I don't imagine he would. Tom
and me, we were always straight with each other, and it
was time I moved on. No regrets. Now me, I've gone
through three wives. One of them I loved, two of them
I was extremely fond of. I have no regrets. Your grandpa,
he loves you boys very much. You're all he has left in the
world now."

"Yes, sir."

"I am sorry what happened to your parents. I'm sorry
I wasn't at their funeral."

"That was a long time ago."

"Yes, well. I should've come. New York wasn't ever that far away. I suppose that is one thing I regret. I could've seen her then. Now it's too late."

Grandpa glanced across the room, and caught our eye. Cloud-shadows passed across his face. He smiled, raised his glass and nodded once.

Carefully, Frank wrapped two cucumber sandwiches in a napkin and tucked them into his pocket. After that, he took out a cigar and unwrapped it. "Don't mind what the world thinks. In the end," he said, gesturing widely to take in the whole reception, "it'll come to this. It always does." He cut the cigar head. "And then, what'll be important?" He patted my shoulder and strolled away. I watched him and Grandpa exchange a few words. The two men excused themselves and exited through the side door leading into the frozen gardens out back.

The reception was starting to wind down. Most of the guests were gone. Earlier, I'd gotten a number of photographs enlarged and put them on display. I went up to one which I'd set on a side table by a vase of lilies. In the sepia-toned image, Grandma sat on a wooden swing beneath a leafy branch, in a paisley dress, her slim legs folded, and an open book in her lap. Someone had stuck wildflowers between her naked, painted toes. It was a candid shot and her expression was one of bemused annoyance. She might've been in her mid-thirties. Not far in the background, you could see Grandpa turned away from the camera, shirtless, fishing lakeside with a cigarette dangling from his mouth, looking for all the world like a young Jack Kerouac. For the first time, I wondered who it was who'd actually taken this picture.

Outside, Frank and Grandpa shared the cigar, their shoulders bowed against the cold like muskox, their breath forming great white clouds about their heads. Beyond them, past the arbour and skeletal apple trees, the unbroken snow glowed amber in the deepening light. I knew I should bring Grandpa his overcoat, but I didn't move. Pat and Liam arrived to stand next to me (Liam looking practically unrecognizable in his jacket and tie). "What's up?" Pat said around a mouthful of food, his plate piled with mini sausages. They followed my gaze out the far window.

"Who's that with Pépère?" Liam asked.

"That's Frank."

Karen and her little sister joined us. Karen rested her hand on my shoulder. "Who's Frank?" Anne asked.

"An old friend." Kitchen staff had begun clearing the scattered cups and saucers. The Miltons and a few others were already helping to wrap tin foil over the potato salads and fancy sandwich trays. "Come on," I said, "we should start packing things up."

"What are we going to do with all these flowers?" Anne asked.

"We can donate them to the home," I replied. I'd already made arrangements with the chaplain and Betty the nursing manager. The staff worked with efficient, easy familiarity. They dealt with receptions like this all the time. I was going to miss this place. We'd been coming to visit Grandma here over ten years. Maybe we could still volunteer our time during the holiday seasons, or at least bring over some of Grandpa's tourtières and sugar pies. They were always a big hit. Then suddenly I found myself wondering where Grandpa himself might be in five, ten or fifteen years. In the photo in front of me, the smooth-limbed youth fishing in the background was barely recognizable. I wondered what I would think if I met this young Tom in the present day, star kicker in high school and crazy in love.

"She's beautiful," Anne said.

"What?"

She pointed at the photograph. "Your grandmother, she was beautiful."

I stared into the photograph. I discovered if I softened my focus, I could actually begin to see Grandma through Grandpa's eyes. "Yes," I said. "Yes, she was." I wondered how it was possible I'd never seen it before. Almost, if I just relaxed enough, I felt I could reach out and step into that picture. In that moment, I felt closer to Grandpa than I'd ever felt before. But it was time to go.

I went to fetch his overcoat.

⌒ The plan for Labour Day Weekend was for Blonde Dawn, Pat, David and me to drive straight up to the Good Medicine Cabin from Toronto, where Karen and Liam and Grandpa would meet us. We'd bring our camping gear and spend three days. Seven adults in all, plus Jackson. Plus Grandma's ashes in a box. For the last eight months, Liam told me, Grandpa had kept Grandma's remains on the pantry shelf, between the sugar and the Metamucil. Before she got sick, the kitchen was her favourite place in the house. Grandpa wanted this weekend to be an end-of-summer celebration, and we did our best to convince ourselves this would be the case. After this weekend, I'd start my second year in med school, Three Dog Run would release their EP, and Karen's sister Anne would move to Toronto. The kid had gotten into OCAD on a full scholarship. The Ontario College of Art and Design was the largest and oldest school of its kind in the country. The coming September marked a new chapter in a lot of our lives.

Liam said he and Grandpa had a surprise waiting for us at the cottage when we arrived. I had no idea what to expect. Unlike Pat, Liam had the best poker face in the world, and there was no hope trying to pry out anything more from him. A week before the road trip, David asked me if I'd come out to Grandpa yet. "No," I said. "No, I haven't had a chance."

We were repainting the main space in our loft. We'd moved all the furniture into the centre, including David's framed Che Guevara poster, a tandem bike he'd been building, a male mannequin (which we'd found in a dumpster out back), my potted palm, and at least a dozen milk crates full of my DVDs, textbooks, and David's comic book collection. We'd covered the floor with tarps Rick had rummaged out for us. David was finishing up with the roller and I was working on the trim. "It'd be nice if you did," he said, "before he meets me."

"It was Grandpa's idea to have you come up." I pried the lid off a small can of paint. "He asks about you all the time. David, he knows."

"Then you should have no problem telling him."

"I'll tell him." I stirred the can and settled down cross-legged by the front closet. "I want to tell him."

"Then why don't you tell him right now?" David picked up my phone and tossed it into my lap.

"What? Right now?"

"Right now. Give him a call." I stared at the phone. "There's no problem, is there?"

"Sure. No problem." I wiped my palms and fingers clean on a paper towel. "But look, can you keep a secret?"

"Totally."

"I mean it. I haven't told my brothers or anyone. I don't want you saying anything to them about this."

"What is it?"

"It's about Grandpa."

"Okay."

"So you know how he built this cottage of ours right after the War, right? Someone named Frank helped him. So I meet this Frank guy at Grandma's funeral. Apparently, he was best man at their wedding. They played high school varsity together. They were like best friends. But Grandpa's never mentioned him, and I keep wondering why."

"Okay."

"Grandpa and Grandma and Frank, they were really close. The three of them would spend summers up at the cottage together. I think, maybe, Frank might've been in love with my grandma."

"Why do you say that?"

"I dunno. There was just something in the way he talked about her, I can't put my finger on it."

"You think he and your grandpa had a falling out? And that's why he's never mentioned him?"

"Maybe. Back then, those two would've been exactly our age, David. They would've been just like us."

"Except straight."

"Yeah, but that doesn't mean nothing ever happened. You know what I'm saying? Can you picture it?"

"Sure. Two young guys, barely out of high school, shacking up with an older woman, in the 1950s. It's hot."

"You see where I'm going with this."

"You think they were a threesome?"

I dabbed at the baseboards by the closet. "I really shouldn't be thinking this way."

"Yeah, you're one sick puppy, Daniel. Come on, it's not that big a deal. Stuff like this goes down all the time. Look, why don't you just ask him?"

"Grandpa? Are you kidding me?"

"Yeah. So hey, Grandpa, did you and Frank ever get it on together with Grandma?"

"No," I blurted, "I am not asking him that."

"Alright." David shrugged and dipped his roller into a paint tray. He hefted the long handle and started on the last patch of cinder block wall. "Well, we'll never know then, will we?"

"No, I don't suppose we will."

"So?"

"What?"

"Are you going to call him or not?"

I realized I still had the phone in my lap. David raised his eyebrows. I put down my brush and speed-dialled Grandpa. On the sixth ring, he picked up.

"Grandpa?"

"Allo, Daniel! Comment ça va?" In the background, I could hear The Guess Who's "American Woman" playing loudly, along with some kind of motor grinding.

"I'm good. Grandpa, what's that noise?"

"It's a blender, Daniel. I'm making drinks."

"I didn't know you owned a blender."

"I don't," Grandpa said, laughing, "or I didn't. I own one now! I am making piña coladas. Now what the hell a piña colada is, I have no idea. But there's a first for everything, eh? Is everything good?"

"Definitely. Everything's fine." I scratched my head. "Grandpa, about this weekend."

"We're looking forward to all you kids coming up. We're going to have some good times. Don't forget your swim trunks."

"No Grandpa, we won't. Who's we?"

"Oh, I'm bringing a lady friend. It's someone I've been wanting you kids to meet for a while."

"A lady friend?"

"I'll introduce you when you arrive. How's David, by the way?"

"David's fine." I glanced at David who was wearing his boardshorts slung low over his hips. His T-shirt kept riding up as he worked with the roller. "He's kind of why I called."

"You didn't break up, did you?"

"What?"

"You're still boyfriends, right?"

"Yeah." I leaned back against the door. "Yeah, Grandpa, we're still boyfriends."

"Good. We look forward to meeting him. Say allo. We've got some tourtières in the freezer for all of you to take home. You'll be able to swing through Sudbury on the way back, won't you?"

"Um, Pat and Blonde Dawn are driving." Still painting, David pulled down his shorts with one hand and mooned me. "But I'm sure we can do that."

"C'est bon. We'll see you Friday, then."

"Yes sir."

"Au revoir."

"Bye, Grandpa."

Grandpa hung up. I set the phone down. "He says hi."

"Is everything okay?"

"Yeah. Yeah, he was really cheerful. He's looking forward to meeting you." I stuck my legs straight out in front of me. "He's bringing a friend."

"You mean Frank?"

"No. A lady friend."

"A lady friend? Who would that be?"

"I have no idea. He knew you and I were boyfriends."

"So I heard."

"It's weird."

"How are you feeling?"

"Relieved, I guess? He made it all seem so normal."

David nodded contemplatively. "Should I thank him for your grandma's douche kits when I see him?"

"No, David, you won't."

"No?" David smiled. "You sure?"

"No."

David came over and straddled me. "Merci beaucoup, Monsieur Garneau," he growled like René Lévesque, "pour touts les douche kits."

"I will beat you with this brush."

"Oooh, mister." David leaned on my shoulders and ground his crotch against mine. "That might sound fun."

"What do you think he meant by a 'lady friend'?"

"Dude. C'mon. What do you think he meant? It sounds like your grandpa's seeing someone. You should be happy for him."

"We're scattering Grandma's ashes this weekend."

"Yeah, and?" He took the brush from my hand and set it aside.

"Don't you think it's a little inappropriate for Grandpa to be bringing a date? I didn't even know he was seeing anyone at all."

"Whoa there, cowboy. It's been, what, eight months since your grandma died."

"They were married fifty-nine years."

"Okay. And what's your point?"

"You know what my point is." I pushed David off me and stood up. "I don't think it's right."

"Daniel, your grandpa has a right to keep on living. He took care of your grandma for, what, like the last twenty years of his life. That man has a right to move on."

"Moving on, okay." I paced the room. "But this is Grandma's ash scattering."

"Yeah, you keep saying that. But it's not a funeral. You had the funeral already. Your grandpa wants this to be a family celebration. Isn't that what you keep telling me?"

"I suppose." I stood in front of the open fridge, a vision in my head of Grandpa in a Hawaiian shirt, slurping piña coladas, overmedicated and dishevelled, bouncing Playboy Bunnies in his lap.

"Then consider what family means." David sat back. "It's the people we love, and who love us. He knows what Karen and Blonde Dawn mean to Liam and Pat. He knows what I mean to you. He's gathering us all together to celebrate family, to celebrate life. Wouldn't your grandma want that?"

I thought of the photograph of Grandma on the swing. The book in her hands was the same book Grandpa had passed on to me last Christmas, Walt Whitman's *Leaves of Grass*. Grandma had loved her poetry.

"I wish I'd known her," I said.

"By the way," David said, picking dried paint from his shins, "I've been meaning to mention something."

"What is it?" I rummaged out two Creamsicles from the freezer.

"My ma, she wants to go back home next year. Her parents are getting older and she wants to spend a summer with them, while they're still well. She wants me and my sister to come with her. It's important."

"To Italy?"

"It'll be for two months. Don't worry about subletting the place. I'll cover my half of the rent. You'll just have to cook for yourself."

"I can cook for myself, David. I won't starve."

"You won't miss me, then?"

"You'll be gone all next summer?"

"We're just talking about it now, but yeah, that's the plan. She'll pay for our tickets. We've got relatives all over Italy."

"Italy." It was just starting to sink in. "Wow."

"The last time I met my grandparents, my sister and I were little kids. I barely remember them."

"How old were you?"

"I was five. She would've been ten. I remember Nonna

letting me sip some beer, and Nonno carrying me on his shoulders in their olive grove. It was nice."

"How's your Italian?"

"It sucks."

"Right." I handed David a Creamsicle and sat myself down next to him. Of course I would miss David, but at this point, next summer still seemed so far away. "Well." I wiped away a drop of paint on his cheek. "You better start brushing up then."

⌒ Road trips with Pat were an exercise in patience. With all our gear, we barely managed to fit into Blonde Dawn's car. During the five-hour drive up the 400, we played Twenty Questions, the License Plate Game, and our own version of punch buggy based on spotting inuksuit along the side of the highway. When we were kids up at the cottage, we'd spend whole afternoons building inuksuit, hauling rocks right out of the lake if we had to. The four of us took turns playing our favourite tunes. At one point, Pat stuck himself out the window for an air guitar version of BNL's "Wind It Up." He agreed to come back inside only after we all sang "One Week" with him. When we stopped for gas in Parry Sound, we ordered homeburgers, sloppy joes and poutines, extra-large Timmy's coffees and a dozen assorted donuts. In the parking lot, after Pat wouldn't stop begging, Blonde Dawn threw him the keys and let him drive the rest of the way. It was late in the afternoon by the time we pulled off the highway onto our family property. The cottage itself was accessed by a two-kilometre stretch of private road. I jumped out and unhitched the rusted chain at the top of the drive. A PRI-VATE NO TRESPASSING sign had been freshly painted and nailed to a maple tree that I remembered being a whole lot smaller. Pat drove through and I re-hitched the chain. Liam had been coming up regularly over the years. The last time I'd visited, Grandpa had piled us kids into the back of his pick-up, and we'd driven up with Mom and Dad.

Our property lay just inside the Sudbury Basin, a 1.85 billion-year-old asteroid impact crater, forty acres of old-growth east of the airport. On a clear day, you could spot the plume from the Inco Superstack, sitting on top of the largest nickel smelting operation in the world. The closest town was Skead, a sawmill community half an hour away. It wasn't what you'd call deep bush, but it was good enough for us. Pat swerved around potholes on the narrow dirt road, low hanging branches whipping past. When we rounded the final bend, the cottage came into view. To-day, the sun blazed in a cloudless sky, and the lake spar-kled in the breeze. Liam's Jeep and Grandpa's truck were parked out front, so I knew we'd come to the right place. But the cottage itself was almost unrecognizable to me. A two-storied A-frame extension had been built onto the original single-room structure. A brand new cedar porch wrapped around the whole cottage. By the time Pat parked the car, Karen had appeared on the front stoop with four beers in hand. As we piled out, Jackson bounded around the cottage barking and pushing his nose into our hands, his tail thrashing. Blue jays shrieked their alarm call over-head: *Jayer! Jayer!*

"Welcome to the Good Medicine Cabin," Karen said, handing out bottles like they were keys to the city.

I drew in a lungful of air fragrant with pine, fresh sawdust, and wood smoke. "Karen, did you know about this?" I demanded, scanning the new addition.

"Mm-hm," Karen nodded. She wore a black bikini top and an ankle-length, rust-coloured skirt that showed off her silver toe-rings. "I've come up with Liam a bunch of times in the last few years."

I turned to Pat and Blonde Dawn. "And what about you guys?"

"Yeah, we helped your grandpa put down the stone-work for the new fireplace," Blonde Dawn said, hauling our gear out of the trunk.

I was flabbergasted. "Am I the only one who didn't know about this?"

"Surprise," Karen said.

Liam emerged barefoot from the cottage wearing khaki shorts and a tool belt, wiping his hands on a greasy rag. He was tanned and looking more fit than he had in years. "Hey, guys," he called out, "you made it. So." He grinned and flipped the rag over his shoulder. "What do you think?"

"It's brilliant," Pat exclaimed. "Bloody brilliant. It's exactly how I pictured it. Bloody fucking brilliant." He high-fived Liam. "Congratulations, man."

"I finished the deck last week."

"Yeah," I said, "congratulations. Why didn't anyone tell me about this?"

Liam squinted at me. "I did tell you, Daniel. Lots of times. Like I said, Pépère's had a few projects on the go. That's why he's been spending so much time up here. I've been driving up from Manitoulin to help out when I can.

Check it out." He backed away and pointed. "I just put up the weather vane this morning."

"Sweet," Pat said.

"It's a cock," David said, elbowing me in the side.

Liam folded his arms in satisfaction. "So it is."

"I could've helped out," I said.

"Daniel, you've been in Toronto. You've been busy with school. It's all good. The main thing is, we've put in a septic system and a tankless water heater. The outhouse is still there, but we've got a working washroom now. We've kept the wood stove, but we've also got a gas generator out back, mainly for the heater and the fridge."

"Holy shit," I said. "And I thought you've been coming up here and roughing it."

"It is pretty luxurious," Karen said, "compared to what it was like before. Some of us might still want to camp outside this weekend. But you can take hot showers now."

"Who needs a shower when you got a lake?" Pat said, laughing. "I'm going in! Who's coming with me?" Without waiting for an answer, he ran hollering around the cottage, stripping off his T-shirt and shorts along the way. Blonde Dawn and David followed after him.

"Where's Grandpa?" I asked.

"He's out getting dinner with Betty."

"Betty?"

"You've met Betty," Karen said. "She's the nursing manager at the home." When I stared blankly at her, she poked me in the chest. "The redhead, Daniel. The nurse you always said you liked."

"Grandpa and Betty?"

Liam slapped my shoulder. "Come on." He led the

way down a flagstone path. When I didn't move, Karen took my hand. Out back, a spacious two-level deck enclosed three towering pines. Red squirrels chased each other along their gnarled branches and leapt onto the cottage roof. A tablecloth covered a table set with placemats and cloth napkins, silver cutlery, gleaming wine glasses, and white plates. Nine settings in all. A glazed vase in the centre spilled over with colourful wildflowers. Pat, Blonde Dawn and David scrambled down the dock and cannonballed into the lake, splashing and shouting. Beyond them, far in the distance, I could make out two people approaching in a canoe.

Liam shaded his eyes. "They'll be here in ten minutes. I better get the grill going." He padded back into the cottage through a sliding screen door.

"You want to see the inside?" Karen asked.

"What?"

"You won't guess where Liam put that moose skull of his."

"Yeah, in a minute," I murmured. "I just want to take this all in."

"When was the last time you were up here?"

"Thirteen years ago. It was just this old shack back then. This is unbelievable."

"Yeah, well, Liam and your grandpa, they've been working hard these last few years to restore this place. It was important, Daniel, for both of them."

"I had no idea."

Liam emerged hefting a bag of charcoal and a spice rack. He descended to the lower deck, Jackson at his heels, where he began to prepare the barbeque.

"We've got some sweet potatoes roasting," Karen said, "and there's a pasta salad in the fridge already. We'll make a baby greens salad. Your grandpa seemed pretty confident he could catch enough fish for the eight of us. They've been gone all afternoon."

"There's nine settings."

"That chair's for your grandma. It was Betty's idea." I drew a deep breath. Karen plucked a milkweed seed from my hair. "Daniel, you'll like her."

"I hope so."

"Trust me. You will."

I bowed my head. "I've been staying away."

"What?"

"I've been staying away. Grandpa's been inviting me back up here for years, but I've been avoiding this place. I always had some excuse: hockey practice, school, work in Toronto." I lowered my voice. "But he truth is, I just couldn't …"

"What do you mean?"

"I loved this cottage. We'd spend weekends and holidays up here, the whole family, packed into this one-room cabin. Grandpa and Grandma would take us kids out hiking. Dad would stay back and chop firewood. Liam, Pat and me, we'd hunt crayfish and frogs by these logs across the cove. We used to play for hours on a tire-swing by that outcrop right over there. That boulder next to it would get really hot in the afternoons and we'd dry our swim trunks on it. Mom would grill up fish or partridge, and make us hot chocolate. The sunsets over the lake were amazing. We'd stay up and roast wieners and marshmallows. Dad would play his guitar, Grandma would read us poetry, or we'd get Grandpa to tell us his ghost stories. You should've seen the stars at night. It was perfect."

Karen leaned against the railing, turned towards the sun. In that light, I could make out every individual glinting eyelash and crease in her lips. There were lines and freckles on her face that hadn't been there before. "The sunsets are still amazing, Daniel." She gazed sideways at me. "What's finally brought you back?"

"Well, Grandma's ashes."

"I'm glad you made it."

"The truth is, I've been afraid to come back ever since."

Karen studied my face. "Afraid?"

"Yeah."

"And now that you're here?"

I clenched and unclenched my hands. "It's different. It's not what I expected." I observed the shining lake and soaring pines, the silvery birch leaves in the breeze. "It's okay. I'm not sure what I was afraid of anymore. I'm regretting I didn't come up sooner."

"Well, Daniel, you're here now."

"We are."

By now, I could make out Grandpa in the stern of the canoe. He waved to us with his paddle. The red-headed woman in the bow also waved. Together, Karen and I waved back. Grandpa reached down and hefted a chain stringer, raising it high over his head. Even from this distance, we could see that it was full of fish. Blonde Dawn, Pat and David began swimming out to meet them.

"I hope you're hungry," Karen said.

I let the golden light wash over me. "I am."

ACKNOWLEDGEMENTS

I'd like to acknowledge use of the following song titles as chapter titles: "The Hockey Song" by Stompin' Tom Connors; "Working for the Weekend" by Loverboy; "Constant Craving" by k.d. lang; "Underwhelmed" by Sloan; "High for This" by The Weekend; "Lost Together" by Blue Rodeo; "All the Things I Wasn't" by The Grapes of Wrath; "Brother Down" by Sam Roberts; "Wake Up to the Sun" by Limblifter; "Your Ex-Lover is Dead" by Stars; "Five Days in May" by Blue Rodeo; "This Could be Anywhere in the World" by Alexisonfire; "Sudbury Saturday Night" by Stompin' Tom Connors; "We're Here for a Good Time" by Trooper; "Rockin' in the Free World" by Neil Young; "We're All in This Together" by Sam Roberts. I'd also like to acknowledge the quote taken from the film *The Blues Brothers* (1980; written by Dan Aykroyd and John Landis).

My personal thanks go out to Mary-Jo Dingwall for setting me on the writer's path; to my partner Daniel and his family, whose loving spirit is the spirit of this book;

and to the Pride & Prejudice team at Central Toronto Youth Services, for the opportunity to learn and grow in so many ways.

I'd like to express my gratitude to Michael Mirolla at Guernica Editions, for seeing something relevant in this work of fiction and opening the door; to my editor Julie Roorda for her kindness and expertise; and to my book designer David Moratto, for his openness and creativity.

Most importantly, I'd like to thank the queer, trans and two-spirit youth who have guided me over the years, for their courage, their heart, and their truths.

ABOUT THE AUTHOR

David Kingston Yeh holds his MA in cultural sociology from Queen's University, is an alumnus of George Brown Theatre School, and attended Advanced Post Graduate Studies in Expressive Arts at the European Graduate School in Saas Fee, Switzerland. Since 2004, he has worked as a counsellor and educator with LGBTQ2S youth in downtown Toronto. David resides in Toronto's east-end neighbourhood of Leslieville, up the street from a circus academy, along with his husband and a family of raccoons. His short fiction has appeared in numerous magazines. *A Boy at the Edge of the World* is his first novel.

Printed in March 2019
by Gauvin Press,
Gatineau, Québec